John William De Forest, Wilmer, Richard Hooker

The bloody Chasm

A Novel

John William De Forest, Wilmer, Richard Hooker

The bloody Chasm
A Novel

ISBN/EAN: 9783743344877

Manufactured in Europe, USA, Canada, Australia, Japa

Cover: Foto ©Andreas Hilbeck / pixelio.de

Manufactured and distributed by brebook publishing software (www.brebook.com)

John William De Forest, Wilmer, Richard Hooker

The bloody Chasm

THE BLOODY CHASM.

CHAPTER I.

THE war of secession was ended—lately ended; and Mr. Silas Mather was once more in Charleston.

It had been many years since he was in that notorious city—so much more notorious even than when he quitted it, when he shook off the dust of his feet against it. Over and over he had said to himself and to others that he would never again go there. Over and over, too, he had resolved that he *would* go there—would somehow or other force an entry into the accursed place; would visit it in enmity, and trample it with his triumph. As a man who had suffered from its social pride, and as a citizen whose patriotism abhorred its counsels, he had regarded it with vindictiveness and with deep hatred.

Now he stood amid its ruins. He saw its few and fallen burghers walking meekly to and fro, decimated, impoverished, humbled, and disconsolate. Their raiment was homespun, or, if they still had broadcloth, it was wofully stained and threadbare. Four out of five of the lounging and laborless passers-by were negroes of extreme raggedness. There was no stir of business or sound of prosperity in the streets. The great majority of the shops and warehouses were closed. The great majority of the dwellings showed no sign of habitation. Here and there, through the interstices of the neglected pavements, sprouted thin grass and long weeds. The upper town, the part where he now stood, was little better than a desert and a silence.

As he strolled on toward the Battery, the desert became a desolation. The well-remembered Huguenot Church was a ruin. The Catholic Cathedral was a ruin. Crumbled and flame-blackened fragments of buildings —many of them once superb mansions—covered a space of many acres. This was the quarter where, for month after month, Gillmore's shells were the only possessors and tenants. There they had rioted at will, crashing through walls, tearing open roofs, and prostrating steeples. To this solitary abolitionist and patriot from Boston the spectacle was fascinating, solemn, and satisfactory. He had never before seen ruins which had been wrought by the hand of war. He had never before seen half a city in ruins. He thought of Babylon, her haughtiness, her violence, and her desolation. At that moment it was a keen pleasure to remember the prophecies against Babylon, and their fulfillment.

Then a gentler remembrance came to him. He halted before a large brick mansion, stained nearly to blackness by time and the damp of ocean air, and fenced in by a lofty wall garnished with spikes of iron, all reminiscent of the days of grandeeism and of slavery. In that dwelling, now evidently untenanted and fallen to neglect, he had won life-long affection, and an ill-will at least as durable, if not as fervent. There he had been

a meek and laborious tutor; then a dazzled, an audacious, and a successful lover. Thence he had gone
forth, almost penniless, to struggle manfully with the
world for its pelf, and to set his bosom's jewel in gold.
The half, or perhaps a quarter, of his present income
would obviously purchase that mansion now. But he
was not thinking of that; his thoughts were in another
world. After standing a long time with bent head, like
one who stands beside a bier or a grave, he lifted a face
wet with tears, and walked feebly away.

He was still wiping the dimness from his eyes when
he came upon another mourner. This companion in
grief, however, was clearly sighing over Charleston.
He glanced sadly around the field of ruins, and then,
settling his gaze upon the shattered Huguenot Church,
folded his arms with an air of submission to final and
crushing calamity. He was a man of over sixty, thin
in figure and haggard in countenance, with long, white,
neglected hair. His clothing was a suit of black alpaca,
glossy with long wear, and pathetically brocaded with
darns and patches. His attenuated figure, showing
plainly through the fluttering raiment, made confession
of either illness or starvation. A white cravat, deco-
rously clean, though frayed along the edges, seemed to
indicate that he was a clergyman.

Mr. Mather, who had not yet learned to be pitiful
toward Confederate distress, at first surveyed this specter with mere vague curiosity. But presently his careless gaze changed to sharp inspection, and eventually
to recognition. Yes, there could be no doubt of it, he
had before him the minister who had married him—the
minister of the Church of the Huguenots. Advancing
eagerly, he said in a tone of sympathy—and also par-

tially of inquiry, so changed was the man by years and misfortune—"The Reverend Joseph Roget, I believe?"

The clergyman turned slowly, gazed at him a moment with dull, watery eyes, and replied in a feeble, disheartened tone, almost devoid of human interest, "Yes, sir."

"I am one of your old parishioners," said the Northerner, putting forth his hand. "Silas Mather, formerly of Charleston, latterly of Boston."

The specter accepted the proffered hand, and forced a feeble smile. "I am glad to see you," he murmured. After an instant of hesitation, much like that of a man whose mind is wandering, he added with impressive pathos: "I am glad to see you alive. It is a surprise. The majority of the people whom I know are in the graveyard."

Mr. Mather realized all at once, and for the first time, that he was in a land of bereavement and mourning. His instant impulse was to resist this unexpected claim upon his pity. "It is the usual experience of men of our age," he said. "Death is everywhere."

Mr. Roget shook his head—shook it pensively and repeatedly—as if seeking to repulse many sad recollections. "But here," he sighed, "it has been a whirlwind of death."

Mather shook his head also, but somewhat with an air of sternness, as if dispensing judgment. "You sowed the wind," he said, "and you reaped the whirlwind."

The clergyman made no response in words. He merely glanced in a meek, troubled way about the field of ruins. He had the air of thinking that the whirlwind was enough, without joining to it the exultation of a foe. Mather followed his wandering, sorrowful gaze, and then looked at the shattered, tattered man himself. "I don't reproach you, sir," he added. "I think I heard that you personally did not accord with the fiendish madness of secession. I was thinking of the wicked leaders in the movement and their crazed followers. They brought their doom—the doom of this destruction—upon their own heads. You surely owe *them* no sympathy."

"I could not help suffering with them," groaned Mr. Roget. "I can not help grieving with them."

"Ah, well, I will say no more about it—no more of it to *you*," returned Mather. "There is sorrow everywhere—unavoidable sorrow. I have had my own."

The clergyman bent upon him a look of interrogation, compassionate with the habit of compassion.

"My wife—" continued Mather, and there stopped suddenly, his voice gone.

"Ah!" said Roget in a tone of comprehension and pity. Then he put forth his hand, and added, "The Lord gave, and the Lord hath taken away."

His manner was that of one who understands another's sorrow, because he remembers full many of his own. For a few moments the two broken and bereaved men stood with clasped hands in silence. At last Roget added: "I shall never forget her. She was the sweetest of her race. Have you children?"

Mather shook his head; it was a great grief to him. But after a little he asked, "Did you know my sister, Mrs. Underhill?"

"Perfectly. I recollect her winterings here with great pleasure."

"And her son, perhaps? He was a boy in those days."

"I think I remember the lad."

"He is *my* son now—the only one I have—the only child. I am doing my best to be a father to him."

"I trust that he will abundantly repay your care."

Mr. Mather sighed. Apparently this nephew gave him sorrow, or at least anxiety.

"I am sure that I shall have your sympathy," he said, looking up sharply into the face of the minister. "I am afraid of his turning papist."

"Is it possible? Has he fallen into the hands of some clever priest?"

"Oh, I could forgive that—almost. If it were an honest change of opinion, however perverted, I could bear that—after a fashion. But this danger comes from a meaner source—one of the pure follies of youth."

He paused, drew a long sigh, expelled the breath with an angry hiss, and then continued: "It is a love-affair, as I suppose. I must really talk with you about it. I remember you as a counselor of old, and I sadly need counsel now. You have, perhaps, seen manias of this sort. This youngster—by-the-way, he is twenty-seven years old—is crazy about a Catholic girl—an Irish Catholic. She is a decent girl, perhaps, but still a commonplace Irish girl and a Catholic. How can I leave him my money?"

The impoverished clergyman stared. The word "money" struck him with something like surprise. There were so few people in his acquaintance who had any money to be troubled about! Protestant as he was, he could not yet feel that the rich man's sorrow was overwhelming, and could not at once bring forth an apt word of consolation.

"They always convert their husbands—those Catholic women," resumed the Boston Puritan. "The Church insists upon that. I can't let my fortune go into that Church."

"Let us hope that it is only a passing fancy," suggested Mr. Roget.

"I don't know," sighed Mather. "I wish I could think so. The girl is very good, I fear—that is, I hope and believe. But so much the worse—that is, in a certain sense. What I am afraid of, you of course understand, is a marriage."

"One can hardly credit that," judged Roget, a Southerner of patrician descent, and not accustomed to expect misalliances. "Is the young person attractive?"

"She is what people call handsome," admitted Mather. Then he shook his head negatively at the epithet and proceeded to qualify it. "She is unmistakably Irish—a pleasing sort of face—that is all. The attraction is that she is a singer, and Harry is absurdly fond of music—foolish about it. I have no ear myself, and I am almost thankful for it, when I see what a snare it is."

The clergyman reflected gravely. Presently, however, there came to him a thought which announced itself by a feeble smile. It seemed a specter of a smile, rather than a real one ; it almost looked surprised to find itself on those wasted lips.

"Would it not be possible," he suggested hesitatingly, "to find for him another singer ?"

Mr. Mather opened his stony-gray eyes with astonishment at the proposition. Then a faint expression of humor stole into his white, wrinkled face, and he answered with an air of assent and hopefulness : "Exactly ! I would give fifty thousand dollars for her. Where is she ?"

"I can tell you who she is, but not where," said Mr. Roget. "It is a young lady whom you would doubtless be interested in looking up. You know of your wife's niece, Miss Virginia Beaufort?"

"I came here to seek out the Beauforts," returned Mather with strong interest. "Where is this girl?"

"I can not say. I have just arrived from my exile in the mountains. My flock was dispersed, and I fled with it. But I understand that she remained in Charleston during the whole siege, or at least the greater part of it. She may be here yet, probably in deep poverty."

"If you hear of her whereabout, please let me know it, at the Charleston Hotel," begged Mr. Mather. "It is an urgent case. I must help the Beauforts, if they need help; yes, yes, I *must* help the Beauforts," he repeated, solemnly.

After a minute or so he began talking of his nephew again. The young man worried him much, he confessed; he had brought him from the North to save him from that Miss Macmorran; and—would it be believed!—he had found her here in Charleston; he had seen her on Meeting Street that very morning. It looked like an arrangement—like a silly or wicked conspiracy.

"Come and dine with me," he said at last. "I shall have a private dinner at two. We will talk everything over. Possibly something can be suggested for the good of the Church of the Huguenots. We will talk *that* over."

The invitation was accepted, and then the two old friends parted, each going his own way through the field of ruins, and each weighted with his own burden.

CHAPTER II.

Not far from where Mather and the clergyman parted, but hidden from them by fragments of ugly and pitiable ruin, a girl of some twenty years stood on the dilapidated sidewalk of Meeting Street, gazing up the long thoroughfare with the air of one who waits an acquaintance or a conveyance.

She had a tall and slender figure, a pale brunette complexion, wavy black hair, and extremely black eyes. Her features were regular and quite handsome, but the jawbones were somewhat more marked than is usual in American beauty, and there was an indescribable touch here and there which indicated the blood of Erin. Her expression was most interesting : it was grave, composed, very sweetly modest, and very sweetly dignified ; it gave one the idea of a naturally pure soul, which had been trained to meekness and obedience. Her dress enhanced this impression : the coarse robe of black alpaca suited the wearer, both physically and morally ; it fitted so neatly as to be an ornament, and yet was plain enough to confess humility or poverty. On the whole, she was an exceedingly attractive specimen of the dark Irish, that mysterious race which was conquered so long ago by the yellow-haired Tuatha na Danaan.

Behind her, emerging from a labyrinth of shattered houses, appeared the Sassenach. He was a young man, blonde, and handsome in face, with short, curling, sunny hair and mustache, and resolute blue eyes. His figure was tall and powerful ; his erect carriage seemed to proclaim the ex-soldier, and his fashionable traveling-costume revealed the Northerner. He had the air of recognizing the girl, and his expression showed pleasure as well as surprise. There was a little pause, as if he were devising some suitable address ; then he advanced quickly to her side, and said, gayly, "Will you please sing me something ?"

The young lady started as if something quite terrible had happened. "O Mr. Underhill !" she exclaimed, turning upon him. "How came you here ?"

There was no doubting the honesty of her amazement and trepidation. Her pale cheek filled with a dark-red blush, and then instantly became paler than before.

"I came by boat," he laughed. "I arrived this morning, and I am delighted to see you, and I want you to sing me something."

"I remember," she answered, shyly, and dropping her eyes to the pavement. "I should have known who it was by those words, without looking round. But, Mr. Underhill"—and here she became very grave— "why did you come ?"

"Well, Miss Macmorran," he said, with a teasing air, "because I knew you were here."

The girl was clearly as artless and unsuspecting as a child ; she obviously believed, or at least feared, that he spoke in earnest.

"Oh, no, Mr. Underhill !" she replied, with a glance of meek reproof. "I hope it isn't true. At any rate, you shouldn't be here for that reason."

"What a dreadful creature you are !" he smiled, continuing to gaze at her steadily. She was evidently a curiosity to him, as well as an object of admiration. "Now, Miss Norah Macmorran," he resumed, more seriously, "what is the need of being so prim ?"

She lifted her eyes to his for a moment, and then dropped them timidly and shyly. This appeared to be a habit with her, and it was almost her only gesture. There was something nunlike in it—something very subdued and pathetic. One might have guessed from it that she had known the discipline of a convent, or the strict and calm schooling of the Sisters of Charity.

"I have to be prim," she said, with a faint, placating smile, meanwhile regarding the grasses which were struggling through the neglected pavement. "I am only a poor chorister—the daughter of a poor woman. I must remember what I am. I told you so in Boston."

Underhill was moved by this appeal of the lowly to the lordly. "Reassure yourself, Norah," he said. "I came here without the least idea that you were here. As to my seeking your society—well, I can't help liking to hear you sing, and I don't see the harm of it."

"Nor do I see the harm of it. But, when people begin to talk and point, I have to say that I must stop— must stop seeing so much of you. You know that your uncle—and he is a sort of father to you"—she added, with a sweet little expression of gravity and reverence— "you know that he dislikes to have you come where I am."

"Such perfect nonsense! It puts me in a fury. I abominate him."

"You mustn't!" protested Norah, with a shocked expression. "You know that that is wrong. You shouldn't say such things."

"I don't mean them," laughed Underhill, greatly amused with her lecture. "What a good little thing you are! I begin to believe that the Catholic Church brings up the best girls in the world."

"Then you should let us stay good," said Norah, lifting her eyes with a look of gratitude, and instantly dropping them under his steady gaze. "You shouldn't want us to do things against our conscience."

"Against your conscience? Don't bring in such grave ideas. It sounds like scolding."

"Now tell me the truth," answered Norah, with another placating smile. "Who is it that is scolding you? Isn't it your own conscience?"

"You are very keen, Miss Macmorran."

"No, I am not a bit keen; but I suppose that I am right, and that you feel it."

"Can't I call to see you?" he begged.

"I wish you wouldn't ask it, Mr. Underhill."

"What did you come South for? To run away from me?"

"I was sent out here on a salary—a better one than I had in Boston. The Church in the North is helping the Church in the South, and a choir was to be started for Saint Patrick's here. It was best for me to come, and also it was a Church duty."

"And also you wanted to run away from me?"

"I did think of that, sir." This was said with a charming expression, partly native modesty and gentleness, and partly disciplined primness.

"You good—horrid—little thing!" grumbled Underhill.

Norah was trying to be grave and severe, but she had an Irish girl's sense of humor, and she helplessly burst out laughing. "You see that you can't help praising me for it," she answered, just glancing at him and then away. "I think that you, too, are good—and horrid."

"I am coming to Saint Patrick's to hear you sing."

"You are at liberty, I suppose, sir," she murmured, looking serious again, as if she were trying to remember a prayer.

"Horrid little thing! I shall sit in the choir."

"I wish you would not, Mr. Underhill."

"Away back, where you won't see me, where I sha'n't divert you from the service?"

"Please don't, Mr. Underhill; please sit below."

"Dreadful little nun! Well, I suppose I must do as you order. Where are you going now?"

Norah glanced down Meeting Street. There had already been an effort to resurrect some of the dead industries of the town; and one of the first to draw the breath of renewed existence, and even of some little prosperity, was the City Railroad Company—so eager were the negroes to ride alongside of white people, and so willing to spend their last sixpence for that privilege. A street-car—ponderous, rumbling shuttle of cheap transit — was traversing the ruinous warp and woof of Charleston, going from the Battery toward the Arsenal.

"I have an errand to the railroad depot," said Norah. "I want to take this car."

"So do I," smiled Underhill.

"Then I—mustn't," returned Norah, after a moment of hesitation. "I think I had better walk."

"Oh, you obstinate little Puritan!" he laughed. "Well, I won't tease you; I won't go with you, though I want to. Good-by," he added, extending his hand. "I wish I could hear you sing before Sunday comes. I wish I could meet you oftener."

She shyly gave him her hand, and replied vaguely,

"Thank you, sir." Then she turned, stepped alertly toward the car as if to prevent him from helping her in, and rode away without looking back.

Underhill followed her with his eyes as long as he could see her. It was a pleasure to him to watch her thin, graceful figure and swift, springy gait. He knew that figure and that gait at any distance. When he saw, at last, that she would not throw him a parting glance, and that the vehicle itself was getting beyond range of distinct vision, he turned away with an air of disappointment, and walked rapidly down Meeting Street, humming one of her solos. It was his purpose to reach the Battery and obtain from there a distant view of Fort Sumter. He had only taken a few steps, however, when he became aware that his uncle was approaching him, and that the old man's countenance was troubled and grim.

"Ah, sir!" he said, with some little confusion of manner. "So you have been studying the ruins?"

"Yes," returned Mr. Mather, dryly. "You have found an acquaintance, I see, sir."

Underhill smiled very slightly. He was too mature a person, and too self-respectful, to be easily perturbed. "It was Miss Macmorran," he said; "the Boston singer you know—the Irish singer."

"I remember," was the elder gentleman's sulky response.

"I met her by accident, quite to my surprise," explained the nephew, not choosing to be misunderstood. "She is a very nice, good girl," he added, a little irritated by the condemnation in his uncle's manner.

"A good Catholic, I suppose you mean, Harry," returned the Massachusetts Puritan, speaking out of a life-long hatred of Giant Pope, and also out of his terror lest his nephew and heir should wed unworthily "I have no confidence in the virtue taught by that Church. It is a superficial, formal, false Church."

Harry tried to joke the matter away. "Oh, yes," he smiled, "it is the mother of abominations, and all that sort of thing." But, seeing that his uncle was only irritated by his attempt at sportiveness, he checked it and spoke seriously. "I am not going to be a pervert, sir, if that is what you fear. I merely admire Miss Macmorran's singing, and approve her character."

It was evident that, whether these two men liked each other or not, there were regard and respect between them, and unwillingness to displease. Mr. Mather looked as if he wanted to speak bitterly, but could not muster courage to do so. Hard words would probably have hurt his own feelings quite as much as they would have hurt Underhill's.

"I have nothing to say against her character," he mumbled, glancing about him aimlessly to avoid meeting his nephew's eyes. "As to her singing, I wish it didn't take you to her church and among such commonplace people."

"I saw very little of them. The chorister was about all."

"What has she come to Charleston for?"

"She came on—in fact, she was sent on—to be soprano in a church here."

"Oh," said Mather, suspiciously. "It's very singular. I wonder if we shall find her in Savannah?"

"Possibly ; she may be on a mission—a musical pilgrimage," returned Harry, ironically.

The elder gentleman had the air of being fretted, if not downright angered, by this trifling. The nephew took note of it, and became serious once more.

"I beg that you will do the girl justice," he urged. "She certainly could not have come here to meet me. She has no money for such adventures, and, I honestly believe, no fancy for them. I am confident that she was entirely surprised to see me."

"Oh, well," groaned Mather. "It is a coincidence, I suppose. I really hope that you won't seek her society. It can't do any good, you know. Are you for the hotel?"

"If you will excuse me, I'll push on to the Battery. I want to get a glimpse of Fort Sumter, and of the fighting arena generally."

Mr. Mather's thoughts took a cheerful turn as he remembered the bombardment of Charleston. "Of course," he said, brightly. "Of course a soldier wants to see all that. You took a part in those matters, thank Heaven! I mean to have a look at Fort Sumter myself. But I take fatigue easily, and I need to get to my room now. Don't trouble yourself," he added, as the young man turned to accompany him. "I can go perfectly well alone. My old complaint," laying his hand tranquilly on his heart, "seems to have left me—for a time."

"Good-by, sir," said Underhill, respectfully, and, touching hats to each other, they separated.

CHAPTER III.

LEFT to himself amid the ruins of Charleston, Mr. Mather soon recovered his equanimity. The widespread spectacle of that flame-blackened desolation was very comforting and exhilarating to him. In all honesty and purity of spirit he compared himself to a prophet walking among the ruins of Babylon.

"I knew it would come," he said aloud. "I knew that slavery and treason and unprovoked rebellion could not conquer in the end. I felt and asserted that, so sure as there is a God above—a God of justice and holiness and awful power—just so surely would the violent South be brought to destruction. This spectacle is the most striking proof that I have ever seen of the might of a good cause, and of the overruling watchfulness of a holy Creator and Governor."

He ended his soliloquy because he became conscious that some one had overtaken and was slowly passing him. Glancing sidelong, he noted that the person was evidently a Southerner—a superbly tall and stalwart man of middle age, with a grave and almost grim aquiline countenance, and an air of dignity which contrasted strangely with his seedy suit of gray homespun. Mr. Mather looked carelessly at the worn face; then he suddenly leaned forward to peer at it eagerly; then he made an effort to get abreast of the stranger. Touching him gently on the arm, he said, in a clear, hard, emphatic voice, "As I was saying, sir, it can't be done."

Both men halted and gazed at each other in silence. The Southerner had an air of non-recognition and of amazement. After a moment he remarked in a deep, mellow bass, and with a singularly collected and courteous demeanor, considering the oddness of the situation : "I beg your pardon, sir. You have the advantage of me. I really beg your pardon, sir."

"Four years ago," said Mather, slowly, "in my office in Boston I told you it could *not* be done."

"Boston? Your office?" queried the other. "Oh, God bless my soul! Is it—is it Mr. Mather? God bless my soul! I remember you now."

"And our conversation?" insisted the Northerner."

"God bless me! I *had* forgotten it. I recollect it now," admitted the Carolinian, with a faint smile. "What a memory you have! Yes, I recall it. I said that the South *would* go out, and you said—"

"That it could *not* be done."

"I see it can't," bowed the Southerner. He laughed, but not blithely, and then shook his head very sadly. "We did our best," he added.

"Or worst."

"Ah, sir! you are victors." This was uttered with a sigh. "You have the right to exult. I would simply ask, my dear sir, is it magnanimous?"

"It seems harsh, no doubt, General Hilton," conceded the Unionist. "I believe you became a general in the rebel army?" he queried.

Hilton bowed gravely, and with a very slight frown, probably at the word "rebel."

"It seems harsh," repeated Mather, "but that one sentence I have kept in my heart for four years. I meant all that time to say it to you, and to say it here. I meant to say it not only to you, but to many others. I meant it as a duty."

Hilton gazed at him with the pathetic composure of

one who has learned to be patient in the school of failure and suffering.

"Well, sir," he replied, "let me tell you in all solemnity, and with such kindness of spirit as I can muster, that, before you have been here a fortnight, you will look upon it as a cruel duty. We are a crushed, beggared, prostrate people."

Mr. Mather surveyed the speaker attentively. There had been a great change in him since that meeting of four years ago. His figure was still tall and upright and imposing, but it looked bony and wasted through his mean raiment. His face had lost its old plumpness and air of confidence ; it was much darkened in color and sharpened in outline ; it was a haggard and weary countenance. His walk had that emphatic and pathetic deliberation, that limp with a strongly marked pause before each step, which indicates an artificial leg. One of his hands, also, was crippled and disfigured, as if by the tearing of a bullet.

"I am sorry to see that you personally have suffered," said the Bostonian. "I have no spite toward individuals."

"I was forty years old when I called on you in regard to the Beaufort properties," returned Hilton. "I was in my prime. Look at me now," he sighed, taking off his hat. "Did you ever before see a man of middle age who was seventy years old ? "

"Ah ! Your hair was black then," said Mather. He scowled slightly, like one who is unexpectedly and painfully forced into pity—who is, as it were, dazzled by a sudden glare of misery. It is doubtful whether he was quite conscious that he took the ex-Confederate General by the hand.

"A gray head is no misfortune," continued Hilton. "But this is a gray head dishonored. I am a bankrupt." He paused a moment; the other could hear, through his closed lips, the grinding of his teeth; then came a deep sigh, and the ruined man added : "But let that pass. It is small business to dwell upon my personal calamities. We are all bankrupts—a people of bankrupts. The South is an almshouse !"

The Unionist, standing on the height of his patriotic integrity, facing this ruin of a rebel, and surrounded by the ruins of Charleston, felt himself driven to apologize.

"I have said my one word of exultation and reproof," he murmured. "I am not ashamed of it. I said it as a citizen, however, and not as an individual."

"If you had been a soldier as well, you would probably not have said it," observed the Southerner, speaking with a gentle pensiveness, like a man who meditates rather than retorts.

Mr. Mather let go of the crippled hand, and asked, with some irritability, "What do you mean ?"

"Soldiers are comrades," said Hilton. "They may fight under hostile flags, but still they are comrades. I have encountered many of your officers since we laid down our arms. We can meet and do meet as comrades. I wish you personally had fought us. You would have liked us better."

"I didn't guess that you cared to be liked."

"The war is over. It would be well to be friends again."

Once more the Unionist took the hand of the ex-Confederate. "So be it henceforward, at least between us two," he said. "I came here to be friendly. I can't forget the past. I am a Union man—a bitter one. But, as for the future, let that be peace. Come and dine with me to-day, General, at the hotel. I want to present to you my nephew, Colonel Underhill."

"I accept with great pleasure, and I shall be happy to meet your relative," bowed Hilton, with Southern urbanity.

"He fought against you, I am proud to say," smiled Mather.

"All the better. We shall have a common ground of sympathy and interest."

Mr. Mather seemed much gratified by this declaration. "I am glad that I met you," he said. "I am glad on my own account. By-the-way, can you tell me anything of the Beaufort family?"

"Ah! your wife's relatives," returned Hilton, becoming quite grave again. "I can tell you much, sir, in one word—gone!"

"What! All gone? Do you mean—dead?"

"There's not a man of that noble race on the face of this miserable earth," continued Hilton, evidently with strong feeling. "I *must* call it a noble race, sir. It had furnished many gentlemen to South Carolina, and it ended as a line of gentlemen should. Every one of those four Beaufort boys fell in the fore-front of battle, with his back to the field and his face to the foe."

"May God forgive them!" said Mather, solemnly. "They have gone to their account."

For a moment the General seemed to forget his elaborate Southern urbanity. "It strikes me, sir," he observed, dryly, "that God may find it easier to forgive than a New England Puritan can."

"I trust that I remember, sir, that I am not the Judge of all the earth," retorted Mather, with equal dryness.

2

Hilton became pensive and reflective again. "You forget one thing," he smiled, sadly. "You forget that you Northerners stand to us in the place of a divinity. Your foot is upon our necks."

"I had hardly become aware of it," murmured Mather. "One can scarcely believe yet that that terrific resistance is over. Well, as I said before, I came to be friendly. Isn't there one Beaufort left? I heard of a daughter."

"Yes—Miss Virginia Beaufort," said Hilton, with a bright smile. "The flower of the low country. Heaven help her! Yes, she is here in Charleston, entirely alone and very poor. I presume she will see you—I don't know. Four brothers gone! She is very bitter. Our women are all in black or in rags, and they are very bitter. God help them!"

"Do me the favor, General, to tell me where this young lady lives."

"I shall take great pleasure in so doing," Hilton bowed, almost gratefully. "It is only a step. But let me beg of you, sir, to be prepared to show patience. You may find her very bitter."

"I know the Beauforts," Mather returned in a tone which was full of significance, and which had a slight twang of vindictiveness. "I have not been accustomed to expect much courtesy from them. You are aware, no doubt, of the nature of our domestic relations. They never forgave my wife for marrying a Yankee tutor—not even after that Yankee had surrounded her with prosperity."

"Old blood, Mr. Mather—very proud old blood—rather grim blood," was the General's somewhat awkward apology. "All the same, noble blood."

"Thank Heaven, my wife was unlike the rest!" exclaimed the old man, his voice suddenly tremulous. "She could forgive. I am here by her wish."

The General respectfully lifted his shabby Kossuth hat, tattered with long field service and a bullet-hole or two. "Faithful and true—not so much unlike the rest," he said. "Mr. Mather, I tell you that it was one of South Carolina's grandest lineages of men and of women. I was educated in reverence toward it. May I exhort you once more to long-suffering and mercy for the last one who bears its name? This very lovely young lady needs friends. She is very poor and very sad."

"No doubt of it," sighed Mather. "God help me to comfort her! She is terribly alone."

There was so much emotion in these final words that Hilton turned and gazed at the speaker with compassionate inquiry. For the first time he noticed that Mather's fresh and prim hat was encircled with a broad weed. "God help her to comfort *you!*" he murmured. "There is grief everywhere."

Then they walked on in silence until the General stopped before a small shanty of unpainted boards, sadly rent and stained by time and the weather.

"What!—here?" asked Mather in an awed and pitying whisper, like that of a man who gazes upon a coffin. He seemed to himself to be standing by the funereal receptacle of a whole family.

"This is what remains to the Beauforts—the house of one of their slaves!" said Hilton. "You will probably find her there, washing and ironing with Aunt Chloe. Or perhaps she has gone to carry the laundry-work to the hotel. She sometimes does that when the old woman is rheumatic and Uncle Phil is looking up a job. I have helped her along the street with her basket."

"Father of mercies!" muttered Mather. "Why didn't I come before?"

The General, turning quickly away, and tottering a moment on his wooden leg, raised his eyes desperately to heaven, covered his face with his battle-scarred hand, and uttered a sob.

"O my God!" he groaned, "how crushed and defiled we are! Trampled into the dust and dishonored! This is only *one*. There are hundreds more—the flower of South Carolina—reduced to this, or worse!"

He limped onward up the deserted street, and Mather prepared to enter the ruinous shanty alone.

CHAPTER IV.

INSIDE the shanty, on a wooden bench, such as daughters of toil stand their tubs upon, sat an elderly colored woman.

She had the mild eyes, the bright and adroit expression, the regular and almost delicate features and the maroon complexion of the Fellatahs—a brown race of north-middle Africa, far superior in parts and comeliness to the pure negro. In spite of a few wrinkles, and of ravages wrought by privation and illness, her face was still an agreeable one, and in its kind handsome. Her attire was as singular a mixture as poverty could well gather out of the wreck of opulence. On her head, folded in the manner of a turban, glared a Turkish towel of red-and-white stripes. Her waist, or jacket,

wofully frayed and split by long use, was of checkered
black and crimson, and had evidently been made out of
a table-cover. The diapering in her white skirt—white
only by extreme courtesy of speech—showed that it
had once been a sumptuous bed-counterpane. A single
glance at her leathery and hardened feet was enough to
reveal the fact that she had not for a long time worn
shoes and stockings.

This was Aunt Chloe, otherwise called Mauma Chloe,
the last faithful remnant of the feminine property of
the Beauforts. She was obviously in bodily pain, and
also in dejection of soul. With her crumpled and horny
right hand she rubbed one thigh and knee, while her
patient eyes gazed mournfully at an empty and fireless
hearth. Meantime she muttered in a slow, dislocated
fashion the following soliloquy : " 'Pears like dese yere
pains 'ud breck me up some day. Ain't no 'count much
longer, I'se afeard. An' Phil—he's a kind o' no 'count
nigger, too—don' fotch in mos' nothin' lately. Ef me
an' him doos breck up, what's to come o' Miss Ginny?
Oh, Lordy ! "

At this moment Uncle Phil, the brother of Mauma
Chloe, a curiously little old brown man, not unlike to
a withered sweet-potato, and dressed in such shabby
raiment that it seemed to stay on him only by miracle,
meekly entered the rear doorway of the shanty, and
seated himself wearily on the broken sill. In response
to an impatient glance from his sister, which obviously
reproached him for not being at work, he muttered in a
feeble, grunting tone : " 'Pears like dar ain't no jobs at
all, nowhar. Nothin' to give away, nuther. Could'n
fotch nothin' along, nohow."

" Oh, you brucken-down nigger ! " groaned Mauma

Chloe. "What d'ye come home fur? 'Spec's ye's gwine ter find chickin an' sweet-pertater? How's I to cook dinnah without vittle?

"Ain't dar *nothin'* lef'?" asked Uncle Phil, who looked weak and famished. "Whar's Miss Ginny?" he added, as if there were some help in that presence—the presence of a Beaufort.

"Gone ter kerry de cloes," grumbled Chloe. "*Would* kerry 'em, 'cause I was limpin'. Jess been cryin' 'bout it myself. Every time she goes out on the public street with dat ar basket, I'se ready to die o' shame. I'd like to butt my ole head agin a stone wall."

"So *I* would," assented Uncle Phil. Then, remembering his hunger once more, he added desperately, "Ain't dar no dinnah at all?"

"Not 'less Miss Ginny gets paid. S'pose she can't eat *us*. Wish she could. Oh, dear! what's to come o' that chile? 'Pears like de Lawd did'n take no notice o' awphans now'days."

At this moment Mr. Mather's knock was heard, and Aunt Chloe fervently exclaimed: "Dar's help! Bet you de Lawd sent dem folks, whoever dey is.—Come in!"

Mr. Mather entered with a gentle step, looked around him in vain for a Beaufort, and then courteously saluted the two colored people.

"Evenin', Masr," responded Aunt Chloe, although it was but a little after mid-day. "Walk right in, Masr. —Phil, brush out Miss Ginny's chair, an' han' it to the gen'leman.—'Scuse *me*, Masr; I'se tarrible rheumatic, an' it makes me kinder slow."

Uncle Phil, without ceasing to bow and grin, did as he was bidden. The visitor seated himself with an elderly person's deliberation, and then glanced again about the cabin. It was a contracted and shabby place of abode, discomforting to the sight, and not entirely pleasing to the sense of smell. The room in which he sat could not have been more than twelve feet square, and was barren of all furniture except a rush-bottomed chair, a rickety pine table, a wash-bench, and two tubs. In the fireplace stood a battered tin coffee-pot, a small iron stewpan, and three or four plates of common crockery. An open door, cut through a partition of unpainted boards, disclosed a sort of sleeping-closet, in which there was a bed made up on the floor. A rude stairway, as narrow and nearly as steep as a ladder, led up through a hole in the unfinished ceiling to a low attic. Mr. Mather surveyed every item of this poverty minutely and gravely, and shook his silvery head in compassionate protest.

"My good people," he said, turning to the old couple, "I came to see if I could be of any service to you."

"Oh, laws! I know'd you did, Masr," returned Aunt Chloe, breaking into a whimper, but smiling as she whimpered. "De Lawd he sont you. You's one o' dem Nawth'n gen'lemen."

"Gin us our freedom, Boss, you folks did," meekly smirked Uncle Phil. "We knows it, Boss, an' 'members it."

Mr. Mather glanced at the dinnerless fireplace, and sighed, "I fear it hasn't done you much good so far."

"Mighty starvin' times sence de wah, Boss," conceded the hungry uncle. "Niggers is dreffful poo' folks dese yere days. All de same, we'd ruther be our own poo' folks, an' not somebody else's."

Mr. Mather put his fingers into his vest-pocket and

banded the old man a small roll of bills. There were copious and humble expressions of gratitude, to which he listened with a half-pitying, half-impatient smile.

" You used to belong to the Beauforts, didn't you?" he asked, as soon as he could get a chance to speak.

" Yes, Masr," returned the old woman, and she was clearly very proud to say it. " I'se Mauma Chloe, an' dis yere's Phil, my ole brother. We was Beaufort niggers, an' no mistake. Lived down on de island plantation, befo' de wah."

Mather seemed to care little for their history. He had the abstracted, cheerless countenance of a man who is recalling a happy past which ended in calamity. Presently he inquired, with a fitfully twitching mouth, " Do you remember Elizabeth Beaufort?"

" 'Member her!" exclaimed Aunt Chloe. "I was *her* gal. When she was down to th' island I was her pertickler gal. I was older'n she was, but I tended her. 'Member her? I loved her best of all till little Miss Ginny come. Wasn't she grand, though! She was jess Beaufort from head to foot—only sweeter. But who *is* you, Masr?"

Mr. Mather's head had sunk on his breast, as if oppressed by these reminiscences. Without lifting his face he now responded in a low, unsteady voice, " Did you ever see her husband?"

" Oh! *is* you him?" cried the old woman, breaking into a whimper and lifting her hands in thanks. " O Masr, you's come to help us, fur sartin—you's come to help Miss Ginny. I know'd it befo' you opened the do'. Praise de Lawd, what sont you!"

The bereaved man made a great struggle for speech

and answered slowly, " Yes, he sent me, by one of his angels."

" An' Miss Lizabeth, whar is she ? " asked Aunt Chloe, little guessing how terrible was the query to her visitor.

The widower did not reply at once. Just at this moment he felt all the might of his sorrow, his years, and his invalidism. His thin white lips moved repeatedly before he could send an audible word through them. At last he said, with unexpected and spasmodic and almost startling force, " She is gone ! "

" O Masr ! " exclaimed Aunt Chloe. " Oh, 'tain't possible, Masr ! " Then, stricken with sudden pity, and with a desire to give consolation, she added, " De Lawd he wants his saints near him."

Uncle Phil, rubbing his horny hands apologetically, ventured to offer his mite of compassion. " Boss, it's hard times for all of us, ain't it ? " he mumbled. " But you has the hardest."

There was a brief silence, during which Mather rested his elbow on his knee and his chin in his hand, while he gazed fixedly at the floor. At last he answered, with a deep sigh : " Yes, I have the hardest. I am worth a great fortune, and yet I am, perhaps, the poorest of us three—the poorest in happiness. Ah, dear ! Separations are too much for the old and feeble. The young and strong can bear them. I *can't*."

" Masr," said Aunt Chloe, " jess now I thought we was powerful mis'able—the mis'ablest of all the mis'able. The Lawd has show'd us greater trouble than ourn."

There was nothing extraordinary in the poor, rheumatic creature's lack of egoism. From childhood she had been ruled and drilled into subordinating her own thoughts and feelings to those of white people. Nevertheless, Mather seemed struck as well as touched by hearing so much sympathy out of such an abyss of indigence. He looked up at Aunt Chloe with an air of surprise, and made an obvious effort to recover his self-possession. "Your trouble can be helped, I trust," he said, gently. "My wife's last charge was to care for her people. What can you tell me about her flesh and blood ?"

"Done gone dead, Masr—all but Miss Ginny, an' her aunt, Miss Anna, if so be *she's* alive. De ole Curnel, Masr Laurens Beaufort, Miss Ginny's father, an' Miss Lizabeth's brother, ye know—he cotched fever buildin' fo'ts in de swamp round Georgetown, an' come home to die. He was a gen'leman, Masr. His mem'ry got mighty poo' at las', but he allays 'membered he was a Beaufort—never stopped sayin' it. His four boys was killed in battles. Miss May, what married Curnel Manross, she died up to C'lumby. Only Miss Ginny left, I 'spec's."

Mather inquired where Miss Virginia was, and, being told vaguely that she had gone out, stated that he would wait for her.

" But, Masr—" began the old Mauma, with an air of embarrassment—"had'n I better see her firs'—jess to break it to her, kinder ? "

" Break it to her ? " stared Mather. " Won't she see me ? "

" Reckon so, Masr," hesitated Aunt Chloe. " Only, she's mightily stirred up, she is. She dŏn jess have much patience, when she 'members it all."

" Ye see, Boss, she's had a heap o' trouble," put in Uncle Phil. " You mus'n mind her, Boss."

"Is she crazy?" asked the visitor.

"No, Boss—she has her senses," explained the old man. "But she's kinder mad—mad agin Yankees. She calls 'em hard names, and keeps kinder clar of 'em. Dōn ye see, Boss? it's Beaufort style, dat is. Dey was allays powerful fur sperrit."

"Oh, I know the family," said Mather, bitterly. "Not ten letters to my angel of a wife in her thirty years of marriage! But won't this mad girl speak to an old man who wants to befriend her? It passes all belief."

"Ye see, Masr, she's los' so many!" pleaded Mauma Chloe. "It's 'mazin' how dat ar fam'ly has gone up. Reckon nobody ever did have s'many uncles 'n' aunts 'n' cousins as d' ole Curnel; an' now d' ain't a single one of 'em outside de grabeyard-fence. An' dey all fotched her up to be so fierce agin Yankees! Oh, de sperrit dar was in dat ar fam'ly! Dey was powerful livin', an' powerful dyin'."

"Miss May, now," suggested Uncle Phil. "Tell him 'bout Miss May."

"Does ye 'member hearin' of her, Masr?" began Aunt Chloe. "She was older sister to Miss Ginny. Her husban' was killed, 'bout the end of the wah, fightin' 'long with Gin'ral Lee. Dey mostly called her Raven— Raven Beaufort. It was a kind o' joke dey had, 'cause she was so white. She was jess de whitest thing ever you see—real milk skin, an' hair like sunshine in de mornin'; an' sech eyes—blue as de good Lordy's heaven. Well, she was in C'lumby—we was mostly in C'lumby— when Gin'ral Sherman he marched in. De cullud folks had been lookin' fur him, Masr, like fur de glory of de Lawd; but his chariot was a good while in comin', an so we'd flopped down to sleep. Reckon 'twas after mid-night a spell when I heerd de scared white folks a racin' by, an putty soon a gret, solemn rumblin' an' trampin'. Miss Raven she was fast asleep, an' her baby 'longside of her. I was so wild an' full o' joy I never stopped to think how she'd take it—never thought to 'member what sawt o' sperrit all de Beauforts had in 'em. I shook her, an' says I, 'Miss Raven, yere's de Yankees.'"

"Wish you wasn't thar," struck in Uncle Phil.

"So *I* do," groaned Aunt Chloe. "But what's did, 's did. Well, she got right up, in her night-cloes, long yellow hair down her back, an' took a pistil out from under her pillow."

"Dat's so—so did," murmured Uncle Phil.

"Looked awful," continued Aunt Chloe. "Her eyes was a-shinin'—an' she was all white, like a sperrit—white cloes an' white face. Next thing, she was out o' do', befo' I could cotch her. Dar was de Yankees—you could see 'em by de light of de burnin'—great black column from curbstone to curbstone—dar dey come! tramp, tramp, tramp—couldn' see no end to 'em."

"It was kinder skeery, Boss," shuddered Uncle Phil. "Seemed 's though the yeath was full of 'em—like the las' day come, an' the dead risin'."

"So did, Masr," assented Aunt Chloe, solemnly. "Believe I shouted—I was so possest. An' den she fotched a scream, Miss Raven did—never heerd no such a scream befo' or sence—an' up with her pistil an' fired —yes, Masr, fired right into 'em."

"The—mad-woman!" exclaimed Mather.

"Beaufort grit, Boss," said Uncle Phil. "Dey was all like dat—was so."

"Did the troops fire back?" Mather inquired, eagerly.

"No, Masr," returned Aunt Chloe. "Didn' fire, nor stop, nor dodge, nor speak, nuther. Dey jess come on, all de same; come on like a gret black flood—slow an' silent an' steady. Didn' take no notice of her; didn' take no notice of nothin'. Seemed like it was a black, monsous dream."

"An' den Miss Raven—" put in Uncle Phil, urging on the story.

"Yes, Miss Raven," said Aunt Chloe, "she dropped dead—right dar in her tracks; yes, Masr—dead!"

"What!" gasped Mather. "Did any man fire?"

"No, Masr; didn' fire; didn' look at her; tramped right by without noticin'; an' she lyin' dar till we kerried her in. It bruck her heart to see de Yankees; her heart jess bust right dar an' den."

"Dat's de kind o' stuff Beauforts is," commented Uncle Phil. "Grit to de las' bref. If dey can't whip, it kills 'em."

There was a silence of some seconds. Then Mather muttered, as if speaking to himself: "Well—I *shall* find the girl bitter. I shall do little good here."

"Masr, I hopes you'll see her—arter we's tole her 'bout you," pleaded Aunt Chloe. "I *wants* you to see her. She's mighty poo' and mighty pitiful. An' she's mighty han'some an' peart too; peartest Beaufort gal sence Miss Lizabeth. Some Beaufort women has been peart an' some hasn't; 'peared like it took putty much all deir senses to 'member dey was Beauforts; had'n no liveliness leff fur anythin' else. But Miss Ginny ain't tiresome; she kin say things an' do things. Laws, masr! if you should see her—ef you should hear her sing jess once—you'd want to make up with her; you'd set you' heart on it."

"Yes, I must see her," assented Mather. "A charge has been laid upon me. I must keep it."

At this moment Uncle Phil pricked up his ears, walked hastily to one of the two little front windows, and then whispered, "Heah she is!"

Mather started; the idea of facing the last of the Beauforts seemed to cow him: he glanced toward the yard in rear of the shanty and asked, "Shall I go?"

"No, Masr—too late now," murmured Aunt Chloe. "We mus' all talk to onct, an' talk de bes' we kin."

CHAPTER V.

THE young lady who entered the shanty looked a very suitable person to bear the character of the last of a notable family.

She was handsome enough to justify Aunt Chloe's affirmations as to her beauty. Her dark hazel eyes were brilliant, her chestnut eyebrows were delicately penciled, and her brown hair was thick, glossy, and wavy. Her features were as regular as one often sees in real life, and her complexion—a medium brunette—was slightly flushed with color. Throughout the whole fine oval of the youthful face, moreover, there was a high-bred air which greatly increased its charm. The figure, too, was admirable, and showed to great advantage through a simple "baby-waist," although the stuff of the dress was the very coarsest and cheapest calico. In age she was then nineteen; but a girlhood of agitations and sorrows had matured her early; and she had the expression, if not the appearance in all respects, of being two or three and twenty. All through the singular scene which follows we must remember that she was still in a period of life which is ruled by emotion rather than by judgment.

Aunt Chloe spoke first. "Is you come, honey?" she said, with a wheedling tone and a placating smile. "I'se so glad! We's be'n a-lookin' fur ye."

Virginia Beaufort bowed slightly to the stranger, quietly set down her large, shabby clothes-basket, and then turned to the old woman with a grave gaze of inquiry. Her manner was entirely self-possessed and dignified, and her expression had a seriousness very pathetic in one so young.

"Yere's a gen'leman wants ter see ye," continued Aunt Chloe, still seeking to smile away the gravity of the situation. "One of your uncles, Miss Ginny."

Mr. Mather advanced with an air of hesitation, but resolutely extended his hand. "I am most happy to find you, Miss Beaufort," he said. Then, with a sudden revulsion to reserve, near akin to defiance, he added, "My name is Mather."

Virginia had given her hand mechanically, and she now quietly withdrew it. "I have heard of you, sir," was her cool reply. "How is my aunt?"

"She is well—well for ever!" sighed the bereaved, worn old man. He was looking at vacancy now—at least not at Virginia.

"Is it possible!" the girl whispered, comprehending him instantly. After a brief silence, during which she glanced once at his shaken face, she continued in a steady, low voice: "I am sincerely grieved. Be good enough to sit down."

"Miss Ginny understan's," muttered Uncle Phil,

with something like pride. "We's used ter dat sawt o' news."

Mather sank into the rush-bottomed chair, and rested his head against his hand. The young lady gazed soberly at him, and the old Mauma sobbed aloud. After a little silence the widower, an invalid as well as a mourner, we must remember, raised his tearful eyes to Virginia's face, and said feebly : "The sight of you recalls so much ! You have your aunt's eyes and hair."

"So have !" exclaimed Mauma Chloe. "Mouf, too, Masr, when she laughs. I hain't done fo'get Miss Lizabeth's little laugh. Never shall."

"I never saw her," said Miss Beaufort, as cold as a statue. It was evident that she had already determined not to be surprised into friendliness.

Mather gazed at her with an air of disappointment, rather than of anger. "There was bad blood," he murmured. "It was not her fault. Well, it was not yours, either. I blame no one now. I have come here in all possible friendliness. The war is over. Everything is over. Let us begin again. Miss Beaufort, I should like to renew amity with your family."

It was now the orphan's turn to be shaken. She sat down upon the washing-bench and covered her face. "My family !" she sobbed ; "where is it ?" Then, looking up passionately, she added in a strident voice, "Don't you know where it is ? Buried on the battlefield ! "

Mr. Mather shook his head softly and waved his hand gently. "I come in obedience to my wife's charge," he repeated. "You can accept the good-will of your own blood, can't you ?—of the dead, can't you ?"

"Oh, yes—I suppose so," gasped the girl. "There

is no other good-will for me.   Every one that ever owed
me any good-will is dead and buried."

"No, no, Miss Ginny !" pleaded Aunt Chloe, touched
and frightened by the grief and despair of her darling.

"I forgot you two," said Virginia, glancing at the
old couple through her tears.

"An' dis yere gen'leman," insisted Chloe.   "He's
come all de way from dem foreign States to look arter
ye, chile."

The daughter of the Southland shook her head in
petulant incredulity.   She was saying to herself that of
course he had his business ; that Yankees always had
money on their minds—the busy, eager vultures !

"I shall not live so very long, Miss Beaufort, as to
be a burden to you," resumed Mather.   "I am likely
soon to be one of those from whom you can accept
good-will."

"I don't wish you dead, sir," answered the girl,
looking him full and honestly in the face, but with no
sympathy in her expression—only suppressed aversion.
"Why should I ?   Death or life, it makes no difference
—none to me.   I never can accept a favor from a
Northerner."

The old Bostonian undoubtedly regarded this as
Southern rant or Southern wickedness ; and his pallid,
prim countenance showed a displeasure which was nearly
akin to disgust.   But he remembered his business training, and strove to be calm, practical, and logical.   "I
should like," he said, "to hear your reasons in plain,
simple English."

"A Beaufort never spoke any other English," Virginia flamed out.   "I should think you would know my
reasons.   The North has ruined my country—"

"Your country!" interrupted Mather, in a tone of argument which he meant to be persuasive. "Where is your country? What is it?"

"South Carolina!" exclaimed the girl, evidently in earnest—defiantly in earnest.

The inflamed Unionist was so angered by this rebellious declaration that he answered with a bitter laugh. "Do you mean the whole of it, or only the low country?"

Virginia vouchsafed no reply beyond a glare of indignation. The two antagonistic ideas of American politics faced each other angrily in the persons of this sickly old man and this passionate, impoverished orphan. The man picked up his hat with a shaking hand, and half rose as if about to depart. Then his eye caught the troubled face of Aunt Chloe, and, drawing a deep breath, he slowly fell back in his seat.

Meantime Uncle Phil sidled up to his young mistress, and said in a hoarse whisper, "Miss Ginny, 'pears like d' ain't no use in dis yere talk."

She turned upon him with a sharp "Be silent!"

"Uncle Phil—" said Mather, his face flushing.

"Sar?"

"We must all be silent in the presence of our born superiors."

"Yes, sar," responded Uncle Phil, entirely in the dark as to the old gentleman's meaning, but knowing by experience that it was good to say "Yes, sar," to white folks.

"Mr. Mather, I understand your satire," retorted Virginia. "I don't know that I owe you any apologies. You are not over-gentle yourself."

The veteran abolitionist and Unionist would, perhaps, have returned bitterness for bitterness, if he had not happened to glance at Mauma Chloe, and noted that her lips were moving as if in prayer. Helped to patience by the pathos of this spectacle, he bowed his silvery head meekly, and said : "I know it. I accept the reproof. I am a sick man, Miss Beaufort—sick and irritable. I was not fit to come on this errand. But there was no one else."

Gentleness is certainly very powerful. The sensitive and vehement girl felt that she was put upon the defensive.

"I want to justify myself," she answered, in a softened tone. "You think very little of my State, and that I ought to think little of it. But how is it with regard to my family? Am I to care nothing for that? Look at it!" Here she sprang up, and stamped her foot with a sudden throb of anguish or anger. "It is ruined and slaughtered! I haven't a brother left. I haven't a dollar in the world. My old father—" But at this point her pathetic declamation broke into sobbing, and came to an end.

"Sit down, my poor child," begged Mather, sincerely affected. After gazing at her pitifully for a moment, he added : "We are both mourners. Wouldn't it be possible for us both to forgive, and to at least strive to forget?"

But the child of the crushed South was implacable ; mindful only of her own sorrows, she retorted, "What have you to forgive?"

"We are both mourners," he repeated, dreamily, as if he were thinking of his dead, and of naught besides.

"Oh, I remember," said Virginia. "Well, I had no quarrel with my aunt."

"No; you were too young. Nor have I any reason for quarrel with you. Indeed, I have a strong reason for seeking your good-will and amity. I desire it most earnestly."

"Do make up, Miss Ginny, please do!" begged Aunt Chloe. "Take all de kindness dat de Lawd sends, if its ebber so much. Mighty poo' bee dat don't make mo' honey dan he wants."

The girl pondered for a little, and then, with a evident effort, asked, "Well, sir, what is it that you wish?"

"Dat's de kind o' talk!" exclaimed Uncle Phil. "Dat's mighty sensible, dat ar is."

"I will be clear about it," said Mather. "I propose to take you North."

Virginia shook her head; then queried, "To come back?"

"I propose to adopt you," continued Mather, "to finish your education, if that is needed; also to leave you a part of my fortune."

"O Miss Ginny! take us 'long with you," besought Aunt Chloe, not doubting but that the offer would be accepted.

But the girl's expression changed slowly from thoughtfulness to sullenness. "I am to be picked up, like a beggar-girl," she muttered. "Yes, and I *am* a beggar!"

"No, Miss Ginny; not s' long 's we kin work," put in Uncle Phil, with exceeding unwisdom.

"Shut you mouf, you big fool, you!" whispered Aunt Chloe, who was ready to cuff and kick her *non compos* of a brother.

But mischief had been done. The high-spirited,

hair-brained child gave Phil a bright smile and thanked him for his stupid devotion.

"Yes, we can all work—so far," she added. "We are not quite beggars. We have nearly a dollar among us," she laughed, with affected gayety.—"There, aunty, take it and get some dinner. We must show Mr. Mather Southern hospitality."

Chloe snatched the money, handed it to the unlucky Phil, and pushed him savagely out of the shanty.

Mather had shown no irritation under the girl's levity, and he was greatly moved by this revelation of poverty. "Had you nothing in the house?" he asked, putting his hand to his pocket.

"Stop, sir!" broke out Virginia, angered by the gesture. "Don't you dare take out your purse! Marion could dine on potatoes," she added, proudly remembering South Carolina's almost mythical hero. "We shall have more than that."

"O Miss Ginny, you's so awful tart!" whimpered Aunt Chloe. Then, turning to Mather, she urged: "Dŏn you mind her ways, sar. She's nothing but a chile."

"Go on and buy the dinner," Virginia called to Uncle Phil, who still lingered in the doorway. "Mauma Chloe, sit down," she rattled on. "I'll get the water.— You will please excuse me, Mr. Mather; Aunt Chloe will entertain you."

This final speech was, of course, a hit at the supposed love of the Yankee for the nigger, and Virginia probably hoped that its sarcasm would irritate Mather into quitting her presence. She was seeking a quarrel; striving to draw from wrath the strength to utterly reject his advances—striving to nerve herself to behave as became a Southerner and a Beaufort.

CHAPTER VI.

Mr. Mather gravely waited while Virginia went out for water and returned with it.

He hoped, of course, that she would tire of her petulant defiance, and voluntarily accord him an opportunity to renew his friendly negotiation. But she paid no attention to him. She busied herself with kindling a fire on her poverty-stricken hearth. If she spoke, it was to Mauma Chloe and about culinary matters. At last his little stock of patience gave out, and, rising tremulously from his chair, he said, in a tone which he vainly sought to render calm, "This means, I suppose, that you decline my offer?"

"I never will touch a Yankee dollar—never!" affirmed Virginia, without looking up from her pottering.

"I wish to relieve my soul of all responsibility," he replied, solemnly. "Do you decline the whole of my offer?—the residence at the North?—the education?—the legacy? or do you merely decline some particularly offensive part of it? The word dollar is such a generality."

"I don't see how I could possibly be plainer," said the obstinate child, still pretending to be busy with her fire. "If I should ever touch one Yankee dollar, the dead of all those battle-fields—every brother and cousin, remember—they would haunt me for ever."

"I wish to clear myself," insisted Mather. "I, too, have the dead to remember. I want an explicit and unmistakable answer, and not a figure of speech. Do you accept any part of my offer?"

Virginia rose from her kneeling posture on the hearth and faced him, flushed either with the effort of rising, or with anger. "I have no intention of being vague, sir," she said. "That is a fling at Southern eloquence, I suppose. I will not touch a dollar for any purpose."

"Do you refuse to go North?"

"Yes."

"Do you refuse the education?"

"Yes. I need it. I haven't had a lesson in four years. But I do refuse it."

"Do you refuse the legacy?"

"Oh, that—of course! Certainly!"

"Not a Yankee dollar?" repeated Mather, with a sarcastic and indignant smile.

"Never!" exclaimed Virginia, thoroughly infuriated by his tone and expression. "Look here! I may as well be frank with you. I hate the whole race. I hate everything that they are and have. I can't express to you my aversion. Why shouldn't I hate them? My country in ruins—my family exterminated—*their* work! As for you—well, I owe you thanks for your good intentions, and I ought perhaps to have been calmer and gentler. But I couldn't be—no, I couldn't!"

Mather dropped his eyes to the floor, wearied of this image of rebeldom. Then, as if speaking to himself, he muttered, "I believe I have had all the patience that could be asked of me."

"I haven't asked any," returned Virginia.

"I was not thinking of you," he sighed, without lifting his eyes. "I was thinking of my wife and her charge."

"O Mas'r, dŏn quit thinkin' of it," broke in Mauma Chloe. "You's had a mighty heap o' patience. But dŏn tire on't, Mas'r. Dŏn mind dis yere chile's highty-tighty talk. She's jess a spiled baby, what I spiled myself. She dŏn know nothin' what's good for her; dŏn know nothin' 'bout the world at all, nohow; jess gabbles like she was on a jogglin'-board."

"Don't know the world!" Virginia laughed, angrily. "I know the sorrow of it, at all events."

Mather gazed at her vacantly. He seemed, half the time, to be musing of some one else. It may have been of the wife whom he had lately buried; it may have been of the nephew who gave him so much anxiety. Of a sudden, a fresh light—the flash of a new and startling idea or purpose—came into his faded, dreamy eyes. He looked a little cruel, if not a little crazy, as he settled his gaze on the girl and said, "I will make one more proposition."

Virginia, as if daunted by his expression, made a hasty negative gesture, and replied, "Excuse me from hearing it."

The old man turned his back upon her and addressed himself to the negress. "Aunt Chloe, I will talk to you," he began. "I have a nephew—a young man— young and handsome. He is to be my heir. Of course, I wish him to marry."

"Of co'se you doos, Mas'r," broke out the woman in Mauma Chloe.

"He is rich enough already," continued Mather. "But I shall leave him a large fortune—at least five hundred thousand dollars—so much in any case. If he should marry, and marry according to my choice, I shall double that. His wife will have half a million as a dowry."

"Is dat ar a big heap o' money, Masr?" asked the old woman, trembling visibly, and throwing a glance of piteous anxiety and pleading at Virginia.

"Miss Beaufort will be able to explain to you that it is," said Mather. He paused a moment, drew a long breath, and then added firmly : "I desire to devote it to *her* support and comfort. I desire to see my wife's niece and my sister's son rich and happy together."

A moment of awful silence, during which it seemed as if hearts stopped beating, followed this extraordinary announcement. Then Aunt Chloe exclaimed, in shrill excitement, "Sar ! does you mean to give all dat money to Miss Ginny ?"

"If she ever marries my nephew," he answered—"if she renews between our families the bond of relationship."

The old Mauma limped toward the girl with her hands extended and her knees bent, as if she were about to fall on the floor in supplication. "O Miss Ginny !" she begged ; "oh, please be good an' sensible ! Please hark to ole aunty !"

Virginia stood with her eyes fixed on the floor. Her face had turned to a sort of sea-shell whiteness, with the exception of a small crimson spot in either cheek. She looked very beautiful, but also very obdurate. At last she broke forth, in a loud, gasping whisper, "It is outrageous !"

"Oh, my chile !" besought the negress. "Dŏn be a spiled, contrary baby ! Do stop an' reckon befo' you says another word ! Do have marcy on you'self, for ole Mauma's sake !"

But Beaufort blood, and the pride of ancient lineage, and the intense anger of the beaten South, and the still fiercer wrath of personal bereavement, rose victorious over intercession and temptation. Virginia suddenly

3

ran out of the back door into the narrow, dirty, and evil-scented yard in rear of the shanty.

" *Won't* you say somethin' good ? " pleaded Aunt Chloe, following her to the door and calling after her.

A sobbing voice answered from without, " Tell him *never !*—I *never* will ! "

The unhappy Mauma turned and gazed at Mather with a countenance of despair. The blood had forsaken her wrinkled face, and her reddish-brown color had changed to an ashy yellow. She was crying aloud, like a child in pain.

The old man did not seem to notice her distress ; he was for the moment much too angry to be pitiful. " Not a Yankee dollar ! " he repeated, with a bitter smile. " Not a dirty dollar ! "

" O Masr, dŏn go jess yit," prayed Aunt Chloe through her sobs. " She'll come back. She's jess like all young gals—mighty skittish an' onsartin. She'll think on't ; suah to think on't. I knows she'll come to want to make up ; an' you'll want to, too, Masr. Ef you could see her when she's quiet, an' see how she looks and behaves like her own aunty what's gone to glory, you would'n' let go of her. Masr, you *could'n'.*"

Mather had wheeled toward the street door, but his steps were as unsteady as a sick man's, and he was evidently very much shaken. All at once he put one hand to his heart, sank down feebly into the rush-bottomed chair, and sat in silence with closed eyes. His milky-white face had such an expression of mere weariness and listlessness that Aunt Chloe feared lest she had not moved him, and recommenced her supplications.

" Oh, to think 'at dat ar chile what I fotched up should make me so mis'able ! " she moaned. " I's as

mis'able 'bout it as you is, Masr. But she'll come roun'.
Dar's ever s' much sense in her, way down. Dar's ever
s' much smartness. Never was no Beaufort smarter'n
dat ar hussy. Wish you could hear her talk when she
ain't stirred up thinkin' 'bout de wah. You'd want her
to live in you' own house all you' life. An' oh, ef you
could hear her sing, Masr !—jess hear her sing *once !*—
you'd ask her to stay with you, like Abraham did the
angels."

Mather lifted his face with an expression of desire
and hope which was almost a smile. Virginia's singing,
he recollected, was to have saved his nephew from the
musical wiles of that Irish Lorelei, and from peril of
conversion to papacy.

"Ah, dear ! it seems to me that I have done my
whole duty," he sighed. "Still, she shall have time
to think of it. I will so make my will as to give her
time. She shall have half a million, on the death of
her husband, if that husband is my nephew. When
she comes in, tell her that, and tell her to think of it.
If she wishes to see me again, or to write to me, I am
at the Charleston Hotel."

Aunt Chloe brimmed over with quavering thanks
and benedictions. "You won't never be sorry, Masr,"
she promised. "De young gen'leman won't be sorry,
nuther. Dey makes good wives — Beaufort women
doos—ef dey *is* spunky. *You* knows it, Masr."

"Yes, I know it," said Mather, wiping his eyes. He
glanced toward the back door and listened a moment.
"She won't come in," he added, with an air of disappointment and vexation. Then, rising slowly, he drew
a large pocket-book from the breast of his coat, and
gave it to the old woman. Hide that," he whispered.

" It's full of Yankee dollars—the things she hates. And here is a shake of a Yankee hand."

" God bless it, Masr ! " wept Aunt Chloe. " Bless all de Yankee han's. Dey's as good as dey is strong."

She tried to kiss his hand, but he gently drew it away from her, glanced once more at the back door, and then went forth into the street.

CHAPTER VII.

The next day was Sunday, or, as Mr. Mather preferred to call it, the Sabbath. He attended the Presbyterian service in the morning, dutifully and decently accompanied by his relative, the ex-Colonel, although the latter would have preferred a ritual which offered more music and less doctrine. In the afternoon, finding himself very weary, possibly from the excitement of the previous day, he took a nap, and left the young man to his own devices. Toward supper-time he awoke much refreshed, read a chapter or two in his small traveling Bible, and began to ponder his double duty of converting his rebellious niece to Unionism and saving his bewildered nephew from Popery. He was growing a little nervous and fretful over the double problem, when Underhill returned from a stroll and entered the room. The uncle did his best to smile cordially and to speak in a tone of cheery unconcern ; but, in spite of all, there was an air of suspicion about him as he said, " Well, sir, and where have you been ? "

It so happened that the young man had attended

vespers at St. Patrick's, and he candidly avowed the fact, although he could not have wished to do so.

"What for?" grumbled Mather, his cheerfulness vanishing at once,—so well did he know the reason which he demanded.

Underhill foresaw a disagreeable discussion, but his health and temper were good, and he smiled pleasantly as he replied, "To tell the truth, sir, I went there to hear Miss Macmorran sing."

"Look here, Harry!" broke out the senior, with a face of sincere distress, "I don't like this. I can't bear it. What does it all mean? Is it a flirtation? I must say that I think nothing quite so degrading to the intellect and morals as a passion for cheap conquests."

"My dear uncle, I am not making a cheap conquest."

"No, it wouldn't be a cheap conquest; it would be a frightfully dear one."

"I don't think I quite understand you, sir. Dear to whom?"

"Dear to yourself—very costly to yourself."

"I am glad, at least, that you consider me a foolish fellow, rather than a bad one."

"I don't charge you with being a bad fellow—not yet. But I don't know how it will terminate. When a man courts a woman far beneath him, he may end by being either a knave or a fool. Where do you expect to end? Not in marriage, I suppose and trust. What can a young gentleman of your breeding and education do with a commonplace, uncultivated wife?"

"It hasn't come to thinking of that," interrupted Harry, rather indignantly.

"Don't try to head me off," answered the uncle with

equal heat. "I want to have my say out. Are you prepared to turn Papist? I presume not. Are you prepared to sign a bond engaging yourself to educate your children as Papists? I hope not. Then what is the use of flirting with a Catholic girl? It can't end in marriage."

"I should say not, decidedly."

"In that case, why not let this girl alone? Why do you run the risk of troubling her imagination and ruining her peace?"

"My dear uncle, I have simply been to hear her sing. I didn't speak to her, nor get a chance to."

"It seems to me, Harry, that you, with the surroundings you have, might find your music otherwhere."

"Well, now, not so very easily. I don't know a single young lady in society who sings like this girl."

Mr. Mather rose and walked slowly up and down the room, with his hands twisted together behind his back, and his head bent in meditation. Perhaps he was querying whether a Christian man really had a right to draw his ass out of a pit on the Sabbath-day. Perhaps he was simply pondering how best to introduce his project of marriage between the said ass and Virginia Beaufort. After two or three turns he stopped in front of his nephew, and said in a gentle voice and with a faint smile, "Suppose I should introduce you to one?"

"A singer?" asked Underhill, staring and amused. "I should like it prodigiously."

The uncle took another ruminative walk, halted again and added: "I am trying to tame a beautiful young rebel. I should like you to help me."

"Just give me a chance at her," laughed Harry.

"She is a wonderful singer. So they tell me."

"I'll promise to be attentive to all the wonderful singers that you'll show me. Who is she?"

"Miss Virginia Beaufort. The last of the Beaufort name—the last! It is a very sad case."

"Why, she is a connection! Why shouldn't I see her? I should like very much to call on her."

Mr. Mather was obviously gratified, indeed he was pathetically elated, by this expression of interest. He sat down by the young man and told him the whole story of Virginia Beaufort's calamities and grief—not even omitting her bitterness.

"It is very touching," said Harry, who was as yet far from suspecting his uncle's matrimonial project. "But it looks like a desperate case for reconstruction. All the same, something ought to be done for her—I mean in the financial way."

"I should like to get her married to some well-to-do young Northerner," cautiously suggested Mather.

"Yes ; but what's to become of the young Northerner?" Underhill laughed. "He would have to turn rebel, and bond himself to educate his children as rebels. What I meant was a dowry, and let her find her own husband. Couldn't you and I subscribe—?"

"I have made her an offer," interrupted the old gentleman. "I hope to hear from her to-morrow."

"Anything that I can do in the way of courtesy and attention, sir?" asked Harry.

Mr. Mather fell into profound thought, twirling his thumbs nervously around each other, and moving his lips as if he were arguing earnestly with some one. After a while he looked up with an air of confirmed resolution and said : "I have a plan for her. I think I had better tell you frankly all about it. This girl, my wife's niece, is behaving like a madwoman. You, my sister's son, are behaving like a madman."

"There's a pair of us," conceded the ex-Colonel, smiling.

"I saw her yesterday, and I thought of you," continued the uncle. "I decided then and there what to do with my estate. It is my own, you know—morally as well as legally—my own in every way. I owe no man anything."

Underhill was attentive, but tranquil. He must have divined just then that his uncle's fortune, or a great part of it, was likely to slip away from him. But, as he was well off in his own right, and also very healthy in mind and body, he bore the situation easily. After arching his eyebrows pensively for a moment, he said : "Excuse me, sir ; I think you owe something to the community. To a certain extent we get and keep property through the protection of the community."

"Yes," returned the old capitalist, emphatically and proudly. "When estates are as large as mine, they are not altogether the work of one man. I am glad to acknowledge my debt to my country and my fellow-citizens. The community—that is, its works of piety and beneficence—will have one fifth of my fortune."

" It is a very splendid gift, sir. It is none too much."

"The other four fifths," continued Mather, "a million of dollars, Harry—it is a great deal of money !—the other four fifths will go to you and Miss Beaufort, on condition—"

Here he paused a moment. On the brink of divulging his plan, he trembled at it. There was a possibility that to other men, and especially to the man who was principally interested in it, it might appear like lunacy.

"Well, sir," he somewhat timorously concluded, "what condition do you propose yourself?"

"I really don't know, sir," stammered Harry, who began to see whither the conversation was leading. "Thank you, for your great good-will and generosity. I am sorry to talk of this subject. Of course, I have no right to propose the condition. I should hope it would be possible and comfortable."

"Marriage!" pronounced Mather, as if he were ordering it; and immediately asked, anxiously, "What do you say?"

Underhill looked thunderstruck and antagonistic. He drew a long breath, glanced at the old man's eager face, and then made an effort to gain time.

"Yes; but *she* won't, will she?" he prevaricated. "She's a frantic rebel, you tell me."

"Well—that is, for the present," admitted Mather, who had driven many a bargain in his life, and had the air of driving one now. "I don't want to put off a lunatic on to you. But I suppose a wedding-portion of this magnitude will restore her to sanity."

"Perhaps so," Harry smiled, not very merrily. "It seems reasonable, in a general way, to hope it. But suppose it shouldn't, then how about *me?* What sort of a chance for connubial bliss should *I* have? What if my wife should secede? I can't order a levy of three hundred thousand volunteers to bring her back."

"If a man is a good husband, his wife doesn't secede," said Mather, recollecting his own happy wedded life.

"As a rule, I dare say. But, my dear uncle, this is an exceptional case. Here is one of your high-strung, vindictive Southern girls to be wedlocked with an ex-

Colonel of the Federal forces. The very honeymoon might be a thirty-days' battle. She would hold me responsible for the bombardment of Charleston. I should have to throw up field-works. I couldn't say 'United States,' except under protection of a flag of truce. You wouldn't like to see me driven to turn Copperhead, would you?"

Mr. Mather was not amused at this raillery; on the contrary, he seemed irritated. "The wedding-journey would convert her," he affirmed. "Northern comfort and elegance would make her a good Unionist. One year of married life would turn her into a black Republican."

Harry stared at his potent and resolute relative, and uttered the embarrassed laugh of a man who is at his wits' end.

"I am tremendously scared, uncle," he said, presently. "Couldn't you detail me to lighter duty, and let somebody else storm this battery?"

"I tell you it is not heavy duty," insisted the self-willed old capitalist and fretful invalid. "You will not find it heavy when you come to it. You remember my wife, Harry? You remember our life together? You remember her last charge to me? *I* remember—I *must* remember! It is particularly my desire that my sister's son should marry my wife's niece."

"I understand all that, sir," Underhill bowed, respectfully. "I assure you that I sympathize with your recollections and feelings. But just look for a moment at my side of the case. A man ought to love his wife, sir."

"Wait till you have seen her. She is handsome enough for you—handsome enough for King Ahasuerus. She is a wonderful singer, too—so Hilton and others tell me. Finally, she is a lady—or will be one when this rebel craze wears out. She *must* be a lady—my wife's blood!"

"Ah! well, we'll see," promised Harry, inclining his head thoughtfully, and then laughing once more, like a man utterly nonplused. "Of course, I must have a look at her first. We can't be married by proxy, like kings and queens. I should like just a word with her before the ceremony takes place."

"Certainly you will see her and have a word with her," answered the uncle, pettishly.

"By Jove! I'm afraid I shall have a great many words with her," thought Underhill; but he did not say it aloud, and had the air of being tranquilly acquiescent.

"Harry, I'm obliged to you for your good-will in this matter," resumed Mather. "I can understand that to you my proposition must seem strange and savoring of family tyranny. Let me explain that I am not ordering this marriage. No, no! I simply desire that it may take place, and that you will favor it. Do what you can for it. Oblige me! If it fails through Miss Beaufort's fault, I shall not hold you responsible—I shall not seek to punish *you*. I want to bring this union about; but I will be rational in the business—I am not a madman."

Underhill looked as if he doubted this final statement; but he preserved the courtesy which even the sauciest of us usually extend to wealthy relatives; he simply asked when he was likely to meet the young lady.

"I ought to have heard from her before this," grumbled the old gentleman. "She might have tried to see me, I think."

"Perhaps she couldn't borrow a revolver," ventured Harry.

"She may have expected another call from me," Mather continued. "Well, we will go there, you and I, to-morrow."

"Hadn't we better wear some kind of helmets, to keep off scalding water?"

The uncle smiled, half fretfully, half sadly. "You forget who she is and what she has suffered," he said. "When you have seen her you will stop these jokes. It is a most pitiable case. I was very sorry for her,—as well as very angry with her."

Underhill apologized. Then he suggested that it would be well to use some art in making the call, if only to gain admittance. Why not send a friendly native ahead to ask for a parley? There was General Hilton, for instance, a pleasant-mannered, genial-hearted sort of a man—tolerably reconstructed in politics, and friendly in disposition also—the legal adviser of the Beaufort family in its days of prosperity. Why not engage him to bear a message and ask an audience?

"An ex-rebel General!" growled Mather. "It's hard for a Boston man to trust those fellows, or get on with them."

"The question is here what sort of a fellow a Charleston lady can get on with," urged Underhill. "I feel certain that Hilton can start my suit better than I can start it myself."

Then it was agreed that the whole story should be told to the General in confidence, and that he should be induced, if possible, to befriend and forward the proposed courtship.

"An excellent idea!" said Mather, who considered

it his own invention as soon as he had assented to it. "Hilton and I will call first. Then you will call. You'll take a bouquet, or something of that sort, you know. You know best what to take."

He looked quite satisfied with himself, like a man who has given full and sound counsel, and is aware of it. Next he put his hand caressingly on his nephew's shoulder, and they went amicably down to tea together.

That evening—writing to a friend in Boston—the Colonel expressed an opinion that his uncle's mind was failing—undermined by invalidism, grief, and the long excitement of the war.

CHAPTER VIII.

As early as possible on Monday Mr. Mather looked up General Hilton and communicated to him his extraordinary project of marriage.

The urbane and warm-hearted South Carolinian received the announcement with unconcealable astonishment, indeed, but also with expressions of rejoicing and promises of earnest furtherance. "I will go with you to call on Miss Beaufort," he volunteered. "I scarcely think that she will decline to receive any one who is in my company. Allow me to suggest, by-the-way, that nothing more should be said, for the present, of this matrimonial overture. That will come up in time between the young people, I trust. The utmost that you and I can hope to effect is a reconciliation between the families, and a resumption of intercourse."

Mr. Mather, having first remarked fretfully that

there never had been any intercourse, went on to state that he agreed with the General's plan of operations. The young lady should not be pestered just now about the marriage, and should simply be urged to receive her Northern connections as friends, or at least as acquaintance. "Suppose we call on her this afternoon at four," he said in his positive, business-like way. "Is the hour convenient to you? Will you meet me there?"

"Quite convenient," bowed the General. "But, if you will permit me to say so, I think we had better go to Miss Beaufort's residence together," he added, giving such respectful mention to Virginia's shanty that it almost sounded like a joke. "Your appearance there alone—excuse me for mentioning it—might renew her excitement. With your permission, I will call for you at the hotel."

"Very good—thank you," said Mr. Mather, briefly, but perhaps none the less gratefully. Then he went home to look up his nephew and inform him of the plan of operations. "In six hours from now," he said, looking at his watch, "I hope to know what we are to expect."

"Make it six hours and twenty minutes," replied the young man, with rather a grim smile. "I can wait that long."

But, although Underhill could joke, he was not merry nor tranquil. By the time it got to be a quarter of four in the afternoon he felt as if preparations were being made for his hanging. He was too uneasy to remain in the hotel, and wandered forth to divert his mind. After strolling a few minutes without any definite goal in view, it occurred to him that he might properly look up his proposed bride's place of abode, and lie in ambush for a chance sight of her. Accordingly, he set off in the direction of the shanty, walking swiftly in order to reach it before the arrival of the seniors. His air meanwhile was that of a man whose soul is perplexed and whose intentions are various. It must be remembered that he had Norah Macmorran to think of, as well as Virginia Beaufort. Chance ordained that he should stumble upon the pretty Irish songster as he turned a street corner.

"I am delighted !" he exclaimed, stopping her at once. "I am very, very glad to meet you," he added, with perilous interest.

Norah received him in a manner quite characteristic of herself. She recoiled slightly, colored deeply, glanced at him in her shy way, dropped her eyes to the pavement, and said nothing.

"I should like to tell you something," he went on eagerly. "But I mustn't."

"I suppose it is because I ought not to know it," she answered, gravely. "Of course, I mustn't wish to know it."

"Oh, you lovely little prude !" he murmured, gazing at her with frank admiration and liking. "You are perfectly fascinating."

She gave him a quick, troubled look, and then dropped her long lashes again. "I wish you wouldn't say such things, sir," she begged, in a very low tone, almost a whisper.

"Oh, dear !" complained Harry. "I wish you would hear them with the good-will that I have in saying them."

"I must bid you good-afternoon, sir," she responded without lifting her eyes. Her expression was really

troubled, and her voice constrained and serious. She
had the air of a person who, under pressure of conscience, performs a painful duty. As she spoke she
drew gently to one side and sought to pass the young
man.

"Wait, Miss Macmorran!—listen to me one moment!" he begged. Then, as she persisted in gliding
by, he added, breathlessly: "When can I see you again?
Where can I see you?"

"I don't know, sir," returned Norah, in an utterance
which was so near to a gasp that it betrayed a violently
beating heart. "Please excuse me now," she added,
with a piteous smile which besought him not to be angry. "Good-by, sir."

There was no possibility of detaining her; there
was no chance of doing any further folly. He said
"Good-by," and let her depart, lifting his hat respectfully. Then he walked onward with a perturbed countenance, muttering irrational and contradictory things.
"Little goose!" he fretted. "What does she treat me
in that style for? Probably she has had a lot of advice
from some Sister of Charity. Girls always tell. But
what a pretty expression! Oh, that shy little dropping
of the eyes! I shall fall in love with her yet. Nonsense! I can't afford it. What would Boston say?"

In his meditations concerning Miss Macmorran he
forgot that he wanted to get a glimpse of Miss Beaufort, passed the street which led toward her shanty, and
took one far below it. After a time he discovered his
mistake, and meandered back in a blundering hurry,
only to come upon his uncle and General Hilton. They
had halted at the corner nearest Virginia's humble residence, and the Carolinian was discoursing with an air

of oratory, while the Bostonian listened in silence. Underhill could discern that the old Puritan seemed worried, and was studying his fluent companion with an air of suspicion.

"Is that you, Harry?" said Mr. Mather. "I understood that you were not to be with us."

"Couldn't keep away from this part of the town," explained the young man. "I want to steal a peep, if possible, at Miss Beaufort."

"Reconnoitring!" laughed the General. "That's a good soldier. All's fair in love and in war."

There was something in Hilton's face and tone of voice which indicated that he had followed the too common Southern custom of preparing for an unusual scene or effort by a liberal refreshment of strong liquors. He grasped Underhill's hand and shook it with embarrassing fervor.

"Colonel," he said, dwelling upon and repeating the title—"Colonel, I never meet one of you gentlemen who fought against us but what my heart warms to him. By Jove, sir, you are more of a comrade of mine than any scallawag of a Southron who staid behind in the bomb-proofs and bake-shops."

"Thank you, General," smiled Harry, quite conscious the while that he owed at least a part of this fraternization to the bottle. "Comrade as much as you will, and comrade to every good soldier, Southern or Northern."

"That is the spirit of a gentleman and a Christian," declared Hilton, wheeling upon the bothered Mather. "The men in blue were the noblest and highest-souled part of your population. If you had been twenty years younger, sir, you would have had on the uniform yourself."

"I trust so," fretted the old Puritan. "I thank Heaven that I had a nephew who could wear it for me."

He looked nothing less than disgusted. He had an air of sniffing the atmosphere with his thin white nose for the hated odor of whisky. He suspected the General's mellowness with the uncharitable suspicion of a teetotaler.

"Gentlemen, this is a love-feast," continued Hilton, not in the least guessing Mather's horror of him. "I enjoy it beyond expression. But we have something to do. We must lay out our plan of battle. Colonel—my very dear Colonel—I am with you in this warfare—God bless you, sir !"

By this time the prim Bostonian had quite lost patience ; he interrupted the voluble and fervent South Carolinian. "Sir, I think it would be best to give up this call," he said. "I have a feeling that it will end in no good. My opinion is, that my nephew had better send in his card and try his chance alone."

The General shook his head with energy, and continued to address Underhill. "Your uncle, sir—with that business-like faculty which characterizes him and you Northerners generally—has lucidly and vividly explained to me the object of our conjoint operation. I can't express to you my sympathy with your purpose, and my longings for your success. She is a most lovely and noble young lady, sir. You couldn't have chosen better, nor she either."

"Remember, General, that she hasn't chosen yet," suggested Harry, gently. "We are a long way from that."

"I understand perfectly," bowed Hilton. "Sufferings must be forgotten. Aversions are to be overcome.

Suasion is needed. Time must do its work. My opinion is, Colonel, that you had better keep out of sight—in ambush. Your place, for the present, is in the timber."

"Do you think so?" grumbled Mather, still full of doubt and disgust, though there was evidently sense in the General's talk. "I had hoped that the presence of a young man might have some influence."

"Her brothers were young men," responded Hilton, turning upon him with solemnity. He paused, lifted his mangled hand and passed it across his eyes, as if to brush away the mists of strong drink. There was a tremulous expression of sorrowful reminiscence and of tender sympathy in his masculine and naturally noble countenance. He seemed to become sober at once. "It would not be well to remind her of her brothers," he resumed, shaking his head compassionately. "I wonder that the poor child keeps her reason."

"I will go," said Underhill, touched with awe and pity. "It is a good deal like a funeral," he muttered, as he turned away.

Hilton now took Mather's arm into his own and led him slowly toward the shanty. "We are going to the house of mourning," he murmured, in his deep, mellow bass—a voice something like the low bellow of a bull in pacific mood. "I have had a good deal of whisky to-day—it is one of our unfortunate Southern habits—besides, I am a weak, sad old fellow. But I am perfectly myself at this moment. There are some bereaved persons who are more solemnizing than the dead themselves. I never see this girl without seeing her attended by the ghosts of all she loved."

"Heaven be merciful to her, and restore her reason!"

sighed Mather. "I shall leave the whole interview to you."

They approached the cabin, and were crossing the little unfenced yard which separated it from the street, when Aunt Chloe came solemnly forth and handed Mather a package.

"I'se so sorry, Masr!" she whispered, beginning to cry. "It's de money you gin us. She won't let us keep it."

The Bostonian turned excitedly upon the Carolinian, as if he would hold him responsible for this act of hostility.

"Very well, aunty," said Hilton, urbanely. "The gentleman will take his money. Miss Beaufort's wishes must be respected."

Mr. Mather silently pocketed his plethoric wallet with the air of a man who pockets a very big insult.

"Gin'ral, she's a mighty triflin', spiled baby,' whimpered Aunt Chloe. "Never see no sech behavin' sence I was bawn. Mule's hind-leg longer dan his ears."

"Hush!" murmured Hilton, patting the old creature's shoulder. "Give my compliments to your young missis, and ask her to grant us the favor of an interview."

"She—she wants ter be scused, Masr," stammered Chloe. "She's powerful sorry—oughter be, anyway—but she wants ter be scused."

"Tell her," broke in Mather, excitedly—"tell her I shall soon leave Charleston, and this may be my last opportunity to meet her in this world!"

Mauma Chloe hesitated, and glanced timidly at the General.

"Yes, my good aunty," he said, "step in and tell her that."

The old woman limped eagerly into the cabin, softly closing the door after her. Mather looked angrily at Hilton, and muttered, "The girl is stark-mad!"

"We Southerners have all been mad, sir," was the grave response. "Some of us haven't yet got over it."

"How long shall you need to come to your senses?" grumbled the stalwart Unionist.

"It takes six feet of gravel to cure some frenzies. I sincerely hope that this isn't one of those cases."

At this moment Aunt Chloe reappeared, slammed the door violently behind her, and sobbed out: "She's jess 's stubborn!—jess 's stubborn!—oh, ain't dat chile stubborn! Dōn wanter do nothin'; don wanter see nobody."

"I must say that I am a little tired of being treated in this fashion," declared Mr. Mather, trembling with indignation. "One would think that I was an enemy and an infamous scoundrel!"

"I wish that my apologies could suffice for you," interposed Hilton, with melancholy urbanity. "Can you accept them on her behalf—my sincere and heart-felt apologies?"

"Please, Masr, dōn git outright mad at her," begged Mauma Chloe. "Ain't so bad 's this every day. She'll come round yit."

"Aunty," said the General, "step in once more, and ask Miss Beaufort if she will see her father's old friend Marion Hilton."

———

CHAPTER IX.

AUNT CHLOE limped into the cabin with the message, and another brief dialogue took place between the General and Mather.

"This is the kind of spirit that you raise," charged the petulant Unionist. "The girl is behaving just as the whole South behaved."

"And suffering as the whole South suffers," sighed Hilton. "My dear and good sir, isn't it just possible, in view of our anguish, to have patience with our writhing?"

"Oh, well—when you put it that way—of course one must try," grumbled the old gentleman.

Then Aunt Chloe reappeared, her face beaming with hope, and said in a loud, eager whisper : "She's willin'. Jess you go right in, Gin'ral, an' see ef you kin coax her."

Hilton entered the cabin, and Mather drew Aunt Chloe aside. "See here, my good woman," he muttered, "I want you to take back this pocket-book. I didn't give it to Miss Beaufort ; I gave it to you and your brother. You are free people, and you can keep it."

Aunt Chloe hesitated for a moment. The pocket-book was less of a temptation than we might suppose, for the reason that all through her slave-life she had got on with very little money, and her freedom had not lasted long enough to impress her deeply with the value of it. Nevertheless, in the present bare state of her cupboard, and in her vague consciousness of the many needs of her delicately nurtured young missis, the pocket-book did seem very desirable. She had to ponder a little, therefore, and to set duty against desire, before she could resist temptation and make this high-minded reply :

"I knows we's free, Masr. But we can't abear fur to plague Miss Ginny. Ef you'd a seen how she cried an' took on, you wouldn' blame us, Masr."

"What's her objection to your having something to buy necessaries with?" demanded Mather. "What right has she to object? It's inhuman."

"What we has is hern too," explained Aunt Chloe. "She knows dat ar puffeckly. Ef we has your money, it'll go to buy her vittle, an' den she'd be feedin' off de Yankees, she said."

"But feed off it yourselves, can't you? You are both old, and need good food. Buy little bits for yourselves."

"How could we eat when she wasn' eatin'?" queried the astonished Mauma. "How could we squat down to chickin' an' rice when she only had hoe-cake? O Masr, me an' Phil couldn' do dat ar noways."

"I believe you are all mad together, black and white," snapped the veteran abolitionist.

"Mebbe so," conceded Aunt Chloe, meekly. "Of cose, dey's excepshums. Dar is niggers as dŏn mind 'bout de folks what raised 'em. But dey is gin'rally niggers of no 'count fam'lies ; or dey is niggers what was bawn low an' mean ; dar's a mighty diff'rence in niggers. But, ye see, de Beauforts was gret folks from all time ; an' so de people what b'longed to 'em takes a pride in stannin' by 'em ; for we gits a heap o' things, Masr, from some of d' ole han's—gets taters an' meal an' poke—an' it helps powerfully. Besides, as fur Miss Ginny an' me, she was my own pertickler chile—jess my own own, to nuss an' fotch up."

"And a pretty bringing up you made of it!" sighed Mather.

"O Masr! you hain't seen the las' o' her; you'll see mo' an' better some day; you'll be mighty glad an' proud of her yit."

Then there was a silence for some minutes, the old gentleman walking impatiently up and down the little yard, and the old negress moving her lips as if in whispered prayer. At last Mather halted by the side of Aunt Chloe, and murmured: "The General stays a long time. I can't but hope that he is succeeding."

"Dat's jess d' way I was feelin' myself," responded the Mauma. "I'se been a-layin' it befo' the Lawd. I has a hope."

Presently the General appeared, closed the door softly behind him, and joined the pair. They gazed at him for a moment in speechless suspense and anxiety.

"I am sincerely obliged to you, Mr. Mather, for your patience," he said, with grave urbanity.

"What news?" demanded the old man, who had no patience at all. "Will Miss Beaufort see me?"

"I am extremely sorry to say, and I apologize to you most heartily for it, that she still desires to be excused from an interview."

Mather stared in angry astonishment, and Aunt Chloe fell to sobbing and moaning.

"Run in and talk to your baby, aunty," whispered the General, wiping his eyes with his hand. "She is crying—terribly!"

"O Mas'r! dōn' go yit!" begged the old woman, as she moved toward the cabin. "Wait till I kin say one las' word to her."

"Am I to stay here all night?" exclaimed the offended capitalist, speaking to himself rather than 10 Hilton. "I don't care to be trifled with any longer." Then, recollecting his courtesy, he glanced at the General and added: "I was not alluding to you, sir. You have done your best to favor me, and I am sincerely obliged to you. Let me ask plainly what is your opinion as to this young person's intentions?"

"She means non-intercourse," sighed Hilton. "There is, I am grieved to say, no doubt as to that."

"Did she refuse my offer—the whole of it—every part of it?"

"She declined all assistance."

"'Not a Yankee dollar'—did she use those words?"

The General gazed at him gravely, reflected a moment, and bowed in silence.

"Very well!"—Mr. Mather feebly stamped his foot here—"then I will go."

"Could you wait one moment for Aunt Chloe's return?" pleaded Hilton.

Mather, who had already turned toward the street, paused irresolutely, and slowly faced about. "Oh, I will wait—it's of no use," he mumbled. "What did Miss Beaufort say? What was the tenor of her conversation?"

The General shook his head repeatedly, like one who recalls a very painful scene. "It was dolorous," he said, in a low, compassionate tone. "I had no full idea before of the soreness of her heart. Please excuse me from rehearsing the interview. It can do no good. Moreover, such grief is a confidence—a sacred trust. Here comes Aunt Chloe."

The old negress had no amicable message to deliver.

4

She looked out, shook her head sorrowfully, and closed the door again.

Mather's milky face flushed to a deep carnation, and he said, in a voice trembling with renewed wrath, "I have waited, you see."

"I beg that you will patiently and mercifully look upon this as a temporary insanity of grief," was the meek response.

"General, I thank you for your patience," said Mather, suddenly reverting to courtesy. "You have had need to be patient with me, as well as with her. Ah, dear! I am sadly disappointed. This shakes me. I don't know that I can get home alone. Will you kindly go to the hotel with me?"

Hilton took his arm, and the two walked slowly away in silence, the wooden-legged veteran supporting the invalid sexagenarian. They had barely reached Meeting Street when they were encountered by Underhill, advancing with the swift, strong step of youth, and the smile of health and gayety. He presented an almost painful contrast to the two more or less crippled and entirely disheartened men with whom he joined himself.

"I couldn't go far away, you see," he laughed. "What was the result?"

"We return to Boston," said Mather, grimly.

Underhill glanced at his uncle, as if to see whether he could bear further questioning, and then dropped into silence. But Hilton, who knew less of the old man's feebleness and nervous irritability, ventured to protest, "I sincerely hope not at once."

"It was dreadful!" insisted Mather. "Shocking!"

"It was very sad, Colonel," murmured Hilton.

"The house of mourning doesn't always welcome a guest."

"Not a Yankee dollar!" broke out the old banker, savagely repeating the phrase which at once rejected his good-will and threw scorn upon the intrinsic result of his life's labor. "She wouldn't even suffer those faithful old negroes to accept bread from a Yankee."

He drew out his pocket-book, flourished it as if it were a weapon, and then of a sudden handed it to Hilton. "General, will you favor me by devoting this money to the comfort of such needy Charlestonians as will deign to make use of it?"

"Take it, General—you will oblige him," said Underhill, seeing that Hilton hesitated.

"Thank you for your noble gift to our poor," bowed the urbane veteran. "But, Mr. Mather, let me also beg for a little compassion of spirit toward this unhappy young lady."

"I hope you won't give her up, sir," added Harry. "Time will probably change her opinions and feelings."

The old man shook his head angrily and walked on without speaking. But a minute or so later he looked up at his nephew and said: "I'll grant her a year—perhaps two years. I'll make my will as I told you, and give her a year for reflection. But meanwhile let her take care of herself."

When they reached the hotel Mather retired to his room and sofa, broken down physically by the struggle and defeat of the day. Underhill drew the General to his own room, supplied him abundantly with his favorite refreshment, and catechised him about the Beauforts. It was a subject which Hilton loved; he had many stories to tell concerning it. At first he was stern and sad, like a stoic of the Roman Empire talking of the greatness of the republic, or a prophet of the captivity recalling the glories of Zion. But, when the whisky had a little mellowed his sorrow, a tint of humor and even of compassionate satire stole over his reminiscences, and made him amusing.

"The Colonel, Virginia's father, was not the great man of his race," he said. "There was a declension in the vitality and force of the breed during his incarnation of it. His grandfather, the old General of the Revolution, made the Beauforts. I don't know but that he unmade them also. Every Beaufort since his time has tried to live in his lordly style. That venerable ghost, sir, has been a sort of vampire, sucking the blood of prosperity out of the family. His example and his supposed demands have done much to ruin it. Colonel Beaufort, for instance, when he came to the estate, found himself with three hundred thousand dollars in property and two hundred thousand in debts. He seemed to think, sir, that that made five hundred thousand dollars, and he proceeded to live accordingly. He kept up his city house and two country houses; he held on to both his plantations—some six thousand badly-worked acres; he entertained a score of impoverished relatives, and at least another score of their attendants; he wouldn't sell one of his three hundred head of negroes. All this he did because the old General had done it; but to do it he had to pay interest on enormous loans. The result was that the year 1860 found him in debt to nearly the whole extent of his property.

"Then came the war, with its wastage of substance, and its depreciation of what remained. The Colonel's contributions to the Confederacy were enormous. He gave liberally at first, and the details took the rest. His horses went to the front; his cows, pigs, and poultry followed them; his live-stock was reduced to an old poll-parrot. Even his sweet-potatoes and corn-nubbins took up their line of march for Lee's bivouacs. His carpets were gradually swept off, and cut up into blankets for the soldiers. As for wool blankets such as Beauforts had always slept under, there wasn't so much of a one left as would toss a small abolitionist. The damask window-curtains were made into raiment, and the mulatto house-maids capered about in figured crimson. I remember Uncle Phil looking insolvently sumptuous in a suit made out of a green-and-gold piano-cover. All the carriages went for ambulances, except one venerable coach, the last relic of the old General's personal pomp. It was an amazing spectacle, sir; you couldn't call it anything but a spectacle—there wasn't an atom of use or service in it. You couldn't have ventured to drive it out of the grounds without taking an axe and a coil of rope along for repairs. Its panels needed a barrel or so of paint and varnish, and its top had been much disfigured by the roosting of poultry. However, all that mattered little, for there were no horses to draw it. There were not even any poultry to roost on it.

"At last, sir, just before he died, the Colonel's spirit broke a little. He was driven to sell one of his plantations, which was painful, and, furthermore, he took the pay for it, which was ruinous. When the war ended, the Beauforts had in hand a vast amount of Confederate bills, worth a good deal less than so much brown wrapping-paper. It would have been no waste, but rather an economy, to light fires with them, instead of with

pine-knots.   Then there were the debts; the estate had
fairly wallowed in our Southern credit system; it was
bemired in it and incrusted with it.   The liberation of
the negroes, the only unmortgaged portion of it, left it
absolutely no estate at all.   I judge, sir, that secession
cost the Colonel alone more than he supposed it would
cost the entire South.

"Now, you smile at this story," continued Hilton,
with a sigh.   "I don't know that I blame you.   There
is something ludicrous in building such immense pur-
poses and expectations upon such a small basis.   But it
made a tragedy.   The Beaufort history during the last
four years has been a long tragedy.   It was awful to
see how fast destitution and degradation and battle
swept them into the other world.   The poor relations
died for lack of sufficient nourishing food.   The good
old Colonel—a most honorable and kind-hearted man—
died of a broken heart, rather than of fever.   His boys
fell, you know how.   Of all the breed there are only
two lean and half-crazed women left.   You can pity
them, I am certain.   Can you do anything for them?
Can you bring your uncle to use further patience?"

Underhill was greatly interested and touched.   "I
will try," he promised.   After a little reflection, he
added: "It isn't easy to bend him.   Mild as he looks,
he is amazingly stubborn, once he has come to a decision."

At this moment the pale and haggard face of Mather
looked into the room, and his feeble, monotonous voice
announced: "We shall leave to-morrow morning, Harry.
Be sure that everything is ready."

CHAPTER X.

SOME weeks after Mr. Mather's departure for the North, Virginia Beaufort's only aunt and surviving relative, a widow of some fifty years or so, named Mrs. Dumont, known aforetime as Miss Anna Beaufort, gave up the uninhabitable shanty which she had occupied in Columbia, and sought shelter in the scarcely inhabitable shanty in Charleston.

She brought not a dollar with her, nor any raiment except the rather shabby clothing on her back, and, in short, no possessions beyond her highly-valued birthright in the Beaufort blood and name. It was another hungry mouth to feed, and two more not very skillful hands to work. Meantime Southern prosperity had not revived; the fallen and desolated city absolutely swarmed with poor; there was little labor to be done, and wages were meager. Under such circumstances it may readily be supposed that the two Beauforts and their two faithful adherents were often in straits. Let us glance into their wretched abode, and see what manner of life they led.

On a certain day, which turned out to be eventful, Virginia and Aunt Chloe were ironing. The young lady—who had that morning washed her calico frock and hung it out to dry—wore a dress of black alpaca, which had seen better days, and which was her Sunday garment. The sleeves were carefully tucked above her elbows, revealing a pair of large, round, firm arms, a little reddened by exposure and toil. Her face, though still beautiful, and noticeably high-bred in expression, was thinner and paler than when we saw it last. She had the air of being physically jaded, and also of being depressed in spirit. A shrewd observer would have guessed that she got either insufficient food or food of a poor quality.

Behind her, seated in the rush-bottomed chair, and dabbling masculine collars in a bowl of starched water, was her aunt. A tallish and angular lady was Mrs. Dumont, with a regularly cut but haggard countenance, carelessly arranged iron-gray hair, and fierce, unquiet, coal-black eyes. She had been a handsome woman once, and reminiscences of beauty still lingered about her, though sadly eclipsed by suffering and bitterness of spirit. There was something in the shape of her forehead and in her expression which indicated a very moderate intellectual development. A frequent gesture with her was to put one hand to her breast, draw a quick gasp, and roll her eyes upward. She had had abundant cause during the four past years for this signal of distress.

"Aunt Dumont, what are you sighing about?" demanded Virginia, turning upon her relative with just a little impatience.

"It does worry me inexpressibly, Virginia, to see you going barefoot," complained Mrs. Dumont. Her tone was dolorous, and her enunciation so deliberate as to be nearly a drawl ; but, for all that, the voice had a cultivated cadence, and was full and mellow ; it was the pleasant voice of the South and of Beauforts.

"You must get used to it," said the girl. "I don't want to wear out my one pair of shoes. I don't see the slightest prospect of ever getting another."

Mrs. Dumont (smiting her breast and rolling her eyes at Providence). "Oh, dear, dear, dear !"

Aunt Chloe. "An' she might roll in her coach, jess

like all de Beauforts befo' her, 'stead o' trampin' round like poo' white folks."

Virginia. "Aunt Chloe, you wear my patience harder than I wear my shoes. It will give out, some day."

Mrs. Dumont. "Virginia must conduct herself as a Beaufort, Chloe. She must never forget that she is a Beaufort."

Virginia. "I am not likely to forget it, aunt. I suppose I have had those very words said to me ten thousand times. My belief is, that I began to hear them before I could talk."

Mrs. Dumont. "I'm sure I don't know of anything more proper to say, especially in our present humiliation, when we are so likely to lose heart."

Virginia. "Quite proper, my dear aunt. I didn't mean to be satirical."

Aunt Chloe. 'Pears to me dar's things might be said what 'd fotch in mo' vittle. What we wants is words what has got some nourishment in 'em."

Virginia (with a weary sigh). "Oh, yes, Mauma Chloe, if a Beaufort could say them!"

Aunt Chloe. "Poo' folks ain't reel shu' enough Beauforts. We's awful poo', Miss Ginny. De times hits hard. Kwishins on mules' foots done gone out o' fashin."

Mrs. Dumont (fretfully). "It does appear to me that Uncle Phil might earn more. If I were a man—"

Virginia. "Don't say a word against Phil. Do you know, aunt, why he wasn't here to dinner?"

Mrs. Dumont. "He was asked out; he told me so. Stuffed himself somewhere else."

Virginia. "It was because there wasn't enough for us and him too. He earned our pork and corn-bread, and then went and begged for himself."

Mrs. Dumont (rolling her eyes and sighing). "Oh, dear, dear, dear! The broken-down creature!"

Aunt Chloe. "Dōn you go mournin' 'bout it, Miss Anna. Phil got his belly full, I reckon. (*Aside.*) Dōn know, though. Dar ain't so very many bellyfuls in dese yere parts sence de wah."

Mrs. Dumont shed a few tears, which were rather drops of wrath than of pity. She positively could not help being angry with Uncle Phil for having come short of rations. The knowledge of the touching and worrying fact was but another wound to her already sore spirit. We must not consider her with condemnation, nor even with wonder. Among the miserable, petulance is far more common, and, for physical reasons, necessarily more common, than sympathy. One result of the poor woman's fretful grief was an access of unusual humility. "This is unendurable, Virginia," she sighed. "At times I don't know but that you ought to write to that Mather. I suppose he meant well."

"Why doesn't *he* write?" demanded the girl. She spoke with a very moderate degree of bitterness, as if her constancy had been a little sapped by poverty.

"Bekase you treated him so mean," broke in Aunt Chloe. "Wouldn' speak to him no mo' 'n' ef he was a free nigger. Never was no decent man so treated befo', sence de good ole Dan'l."

"I think Virginia behaved very properly," said Mrs. Dumont, struggling back to dignity of manner and greatness of mind. "I think she behaved like a Beaufort."

"An' here she is bar'foot, like me an' Phil," grunted the Mauma.

"It's a perfect shame to Mather—my own sister's

husband! He's just like all of them. Oh, how I hate those Vandals!"

"He is not responsible for my bare feet," remarked Virginia. "I refused everything."

"I *hope* it hurt his feelings," exclaimed the senior lady, her black eyes sparkling almost savagely. "'Not a Yankee dollar!' It was just the right thing to say to him."

"Mus' hurt him powerful to keep his dollars," scoffed Aunt Chloe. "Reckon he dōn sleep nights, dey worries him so."

For a time there was silence. The ironing went on wearisomely and drearily. Mrs. Dumont soaked and patted her collars, or sighed and rolled her eyes, by turns. After some minutes she resumed the subject of the Boston Vandal and his offer.

"Virginia, I don't know—I am still thinking about it, my dear—I don't know but you made a mistake."

"My good aunt, I can't change my mind half a dozen times a day," replied the young lady, with a mild sarcasm.

"An' it's an awful pity fur you, Miss Ginny," lectured Aunt Chloe. "Women-folks is like niggers—can't have deir way much in dis yere world; gits along easier ef dey *can* change deir minds."

At this moment Uncle Phil, a very meager and withered old darky in these days, wandered feebly up to the cabin-door and sat down on the threshold with a weary sigh. Mrs. Dumont glanced at him fretfully, thinking, no doubt, that he ought to be at work. Virginia asked, "Did you get a good dinner, uncle?"

"Specs so, Miss Ginny," mumbled Phil, evasively. "Would'n' be likely to find a dinnah anyways but good. Never complained of no dinnah yit, when I got one."

The girl eyed him sharply, and was evidently about to question him further, when he suddenly exclaimed : " Fo' God I fo'got. I'se gittin' so em'ty-headed ! Yere's a lettah from de pose-office."

He put his shaky, horny hand into the one remaining pocket of his wonderfully shabby cotton jacket, and produced a large business envelope. Virginia hurriedly tore it open and glanced through the contents of the voluminous inclosure, while the others watched her with the anxious eyes of wretches who dream daily of marvelous interpositions of grace.

"Oh, dear ! " she presently exclaimed. " Oh, this is very sad ! I am sorry. I wish I had given him a kind word."

" What is it ? Who ? " screamed Mrs. Dumont, in the sharp voice of one tortured by suspense.

" Mr. Mather—he is dead ! " replied Virginia, looking at her with a momentary solemnity, and then eagerly returning to her reading.

" As—ton—ishing ! " exclaimed the elder lady, as if Yankees were a kind of monsters who lived for ever.

" Oh, dear ! I wish I had given him a word of kindness," Virginia repeated, her eyes still running along the lines.

" What *do* you mean, Virginia ? " begged Mrs. Dumont. " Has it ended well ? Do, for mercy's sake, speak ! "

" It is amazing ! " exclaimed the girl, her face suddenly flushing crimson. " He has not changed his will. I can still have that money—if I choose it."

There was a brief period of silence. The beating of

hearts was at first too violent to admit of speech. Next
after dumb amazement and mere pulsation of emotion
came the reflection, what should be done ? Then arose
an eager, confused, shrill talk of three excited women,
as wild and dissonant as the vociferation of birds, and
as difficult to understand. It is impossible to report the
first outburst of such a conversation. The speakers con-
tradicted each other and themselves. In one breath,
for instance, Mrs. Dumont alluded to the deceased millionaire as "that Yankee," and in the next called him
"brother-in-law Mather." She had counsel after counsel to give, and differed from herself minute by minute.
There was only one thing that she stuck to : "Whatever you do, Virginia, I trust you will do it like a Beaufort."

"Oh, yes," the girl at last retorted, impatiently.
"How did they do this sort of thing ? "

"I don't know," gasped Mrs. Dumont, as helpless as
a child in face of the question. "But surely whatever
you decide to do you can remember that you are a Beaufort."

Then Aunt Chloe (who had hitherto confined herself
chiefly to praising God and blessing Mather) burst indignantly into the discussion, and, with arms akimbo,
delivered a set speech.

"Miss Ginny, you has got to be sensible now," she
declared. "Dōn go to sayin' dat ar ole-time nonsense
over an' over. Miss Anna here talks like d' ole poll-
parrot. He useter holler 'I'm a Bufor' ! I'm a Bufor' ! '
jess 's loud 's he could screech. Laws ! he'd larned it
's peart 's Miss Anna. Some of the plantin' han's useter think he was a Beaufort, shu enough. Does ye 'member him ? He had a hook nose, an' a limp like your

granpa after he got gouty. Ef dar ever was a bird proud of b'longin' to a fam'ly, 'twas dat ar ole, limpin', towsled poll-parrot. But de fam'ly ain't what it was. Things has mightily changed with it. Dar ain't no sense now hollerin' 'I'm a Bufor'! I'm a Bufor'!' De time am come fur to quit foolin' an' talkin' bird-talk 'bout folks what's done gone to glory. De time am come fur you to think how you's gwine ter git some mo' shoes an' stockin's."

"Do hush, Chloe!" interposed Mrs. Dumont, showing no offense at the Mauma's satire, and indeed taking no notice of it, so preoccupied was she with curiosity. "I want to know more about this letter. Oh, dear! what a loss it was to break my spectacles! Is it the young gentleman who writes, Virginia? I hope his tone is respectful. Of course a Yankee would be in a great rage to see so much money taken out of his hands."

"It is *not* the young gentleman who writes," said Virginia. She pondered a moment, drew herself up to her full height, and added, "And the money is *not* taken out of his hands."

"What!" screamed Aunt Chloe, comprehending with the quickness of fear. "Ain't you gwine ter take anything? O Miss Ginny!"

Here the old creature fell to wringing her horny hands and sobbing like a distressed child.

———

CHAPTER XI.

AFTER a long silence Mrs. Dumont murmured, "It is like a Beaufort"; but she was evidently much dismayed, and a tear rolled down her haggard cheek.

"I should like to read the letter—if I had my spectacles," she added, in a shaking voice. "Are you sure, Virginia, that you understand it? Are you sure that there are conditions?"

The girl read the letter aloud. The purport of it was clear enough—she could have the fortune if she would take the man.

"The question is," sighed Mrs. Dumont, and stopped to meditate—"the question is," she resumed, "what ought a Beaufort to do under the circumstances?"

"Go bar'foot," scoffed Aunt Chloe, loudly and wrathfully.

"Go hungry," echoed Uncle Phil, in a feeble, waspish tone, which gave notice of physical *malaise* and discontent.

Virginia turned upon him, eyed him sharply, and asked: "What's the matter with you, uncle? You look sick."

"'Specs likely d' ole man's dinnah distresses him," said Mauma Chloe, bitterly. "Nothin' sets wuss dan sour grapes."

"O Phil!" moaned the young lady. "Didn't you have any dinner? Didn't you have any at all?"

He tried to smile cheerfully, but there was hunger in his eyes, and Virginia understood their dumb complaint. She sat down on her washing-bench, covered her face with her bare arms, like a desperate infant, and sobbed convulsively. Mrs. Dumont gazed at her with

an air of stately reproof, as if she wanted to say, "My
dear, bear it like a Beaufort." Aunt Chloe, harrowed
by the grief of her darling, made at her brother, and
demanded : "What'n you go an' tell her 'bout havin'
no dinnah fur ? Mus' like to make her cry."

"Fo' God, didn't tell her nuffin of de sawt," protested Uncle Phil, resentfully. "Twas all got up 'mongst
you women-folks. Dat's de kind o' jestice a man gits.
I gits 's much jestice as I do hoe-cake."

"Aunt Dumont," said Virginia, lifting her head
from her knees, "give Phil that fifty-cent piece."

"It's the last money in the house," pleaded the startled lady.   "It was for supper."

"Give it to him," insisted the girl. "We'll eat alike
as long as we do eat.—Phil, do you take that and buy
some food. I won't stop crying till you do."

She was such a domineering, beloved, spoiled, ador-
able pet ! they were all, black and white, accustomed
to yield to her every passionate desire. The old negro's
face was pitiful ; it was full of shame and humiliation
and feebleness ; he had the cringing expression of a
famished dog. He wanted to refuse the precious gift,
but he was dragged toward it by the urgent longing of
hunger ; and then there was the hope, of course, that
some other half-dollar would ere long come on the wings
of happy accident.

"I'se an ole man, or I wouldn' do it," he stammered
as he took the money. "It'll git suppah, too, Miss
Ginny," as he tottered out of the shanty.

"We'll have our supper to-morrow morning," said
Virginia. "We must go to bed early to-night—as we
have done before."

"Something *must* be done," groaned Mrs. Dumont.

"I don't know, Virginia—of course it is very dreadful
—but Providence seems to be driving us to it—I don't
know but you ought to—accept."

"Dar, Miss Ginny!" exclaimed Aunt Chloe, joyfully.
"Do give in! Why, its jess mirac'lous. Never heerd
Miss Anna talk so much sense befo'."

"I shall have to take him," moaned Virginia. She
burst into a hysterical laugh, and added, "For Uncle
Phil's sake."

"Glory to God!" shouted the delighted Mauma.
"Oh, de Lawd bless your innocent, sweet soul, my own
blessed baby! You has some sense, after all, if you is
a bawn lady. Blessed be God dat he fotched us down
to fifty cents! Dar's no cure for an em'ty head like an
em'ty puss."

"And do you really mean it, my child?" asked Mrs.
Dumont, vainly striving to dissemble her satisfaction.

"I—*must*," was the desperate response.

Mrs. Dumont's eyes sparkled joyfully; nevertheless,
she pursed her lips with gravity and dignity; then came
the matured and weighty judgment: "Virginia, I don't
know but you have made a mistake."

"Oh, my dear aunt! let us think one thing or the
other."

"I want you always," pursued the dear aunt, trying
to whimper, "always to think and act like a Beaufort."

"Dar goes d' ole poll-parrot agin," broke in Aunt
Chloe, out of patience with this unpractical gabble.
"Never no Beauforts what I ever heerd of let deirselves
starve when dar was vittle handy."

Virginia uttered one of those bursts of spasmodic
and mistimed laughter which betoken hysteria or desperation of spirit. "I am the first Beaufort that ever

went hungry," she said. "I have fasted enough for the whole breed. I never will keep Lent again as long as I live."

"Vir—gin—ia!" screamed Mrs. Dumont, who was a very churchly person. "How recklessly you talk! I believe you have lost your senses. The Beauforts have always respected the ordinances."

Uncle Phil now reappeared with a large piece of corn-cake in one hand, another not very much smaller piece in his mouth, and something like a buckler of the same under his arm.

"Yere's fur twenty," he mumbled. "An' yere's twenty dollars, Miss Ginny. General Hilton he met up with me an' tole how it was somethin' he collected for ye out'n what was owin' to yer father."

The girl took the bills with hesitation. "Why didn't he keep it himself?" she said. "My father's estate is indebted to him for thousands of dollars."

"Virginia, that has nothing to do with it," struck in Aunt Dumont. "This was owing to you, and, of course, General Hilton ought to pay it, and it is your duty to keep it. His own bill is entirely another matter. When he sends that, we will see about it," concluded the good lady as composedly as if she had thousands in bank.

"It is a pure charity," declared Virginia, who was far from suspecting, by-the-way, that it was a dole out of the Mather pocket-book. "However—it is food—I must take it."

"Aunt Chloe, hand me a bit of that corn-cake," was Mrs. Dumont's next remark. She could have got it herself easily, but she had not altogether lost the stately habit of bygone days, and retained an almost automatic preference for being waited on. "I feel," she added, as she commenced eating heartily—"I feel a little empty-headed."

"'Specs likely, Miss Anna," responded Chloe, whether satirically or not it was difficult to say. She gave a large piece to Mrs. Dumont, and then pressed a still larger one upon Virginia, who was surveying the coarse edible with an interest which any one unused to scenes of hunger would have found wofully pathetic. Lastly, the unselfish soul helped herself, and devoured like an earthquake.

"You didn' miss much in missin' our dinnah, ole man," she said to her brother. "'Twan't enough for one Yankee's dog."

"Greedy Vandals!" mumbled Mrs. Dumont, with her mouth full. "Fattening on our possessions!"

"Ef dat was all dey had," gobbled Aunt Chloe, "'twouldn't make 'em 'possum-fat."

"How food does restore one's spunk and self-respect!" said Virginia, smiling over her slice of toasted dough. "I feel as if I had on shoes and stockings."

Then Mrs. Dumont broke out with a prediction that this payment of twenty dollars would prove to be the beginning of a turn in the family fortunes. If General Hilton had begun to collect, there was no reason why he should stop. She had faith to believe that the Beauforts would recover all they had lost.

"Da 's jess d' way 'tis," corroborated Uncle Phil. "Gin'ral Hilton he said dis yere money wasn' all—said dar was as much mo' a-comin'—anyhow, kinder hoped so."

"As much more!" exclaimed Mrs. Dumont. "I should think so! Ever so much more! Two hundred thousand dollars, at least.—Virginia, I do hope you won't be hasty."

"Dōn you be a spiled baby now," eagerly counseled Mauma Chloe, addressing her pet. "Dōn you go fur to mind Phil's nonsinse. Wish he'd choke hisself with hoe-cake!"

"I wish the Yankee was to marry *you*, Aunt Dumont," laughed Virginia.

"Horrors! I wouldn't have him!" screamed the elder lady, as much in earnest as if the thing were possible, and perhaps much more so.

"And yet you counsel *me*," exclaimed the girl, flushing with sudden passion.

"Nothing of the sort," interrupted Mrs. Dumont. "I did *not*. It was your own notion. What I said was, don't make a mistake. I leave it to Aunt Chloe."

"Oh, what *shall* I do?" cried the haughty, sensitive, vehement, unreasonable child, the product of generations of grandeeism and years of civil war. "The idea fills me with loathing—the mere idea of this match. My very name seems to forbid it."

"Yes," whimpered Aunt Dumont—"all the Beauforts who fell fighting those wretches!—O Virginia, think of them!"

However absurd her talk might be under the circumstances, and whether the poor lady desired the Underhill marriage or not, it was clear enough that she was quite sincere in her grief and hatred. Her emotion aroused all the passion which lay in the ardent nature of her niece.

"Think of them!" she replied, in a high, wild tone. "I *do!* They are never out of my thoughts. I *can't* marry a Yankee."

"Dar ain't no Yankee ast you yit," stormed in Aunt Chloe, trembling with disappointment and grief. "You's got to wait till you's ast."

"I *shall* wait—and wait *after* that!" declared the girl.

The old Mauma collapsed into a whimper. "Ain't you gwine to write to him?" she pleaded.

"No!"

There was a brief silence. Mrs. Dumont, who perceived that she had vindicated her character as a good Southerner at a frightful expense, looked considerably dismayed. "I don't know, Virginia," she stammered—"after all, I don't know—but this may be a mistake. I advise you not to be hasty. You are always so hasty!"

"Haven't I decided like a Beaufort?" retorted the niece, impatiently, not to say scornfully.

"Oh, yes," sighed the perplexed and worried aunt. "But—if General Hilton shouldn't collect—what is to become of us?"

"Just what has become of all the other Beauforts. We shall die, when we do die, honorably."

It was not ranting; it was the sullen utterance of grief and pride and desperation; it had a dismal accent of finality.

CHAPTER XII.

A CONSIDERABLE time slipped by without bringing to the affairs of the Beauforts any change worthy of record.

No further word arrived from the executors of Mr. Mather. They had fully explained in their one letter that they were empowered to advise Miss Beaufort of the conditions of the will, and also to mail her a liberal advance in case she assented to those conditions. Having made this formal and adamantine statement, they had fallen back into silence and mystery.

Mysterious, also, and to an even more perplexing and exasperating degree, remained Mr. Harry Underhill. Far from offering hand and heart, far from throwing himself in hot haste at the feet of the Beauforts, he did not write a line. It began to look as if this irrational, low Yankee did not hanker after the noble alliance which had been arranged for him. Exasperating suspicions arose that he looked upon it as a matter of no consequence, which he might attend to at his leisure, or possibly leave entirely unnoticed. There were shamefaced anxieties lest he had fallen in love with some one else ; there were even unnatural terrors lest the abominated Vandal might be dead.

Meantime, the wolf of poverty went in and out of the cabin at his ease. The heroine of our story was daily driven to marvel and shudder at the bigness of his mouth. Jobs of work were few, and the wage thereof scant. The pocket-book, which had been intrusted to General Hilton, drawn upon as it was by the many-headed pauperism of Charleston, eventually ran empty. As for the Beaufort estate, not only were its debits far superior to its credits, but the latter could not be gathered in by any industry of attorneys. The situation was very like that of the Irish squire who said, " Sir, if I could collect my debts—and by my debts I mean what I owe to other people—I should be in easy circumstances."

Things being thus with the denizens of Mauma Chloe's

shanty, it is not wonderful that they should often discuss the Mather testament. A day came—Virginia and Mrs. Dumont and Chloe being present—when they had an unusually full and decisive interchange of views on the subject.

"I can't help thinking about it," sighed the senior Beaufort lady. "It is dreadful not to know anything at all of a matter which concerns us so much."

Virginia. "It seems like something which happened in my childhood, or to somebody else. It is fading out of memory."

Mrs. Dumont. "Such struggling and pinching! it is enough to fade out everything. Oh, what grubbing and pinching! *So* degrading!"

Virginia. "They talk about the war being over. It isn't over for the widows and orphans."

Mrs. Dumont (spitefully). "No, and never will be! How can it be?"

Aunt Chloe. "Keeps it up deirselves—some on 'em. Blessed is de peacemakers. Does you 'spose wah-makers is blessed, too?"

Mrs. Dumont. "I'm sure God ought not to starve us. We work hard enough—and I've begged, too—actually asked charity—a born lady!"

Aunt Chloe (aside). "An' a bawn goose, too. Lady enough, but goose too much."

Virginia. "Chloe, I wish you wouldn't mutter. Everything irritates me."

Aunt Chloe. "It's dumb ager—comes o' workin' befo' breakfuss."

Virginia. "How else are we to have breakfast? Oh, dear! how are we to have it to-morrow morning? Only a few cents left!"

Aunt Chloe. "Dar's enough fur you to send a lettah to Bosting an' say you's willin' to be richer'n King Solomon."

Mrs. Dumont. "And abandon her commanding position!—O Virginia, your attitude is so noble! No other girl in the South is scorning such a fortune for the sake of Southern principles. Only a Beaufort could do it. Still, you may have to bend, if General Hilton doesn't collect. Why *doesn't* he attend to his business? There are thousands of dollars owing us—thousands on thousands of dollars. Oh, if I were a man!"

Virginia. "General Hilton can't make his own collections, I fear. He dresses very shabbily—nothing but old homespun."

Mrs. Dumont (loftily). "It is the dress of heroes and gentlemen!"

Aunt Chloe. "An' niggers. You dŏn see no Yankees in dose kind o' cloes. Reckon homespun's out o' fashion in Bosting.—Miss Ginny, dere you is barefoot agin! You'll run a nail inter you' foot some day."

Mrs. Dumont (shuddering). "O Virginia! lockjaw! We shall *have* to give up. We shall have to swallow our pride and hate."

Aunt Chloe. "Dar ain't much else to swaller. Mighty poo' feedin' dey is, too. Mule can't live on his own kickin'."

There was an interval of silence, only broken by the dull thump of the irons on the ironing-table, and by the frequent sighs of Mrs. Dumont. Then the dreary, wearisome, contradictory conversation resumed its uncertain course, now flowing in a current of assent to the inevitable, and now whirling into eddies of aversion and revolt.

"Why doesn't he write to me?" complained Virginia, alluding, of course, to Underhill. "Does he mean that I shall say the first word? That is a man's business."

"So haughty and cruel!" snapped Mrs. Dumont. "He means to roll us in the dust. Brother-in-law Mather was decent compared to this creature. He wants to humble the Beauforts. That is Yankee humanity and courtesy, I suppose! I don't believe there is one chivalrous family—not one family at all like ours —in the whole North."

"Miss Lizabeth was a Beaufort," remarked Aunt Chloe. "*She* didn' take no shame to marry a Yankee."

"Oh, my poor sister!" interrupted Mrs. Dumont. "How she must have suffered among those people! What a mistake she made!"

"She was de brightest an' sensiblest of d'hull fam'ly," declared Aunt Chloe, stoutly.

"She was a very superior woman," agreed Mrs. Dumont, proudly. "She must have been a very queen in Boston. Poor Elizabeth! I never saw her but twice after that unhappy marriage. She looked healthier and more cheerful than I expected. She bore up under it as only a Beaufort could."

"Reckon 'twan't no gret affliction in it," opined the Mauma. "Didn' have to live on hoe-cake an' go bar'-legged."

At this point Virginia, who had apparently been carrying on a sad and stern meditation, broke out in her impassioned way: "Aunt Dumont! *shall* I write?"

"O child! what can a relative say? Remember who you are," was the enlightening response.

"An' kinder 'member, too, what you've got," added Aunt Chloe, surlily.

5

"I don't love him," said Virginia, much as if she had been trying to, and regretted that she could not. Then, bursting into a sardonic laugh, she added, "Who ever asked me to?"

"It's a shame," affirmed Mrs. Dumont, with severe emphasis—"it's a burning shame that he treats you so! He ought to have written at once. A South Carolina gentleman would have done that. Well, perhaps not to a Yankee girl," she subjoined, on reflection. "No, indeed—of course not!" she concluded with proper spirit.

"This is such nonsense!" exclaimed Virginia, impatiently. "I mean my hesitation is nonsensical," she explained, remembering her aunt's feelings. "I *must* write, and I *will*."

"Oh, my child! what are you going to write?— what?" asked Mrs. Dumont, pressing her hand convulsively to her breast and rolling up her eyes.

"I shall say that I consent to the marriage," replied the girl, meanwhile searching the drawer of the ironing-table for her meager stock of writing materials.

"Oh, mercy!" gasped the elder lady. "To think of a Beaufort coming to that!"

"Shall I refuse, then?" demanded Virginia, sullenly.

"No, no! I didn't say so. Dear, dear, dear! how shall we put it? On reflection, my dear, I think you have put it very delicately; it is as though the proposal had come from him, the ungentlemanly fellow! Yes, say *consent*—that is the very word."

"I shall not disguise my feelings," continued Miss Beaufort, looking up nobly from her one sheet of note-paper already spread on the ironing-board. "I shall tell him frankly that I accept the alliance solely because of my poverty and that of my family."

"Dŏn' you go fur to tell him no sech foolish non-sinse!" protested Aunt Chloe. "Tell him you likes him; say you's a-dyin' fur him."

Virginia's solemn and lofty tone changed into a burst of girlish laughter, perhaps a little nervous and hysterical in its foundational nature. "Why, you old goose!" she giggled, "I never saw him. He wouldn't believe it."

"Bet you he would. Dey allays doos, de men-folks," asserted Chloe.

"I shall tell him that I demand nothing of him per-sonally," pursued Virginia, resuming her serious mood. "I shall tell him that I leave him his entire freedom."

"What!" stared Mrs. Dumont. "Live apart? That would be very unusual—in a Beaufort. Besides, he might take offense, my dear. Do be careful."

"I thought you had an aversion to the match," said the girl, losing patience. "I thought you objected to it."

"O Virginia, you quite misunderstand my posi-tion," declared the elder lady in that sugared tone of pacification which is so hard to bear, because it inti-mates that the person addressed has an unreasonable spirit and a peevish temper. "What I think is that, under the circumstances—our present dreadful circum-stances—you may have to—to bend. If Elizabeth could bear it, you can, my dear."

"Now dat's human talk, dat ar is," approved Aunt Chloe. "D' ain't no poll-parrot in all dat. As fur Miss Ginny not wantin' to be married, never heerd no gal talk different. Smart dog always allow he can't bear sheep-meat."

"Of course I grieve for you," continued Mrs. Dumont, striving in vain to shed a tear. "Such a sacrifice!   Ah, dear!"

"O Miss Anna! do stop you' mouf," interrupted the old negress, exceedingly troubled and angered. "Wish you was little enough to be spanked."

Mrs. Dumont was horrified; she really did weep now. "I never thought," she sobbed, "to be so addressed by one of our own people."

"I can't help it, Miss Anna," apologized Aunt Chloe, whimpering also. "I'se so mad to see Beauforts hungry an' bar'legged! I dōn bust out so 'cause I'se free. I hain't got no mo' rights nor I had befo' the wah. I allays did have a right to speak up fur Beauforts, even agin deirselves."

"Never mind, Chloe," returned Mrs. Dumont, who was as much of a lady as one well could be with her parts. "I know you are faithful, and mean to be respectful. I shall remember you for it," she promised with an air of munificence.—"And now, Virginia, as to that match. I should be sorry to see it broken off now."

"Oh, of course," said the girl, ironically. "It would be a pity to break it off. Such a scandal!"

"An' you means to tell him you ain't gwine ter live with him?" demanded Aunt Chloe.

"Yes, plainly and firmly; that is what I shall tell him."

The widow shook her experienced head. "I think, Virginia," she hesitated—"wouldn't it be better to tell him so, plainly and firmly, of course, but *afterward?*"

"O aunt!" stared the niece. "What a Yankee trick! You seem to forget that I am a South Carolinian and a Beaufort."

"Fox like to go to church, ef he kin walk home with chicken," grinned Aunt Chloe.

Mrs. Dumont looked extremely confused. There was a silence for a minute or two. Then the fatiguing dialogue dribbled on once more.

Virginia (looking up from her writing). "I—can—not—live with him."

Aunt Chloe (with arms akimbo). "Is you a grown woman, or a baby? Does you s'pose a grown-up man —a man as wears britches an' tail-coats—is a-gwine ter agree not to marry his wife? You two's jess talkin' like folks in a dream."

Mrs. Dumont. "*I* didn't propose it, Chloe. *I* didn't propose this absurd plan. Of course, I hope he will accept it. He may. Just consider what an honor even that is to him! We might concede something. We might allow him to take the Beaufort name."

Virginia (writing). "Aunt, how *could* I live with him? Remember my poor brothers. You loved them. —And you loved them too, Chloe, didn't you?"

Aunt Chloe. "I loves you a heap better, chile. I wants you to write a sonsible lettah, an' not put in no poll-parrot talk."

Virginia (laughing bitterly). "I am writing my offer of marriage. That ought to satisfy you."

Mrs. Dumont (smiting her breast). "Oh, my dear! my poor dear! Are you quite determined?"

Virginia (tartly). "I am."

Mrs. Dumont. "O Virginia! you are always so irritable when I make a remark, but I can't help saying I hope you are not making a mistake."

Aunt Chloe. "Now you wants her to, an' now you dōn want her to. Question is yere, what does *he* want?"

Virginia. "Just so, Chloe. But we shall know that. The letter is written."

Mrs. Dumont. "Oh, dear, dear, dear! *Shall* we send it?"

Aunt Chloe. "A pusson would s'pose, Miss Anna, de young gen'leman was a-gwine ter marry bofe of you."

"There!" exclaimed Virginia. She had finished the letter, and the superscription thereof. As she looked at it, the full sense of what it included and might include seemed to come into her mind, for a deep blush of womanly modesty suddenly flooded her whole face, and her eyes sank to the floor. For a moment she sat shrinking and irresolute; then she rose in silence and put on her frayed and faded hat.

"It *must* go," she gasped, without glancing at either her aunt or her old nurse. "I will mail it myself, to make sure."

CHAPTER XIII.

THE first consequence of Virginia Beaufort's letter was that Underhill at once made a rapid journey to Charleston.

Immediately on his arrival, he looked up General Hilton, the lawyer and devoted friend of the Beauforts, and, not finding him at his office, left a pressing message, begging him to call at the hotel. During the evening, therefore, the wooden-legged veteran stumped into the young man's private parlor.

The meeting was friendly and courteous, but slightly ceremonious. Underhill, naturally frank and easy

and genial in manner, showed a seriousness almost
amounting to anxiety, and spoke with unusual elab-
orateness of address. Hilton, who had not even the
smell of whisky upon him, behaved as if he had gone
into training for the interview. He evidently realized
that he had before him a capitalist, and a person who
could weightily influence the fate of one whom he held
very dear. Self-respectful as a gentleman should be,
and dignified in bearing by habit and by the gift of an
imposing figure, he was even more carefully urbane than
common, as well as more reserved and watchful. He
bowed, shook hands, smiled, and said : "You wanted to
see me, Colonel. I am very much indebted to you. The
wish is a compliment."

"General, you oblige me greatly by calling," was
the young man's response. "I had no doubt, of course,
that you would favor me. You were very courteous to
me during my former visit."

"Don't mention it," begged Hilton.

"You may suppose that I wouldn't have risked putting you to this trouble for any slight matter," pursued
Underhill. "I wanted a long and private conversation
concerning your friends and my connections, the Beauforts."

"I suspected as much. I am exceedingly gratified
to make sure of it."

"You remember my uncle's talk about his will, I
presume. Well, he actually made it—the strangest
will—the maddest—"

"Excuse me ; I hope no offense, but I know all
about it. As the legal adviser and old friend of the
family, you understand."

"Very proper. They did quite right to consult you.

Well, I have received—" Here the young gentleman hesitated; he did not know how much Hilton knew of the matrimonial imbroglio; he found it embarrassing to unveil what might be a young lady's secret.

"Yes, you received an assent from Miss Beaufort," added the General. "Pardon me for being so well informed."

"Oh, very good!" nodded Harry, drawing a sigh of relief and dropping his ceremoniousness. "Glad you know all. Saves explanations."

"And you will try to see her, may I hope?" inquired Hilton.

Underhill pondered. "I am sorry for this young lady," he said at last. "If this marriage doesn't take place, she gets nothing. My uncle did a very strange and very cruel thing. I sometimes think that he was in reality a little insane."

"It is a common saying among lawyers that a man frequently saves up all his lunacy for his last will and testament. Well, it *was* a cruel will, since you permit me to say so."

"Very hard on *her*—his wife's niece—very hard! All the more so as I don't lose my half if I refuse the marriage."

"There was no reason why you should," conceded the General. But he looked very sad, for he could not help discerning that Underhill was not inclined to the match, and a fear came upon him that his pet, the last of the Beauforts, was doomed to a life of penury.

"Well, now," resumed the younger man, "you know the terms of Miss Beaufort's letter, I suppose. Don't you think she rides a rather high horse?"

"I want you to pardon the poor, inexperienced

child, if possible. Please consider how she has been tortured : a girlhood of poverty, and calamity, and mourning ; property lost—brothers lost ! "

"Oh, I know all that. Am I responsible ? "

"It would be useless to open a discussion on that point."

"Oh, quite so. My question was absurd. I will try to look at the matter practically."

The General bowed his thanks ; he continued to be very polite, almost submissive. "I concede that her terms are quixotic," he went on. "But how long will she insist upon them ? At her age people change their ideas easily. Moreover, she is honorable, particularly high-minded. I think she will soon become ashamed of receiving much and giving nothing. It is not Southern fashion ; it is not Beaufort fashion."

"All that is true enough, I presume," admitted Underhill. Then he added with a light smile, "And there would be something poetic, too, in a fellow courting his own wife, if he could make her acquaintance."

The General smiled also, but rather sorrowfully. "I don't like to laugh about it," he said, gently. "It is to my mind a serious and sad affair."

"Well, that depends somewhat upon Miss Beaufort. Do you think she will insist upon her programme—meet, marry, and separate ? "

Hilton gazed at the young man, gravely and without speaking. He clearly knew that the girl would so insist, and dreaded to avow it.

"Very well," Underhill laughed, with some natural petulance. "Then I shall get on as best I can without her."

"I am extremely grieved, sir. I am not surprised, of course."

"This drives me to look up my Irish nightingale, or some other nightingale that is willing to sing," pursued the young man. "I really did and do want a musical wife, so far as I want one at all."

The General made no reply, and appeared so exceedingly cast down, that the Colonel pushed forward a decanter of whisky and urged him to try the quality of it.

"Thank you!" sighed Hilton, shaking his head. "But do me the very great favor to excuse me. I have lately taken a resolution to evade that sort of inspiration when I have serious matters to think of. I have learned that alcohol is a poor counselor, and I begin to doubt whether it is a good consoler. This affair lies very near my heart, and I prefer to treat it without whisky."

But Underhill had apparently determined not to talk any more about the Beaufort alliance. "Miss Macmorran is here still, isn't she?" he asked. "Have you heard her sing yet?"

"Do you mean the soprano of St. Patrick's? I have had the pleasure not of hearing her sing but of speaking with her."

"Ah, General! Lucky dog! Take care! I may make a personal matter of it."

"I have had twenty years of marriage, Colonel," said Hilton, seriously. "When a man alights at the end of such a journey as that he feels like asking if people ever marry twice, just as Lord Chesterfield asked if people ever hunted twice. I don't mean that I was unhappy—far from it! But marriage is a struggle—that is, for a poor gentleman. One such jaunt is enough for a lifetime."

Underhill gazed at him with the vague sympathy

and respect which the novice accords to the tried veteran. "I know nothing of struggles," he confessed. "I feel like a small fellow, compared with those who have had them. Miss Macmorran has struggled, and I admire her for it. What did you think of her, General?"

Hilton could not have wanted to eulogize the pretty Irish singer just then, but he was too honest and highminded to say anything but the truth, or anything short of the truth. "She is a very modest and pleasing young lady," he declared.

"Isn't she!" smiled Underhill, obviously gratified. "What a sweet, nun-like way she has of casting down her eyes, just lifting them shyly to your face when you speak, and then dropping them! It is prodigiously fascinating. I think that girl, in spite of defects of education, might make an admirable wife—such a gentle, meek wife as men dream of."

The General had a troubled air of carrying on a perplexing discussion with himself. There was apparently something on his mind which he wished to say, while he doubted whether it would be fair and gentlemanly to say it. At last, with an apologetical smile, he continued, "I saw her family, also."

"What!" laughed the Colonel. "You went to her house and she let you in! You must have some talisman."

"I was caught by a storm of rain. Miss Macmorran was thoughtful enough to offer shelter to a limping old fellow."

"Lucky storm! I wish I could find one in that neighborhood. You must know that I never have been allowed to call on her. Well, what were her surroundings?"

"The young lady is the pearl of the family, Colonel. She seems out of place in it."

"Oh," muttered Underhill, "the others are rather common, I suppose. I never saw them."

"The mother is a worn woman—has done a good deal of washing, I fancy; her rounded back tells the plaintive story of labor—hard and long labor."

"Gracious! I hadn't guessed a mother—a washer-woman mother."

"There is a sister, also—a hard-featured, strongly built person of thirty—who is at service in a Northern family here, as I understood."

Underhill absolutely blushed. The sister of his St. Cecilia at service! One's own possible sister-in-law! "It's perfectly dreadful," he grumbled, "to think of that sweet girl *dans cette galère!*"

"It reminds one of an angel with human relatives," answered the General, expressing himself with poetic delicacy, though he could not have been ill pleased with the impression which he had produced. "They are entirely decent people, Colonel, and honorably self-respect-ful. I was pleased to see that they were not ashamed of their humble interior, and that Miss Macmorran was not ashamed of her own flesh and blood. But, as a family, they are not of our sort."

"Of course, I might have supposed all this," resumed the young man, after a moment of brooding. "In fact, I did suppose something of the kind, but not with any distinctness or reality; couldn't make a clear picture of it—didn't want to. The truth is, that I have been idealizing that girl, and idealizing everything about her. If you like fine music, you can understand it. Well, I must stop making poetry on that subject. I meant to go and see Miss Macmorran, if the little nun would let me. But I mustn't. It couldn't come to any good."

"No, you mustn't go there," said Hilton, with the smile of a good-hearted senior addressing a hot-headed junior whom he admires for worthy qualities. "You don't want to turn that good child's head merely for your passing amusement."

"It would be shabby, General," Underhill sighed. "I can't be shabby. Once an officer and gentleman, always an officer and gentleman."

"I wish you were a South Carolinian, Colonel," declared Hilton, with honest fervor. "But, merely as a brother man and brother soldier, I am proud of you."

Underhill laughed cheerfully. He was evidently gratified by the compliment. "General, you are too much for me," he said. "You make me want to do something noble. Well, now, since this subject is closed for ever, let us talk once more of my uncle's project."

CHAPTER XIV.

To General Hilton it must have seemed a little like sacrilege to change the conversation so abruptly from the daughter of a washer-woman to the daughter of one of the noblest families of the Palmetto State. He probably had irritable reflections concerning the obtuseness of Northern democracy, and the ingrained lack of delicacy in the Yankee nation. On the other hand, as he was a peculiarly self-possessed and rational gentleman, he no doubt remembered that Underhill must regard Virginia Beaufort as an embarrassing and even hostile personage, and exhibited at least good-nature in being able to talk of her without vindictiveness. At all events, his countenance and demeanor revealed neither vexation, nor surprise, nor impatience. He gazed tranquilly and blandly at the young man, while waiting with keen anxiety for him to speak.

"As for Miss Beaufort," resumed Underhill, "can I see her?"

The General took from his breast-pocket a large envelope, tenderly drew therefrom an "imperial" photograph, and laid it on the table between them. It was his own valued copy, paid for out of his own beggarly pocket, of the likeness of the beautiful ultimate Beaufort. Underhill bent over it with an expression which rapidly changed from curiosity to admiration. Hilton watched him with anxiety, and then smiled with simple, honest, sympathetic pleasure.

"She is handsomer than I supposed," murmured the young fellow. "My uncle said she was very handsome. But this is a remarkable face. It's astonishing how blood tells. That's a wonderfully high-bred air, General. Why didn't you tell me before that she was a Diana victrix?"

"There never was a Beaufort who hadn't that air— at least to some degree," returned Hilton, in a tone of beatitude.

"Yes; she resembles my aunt, the only Beaufort that I ever saw," nodded Underhill, still studying the portrait.

"Your aunt was a most charming lady," said the General; "and a model wife, I believe," he sagaciously added.

"My uncle had no reason to complain," replied Harry, looking up sharply. " But *his* wife lived with him. There is the trouble in this case ; there is to be no living together. I don't want to marry, and then go mad about my beauty of a wife, because I can't win her liking, and somebody else can."

"Oh ! That last idea is insupposable," exclaimed Hilton, looking almost angry enough to ring for pistols. "I *know* this girl. She is a Beaufort and a South Carolina lady."

"Pardon me," said Underhill, but he nearly laughed at the Southerner's heat, and at the general oddity of the situation. "Please observe that absence might breed suspicion, even when there was no reason for it. I can't help insisting that my uncle and my prospective wife have laid a heavy burden upon me."

" Certainly—for the present," admitted the General. "On the other hand, it is proper to remember—you will excuse me, I hope, for suggesting it—it seems proper to remember that you owe your uncle something."

"Oh, yes—everything in reason. But is this reasonable ? "

" I can imagine that he had this match very much at heart. He had loved a Beaufort a great many years."

" Well, let my uncle pass. I owe him too much to want to have the air of saying anything against him. But how is it "—glancing at the photograph—"how is it with this lovely young person ? Is *she* reasonable ? "

"No," conceded Hilton, "Miss Beaufort is not reasonable. But I hope and believe that Mrs. Underhill will be."

The Colonel uttered a laugh of incredulity and impatience. "I should like to know what chance you can see of it," he retorted.

Once more the General explained that Virginia was a baited and irritated woman ; that she was high-spirited and not to be put down by baiting—only angered by it. What she needed to soften her and render her sympathetic, he argued, was a taste of prosperity. He believed that to noble souls prosperity was humanizing ; it brought them to want to bestow happiness upon their fellow-creatures.

"Of course, I hope so," assented Underhill. " But I don't know that it will turn out so in this particular case. I am afraid Miss Beaufort has suffered too much ever to forget or forgive."

" She must be got out of this atmosphere, no doubt," said Hilton. " The very air of South Carolina is loaded with sorrow and wrath. She hears words of vindictiveness every day, here. But let her once go North, or to Europe—let her abide only a few months afar from our desolation—she will be unable to keep up her vivid remembrance of injuries. When she once begins to forget, she will begin to forgive."

" Forgive *me*—her husband ! " Underhill laughed with comprehensible bitterness.

" My dear sir, I envy you," the General declared, not only with seriousness, but with something like enthusiasm. " It will be a fine moment—that moment of reconciliation."

" Yes ; I see all that. I have an imagination." The young man smiled, rather amused by the senior's tone of romance. " But there is the previous humiliation ! Just think of it—dismissed at the church-door—like the sexton, or a beggar ! Obliged to sue humbly, for years perhaps, because somebody else ate forbidden fruit, or didn't eat it ! Forgiven at last for nothing ! Really, the programme is almost alluring through its oddity—through its unlikeness to anything out of ballads and fairy-stories. Such a chance doesn't come once in a man's lifetime."

"Colonel, such a chance doesn't come to one man in a hundred millions," returned Hilton, fervently. "It is a sacrifice of pride and of feeling, I admit. But it is a sacrifice worthy of a chivalrous gentleman and of a great soul."

"And you would do this?" stared Underhill. "Word of honor, General!"

"Word of honor, Colonel!" declared Hilton with solemnity; "if I were in your place I would not let the opportunity slip. As Heaven is my witness, I would seize it!"

The young man meditated for some moments in silence; when he spoke again it was in a tone of profound seriousness. "If I don't do this, she will have nothing," he murmured. "And if I do—"

"You will have your reward somehow," interposed the General. "Depend upon that, my dear Colonel—you will have your reward."

"In the next world, perhaps," said Underhill, shaking his head gravely.

"Certainly there!" returned Hilton with emphasis. "And here, too! It is worth something in this life to be conscious of a deed of singular mercy and self-abnegation, even if it brings no recognition from those whom it benefits. The greatest names in earthly history are the names of those who have suffered for the uncomprehending and ungrateful."

Underhill rose slowly from his chair and walked the room for some minutes in silence. At last he halted in front of his anxious companion, gave him his hand with a bright, cheerful smile, and said, in a tranquil voice, "Very well, let it be done."

The General started up with a vivacity which made his wooden leg creak, and burst into a passion of thanks and joy—of congratulation and panegyric. With pathetic fervor and with unhesitating confidence he promised the Colonel his reverence for life, and the reverence of every chivalrous gentleman and of every true Southerner. He looked him straight in the eyes, and called him the Bayard of the age. He said all these things without being absurd, and without seeming to be extravagant. His Southern fluency, and the fervid beating of his Southern heart, made his very hyperbole convincing and touching. It was evident that the man was an orator, and that Nature had done more than art to make him one.

At last Underhill found opportunity to reply: "Thank you, thank you exceedingly. I hope it will turn out as you predict, and I wish I were as grand a fellow as you say."

Then, after they had resumed their seats, he picked up the photograph and studied it intently, as if seeking to discover some softness and sign of pliability in the high-bred features.

"I shall keep this," he observed; "so much, at least, is mine."

"I feel at liberty to leave it with you," bowed Hilton, who clearly had not been commissioned so to do. "May I suggest that it might be well to send her yours?"

Underhill did not answer for a little; he seemed to be meditating earnestly. At last he said, "She will see me."

It was now the General's turn to hesitate and ponder. "Possibly not," he finally explained. "Perhaps I ought to tell you that the church is to be darkened."

"Oh!" exclaimed the young man, surprised and indignant, as well he might be, "so we are not even to see each other? In that case I had better send her my portrait. She'll be wretched without it."

After further thought he went to his trunk, took out an elegantly mounted photograph, and brought it to the General.

"Thank you," bowed Hilton; but he had scarcely glanced at the picture when he added, "Excuse me, there is some mistake here—this is another person."

"It will do—for her," was the reply. "It is the likeness of my brother, who fell at Gettysburg. She shall have mine when she makes peace with the original."

With a very gentle hand, but with a resolved countenance, the General laid the photograph on the table.

Underhill took up a pen and wrote his name at the bottom of the card. "That will save explanations and prevarications," he said. "You can simply give or send it to her."

"Would you kindly do me the favor to transmit it by some other hand?" requested the South Carolinian.

"Oh, certainly," answered the young man, coloring. "I really beg your pardon. I, of course, had no right to ask you to play a part in my—my bit of finessing."

"Pardon me, if I had the air of taking offense," bowed Hilton. "But in such an affair a man had better bear his own responsibility. Well, it is all settled, I believe," he added. "You permit me to say so to Miss Beaufort?"

"Yes," sighed Underhill, and then thanked the General for his patience and courtesy; for, in the presence of this urbane Southron, he also became elaborate in manner and complimentary in speech.

"Colonel, you deserve all the courtesy that I or any other man can render," was the fervid parting utterance of the fast friend of the Beauforts.

CHAPTER XV.

GENERAL HILTON, of course, carried report of Underhill's decision to Virginia; but we will not relate the particulars of the remarkable interview which ensued; we will simply state that the engagement became a fact.

This point once established, events marched rapidly. It was the young lady's purpose that the marriage should be kept as secret as possible; and, to increase the chance of securing privacy, she fixed an early day for the sacrificial rites. Meantime she remained quietly in Aunt Chloe's lodgings, and made there all her few and mysterious preparations. She had money enough at command to do otherwise, and even magnificently otherwise. Underhill had promptly transmitted to her a large check, signed by the Mather executors, and she might have taken rooms at the hotel, or rented the grandest house in Charleston, both of which plans were suggested to her at random moments by Mrs. Dumont. But, partly through whim, and partly to be more sure of escaping gossip and publicity, she continued to abide in the tattered shanty, and scarcely modified her humble style of living.

All this while the amount of agitation and discussion in the little household was something indescribable. Notwithstanding that the three women were now better fed than they had been for years, they positively palpitated and talked the flesh off their bones. Aunt Chloe, in particular, went nearly wild, prattled incessantly and with continually rising vehemence, and was specially copious in denouncing the manner and method of the marriage.

"It's jess like a weddin' of mad folks," she lectured. "Married without co'ting! Never heerd the like, 'cept among slave niggers or dumb crittahs. Wha's d' young man all dis time? Why dōn *he* come 'long? We don 's much 's see him gwine by. Wouldn' know him from Adam ef 'twant fur his poetrait. What's dat, Miss Ginny? *You* dōn look at it? Yis you has looked at it; you's seen it onct, anyway—got up las' night an' looked at it by moonlight. I seen you trew de cracks in de flo'. You jess couldn' go to sleep without one peek. No, I ain't shamed to lie awake spyin' on ye. How kin I shet an eye, with all dese yere crazy doin's? I's a mos' gone loony with a fearin' you should back out, an' with mournin' an' tremblin' 'bout you bein' married in black. Ugh! black-crape dress! All de Beaufort ladies ever I heerd of stood up in white satin.—Miss Anna, you was married in satin—powerful satin—fit to stan' alone an' be married all by itself."

"We don't see such satin nowadays, Chloe," responded Mrs. Dumont, warming up at the recollection of her bridal glories.

The worthy lady, by-the-way, was much improved

in appearance since we last saw her, and had such a gloss of prosperity that it was not difficult to imagine her in wedding-garments. The purchasing power of "Yankee dollars" revealed itself in dainty bootees, a well-fitted black-silk dress, and a becoming little cap on her now carefully brushed hair. In her expression there was that wonderful embellishment and refinement which handsome attire and a consciousness of well-being bring to humanity, and especially to womanhood. She had lost the hard and hungry glare which once made her eyes pathetically displeasing—that glare of eagerness and bitterness which caused her to resemble a "sand-hiller" rather than a Beaufort. She looked a lady—decent, even-tempered, high-bred, and dignified—though not intellectually powerful.

"I dōn' keer ef we dōn' see no sech satin nowadays," grumbled Aunt Chloe. "You could git *somefin* white. Ugh! black-crape dress! Jess 's ef you was gwine to a fu'nal!"

"So I am, aunty," said Virginia. "It's only a funeral to me."

"I must say that I shouldn't object to white," put in Mrs. Dumont. "Black will look—well, it will look ungrateful—I mean to brother-in-law Mather."

"So I *am* ungrateful," declared Virginia. "Am I to shine out in thanks for this bondage? What have I to be grateful for?"

"It is a great deal of money, Virginia," said the elder lady, eagerly and pleadingly, as though she still feared lest it might vanish. "We shall be comfortable for life."

"Ah, Aunt Dumont, you have been bought over," the girl laughed. Then, seeing that her relative looked annoyed, she added : "Never mind what I say, aunt. I have been bought, if you haven't."

"I don't like to hear you talk of it so lightly," murmured Mrs. Dumont. "After all, whether we are thankful or not, it is a wonderful providence, and seems like a direct interposition."

She spoke in a low and as it were awe-stricken voice whenever she alluded to the Mather inheritance. It seemed as if she remembered the tales of treasure-diggers who have seen the iron chest disappear because some one uttered a loud word.

"Of co'se it's a providence," affirmed Aunt Chloe. "An' you goes to meet it in a black dress ! Dar was a man in Scripter what went to the Lawd's feast without any weddin'-garment, an' got hisself cast inter outer darkness fur his impidence. Da's what'll happen to you. Such behavin' 's shuah to bring ill-luck."

"The ill-luck has come," said Virginia. "The marriage is the ill-luck. There can't be any worse."

"An' de bridesmaids?" queried the old woman. "Is dey to be in black, too—like mourners?"

"There won't be any bridesmaids, aunty ; nor groomsmen, either."

"No bridesmaids ? An' is dis yere young gen'leman to stan' all dese cracker 'rangements? I 'gin to b'lieve, fur true, d' Yankees has'n' got no sperrit. An' no groomsmen, nuther? You two stan' up alone, like poo' white folks? Oh, *you* wait ! *You'll* see ! *He'll* have groomsmen. D'aint no rich young man gwine ter be 'posed on dat ar way. He'll fotch on his own grooms-men, an' bridesmaids, too—bawn Yankees, every one of 'em—jess to punish ye."

"Then there won't be any bride, not if I have my senses," declared Virginia.

"Well, you has'n' got 'em," retorted Aunt Chloe. "Dar has'n' been no sense in Sou' Carliny sence d' wah —no, nor fur a good while befo' d' wah. De hosses has a heap sight mo' gumption nor de folks. Why! how's you gwine ter look, stannin' up without bridesmaids, an' towsled with black crape?—What's dat you say? No lights in de church! What! married in the dark? I shall jess go 's crazy 's a bawn Beaufort. Married in the dark! How's you to know which is you' husban'? How's he to know which is you? You'll jess git you'self married to Gin'ral Hilton, an' never find it out till you sees it in de papahs."

"Aunty, I think I could stand that better," said Virginia, half laughing, half groaning.

"Why! you' husban' won't see you," pursued the scandalized Mauma—"won't see what he marries— black, or white, or yaller gal. Dōn' you mean he shall ever see you' face? What, never? Not in all you' life? Ef dat young man puts up with all dese yere tomfoolcries, I'm done with him. I mos' dispises him now. Why dōn' he behave hisself like a gen'leman? Why dōn' he come here, an' fo'ce hisself in? Who's to hender?"

"He wouldn't dare—he has no right!" exclaimed Virginia, coloring with alarm and indignation at the mere thought of such an intrusion.

"Right! He'll have right enough when d' words is said an' de ring is on. He kin fotch along de police an' break in. Reckon he will, too; anyway, he oughter."

"O Chloe!" murmured the girl, her fears getting the upper hand of her defiance. "You scare me out of my wits."

"Wish I could skeer you inter 'em—wish I could now. Hain't been in 'em fur fo' yeahs."

"I half think so myself when I remember what I am doing," sighed Virginia.

"An' how you's a-doin' it!" snapped the Mauma. "Never was no sech loony business sence Adam an' Eve ate the apple. It's wuss 'n crazy. It's jess like a weddin' in de bad place—a weddin' 'mongst Satan's angels an' fallen sperrits—all blackness an' darkness an' hatred an' lies. Ef d' Ole Boy hisself dōn' come to 'tend it, it's bekase he's acsumdentally got outside o' Sou' Carliny."

"O Chloe!" screamed the churchly Mrs. Dumont. "How *can* you! I think you are awfully profane—and so cruel and discouraging, too! It all comes of freedom. You didn't talk so in the good, quiet old times."

"Didn' dast to, Miss Anna; wanted to, lots o' times —wanted to talk wuss."

Just here Mrs. Dumont observed through the window that some one was approaching the house, and, with the indolent dignity of a person accustomed to be waited on, directed Chloe to see who it might be.

"Da's d' i'nin'," explained the old woman. "Da's d' young lady what fotches d' i'nin'."

"Young lady! young lady that fetches the ironing! What are we coming to?" gasped Mrs. Dumont, with an upward roll of her eyes.

"Dis yere's mighty 'spectable, an' a powerful fine singer, too, as I heern tell," added Chloe. "She on'y fotches when her mother's out o' sawts, like Miss Ginny useter when I was rheumatical."

"A Beaufort is a lady, whatever she does," declared Mrs. Dumont, tartly. "I really don't like your comparing my niece with a common-born Irish girl."

6

Thus speaking, the rehabilitated grandee passed into her wretched little sleeping-closet with as august an air as if it were a withdrawing-room of lordly dimensions and furnishings.

Mauma Chloe now opened the door and courtesied in Norah Macmorran, bearing a basket of fine linen daintily starched and ruffled. Virginia glanced at the modest and pretty girl with the surprise which we accord to unexpected refinement of expression and bearing, and with the interest which one handsome young woman usually grants to another. When Norah spoke, too, she turned and looked at her with something like admiration, so delicious was the voice and so neat was the utterance.

"The heavy pieces will be done to-morrow," explained Norah. "I brought the small things because mother said you wanted them directly."

"I am very much obliged to you," returned Virginia, with an instinctive civility which did her honor. "Please sit down while I look them over."

In another instant she had forgotten Norah in her finery. She picked up the basket, hurried with it into the sleeping-room, closed the door behind her with a push of her foot, and proceeded to take out the rustling delicacies of raiment. The lowly bed was soon covered with glossy cuffs and collars, snowy handkerchiefs, and other fine linen. The two ladies bent over them and fingered them and counted them with a joy which was almost great enough for tears. It was a long time since they had been able to look upon such a pageant as their own.

Meanwhile Aunt Chloe, left alone with Norah, seated her in the arm-chair and began to babble. "You's just in time, miss," she chuckled. "Things is mighty pressin'."

"So I understood," was the tranquil reply.

"Oh! then you heern of it?" stared and smirked Aunt Chloe.

"My mother told me," said Norah, meaning simply that her mother had told her that the washing was needed promptly.

"Laws! so it's all out," giggled the old woman, delighted that the fact should be so, since it left her free to talk. "Yis, Miss Ginny's been spoke for," she went on. "Wonder ef you knows de young gen'leman?"

"I suppose not," answered Norah, with her sweet smile, for the subject of nuptials interested her pleasantly, as it does many young women. It was surely a pathetic speech, when one remembers how well she did know him, and what scenes had passed between him and her. "But you misunderstood me," she added, quickly. "I didn't mean to say—"

"Perhaps you knows him," interrupted Chloe, altogether heedless of Norah's explanation, so eager was she to learn something about the mysterious groom. "He's from the Nawth, whar you comes from. His name is Underhill, an' he's a Yankee colonel."

The girl quivered a little, like one who has been stabbed mortally, and who can only quiver. Her lips parted slightly, but did not give forth a word, not even a sigh. Her eyes dropped to the floor.

"So you dōn' know him?" queried Aunt Chloe, disappointed. Then, staring vaguely at Norah, she noted that her face had turned very white, and broke out with "Law sakes! wha's de mattah?"

"Nothing," murmured the girl; but she was clutching the arms of her chair, and seemed to be struggling against faintness.

"Why, you looks dead sick," insisted the Mauma, and began to call aloud, "Miss Ginny! Miss Ginny!"

"Oh, please don't call her!" gasped Norah. "Have you got any water?"

But Virginia had already entered the room and divined the situation, at least so far as concerned the fact of faintness. She hastily filled a tumbler with water and brought it to the invalid.

Norah drank eagerly, without raising her eyes, and then whispered: "Thank you. It is nothing. I have such turns sometimes. I haven't been well lately."

"Let me help you into the other room," said Virginia. "You must lie down a minute."

Norah merely shook her head and tried to smile. After a moment of waiting and silence, compressing her lips for a desperate effort, she grasped the arms of the chair and rose to her feet.

"Take care!" exclaimed Virginia, catching hold of her arm to steady her. "Don't go yet; you might fall in the street."

For the first time since the revelation of the engagement the girl glanced at her. It was a quick, furtive, strange look; it seemed to express fear, humiliation, and resignation; it was a look which the other probably never forgot.

"I must go," she murmured. "I am quite able. Thank you."

Next, without lifting her eyes again upon any of them, she seized her basket, opened the door hurriedly, and passed out.

"What does all this mean?" demanded Mrs. Dumont, appearing from the sleeping-closet. "What's that girl fainting about?"

Then, little by little, the whole story came out—how Aunt Chloe had blunderingly given up the secret of the engagement, and how thereupon the girl had come nigh to swooning. It was obvious that all three of the women suspected a love-affair between Norah and Underhill.

"Reckon she ain't strong-like," urged the subdued and alarmed Mauma. "Some women has watery blood, and turns white fur nothin' at all."

"It is not worth minding," asserted Mrs. Dumont, glancing with anxious eyes at her frowning niece. "The world is full of cases of misplaced affection. Those commonplace girls, I suppose, are always reading trashy novels, and dreaming about impossible marriages. Or, it may be as Chloe says—some girls are for ever fainting. My opinion is, that it comes from an irregular circulation."

At last Virginia spoke. "I suppose he has trifled with her," she said, sullenly. "I think he is a bad, cruel man. Well, it is what I expected. They are a mean race."

"My dear, I really hope you will do nothing rash," implored the aunt, fairly trembling with terror lest the marvelously found treasure should vanish away.

"'Sposin' he *has* behaved bad," put in Aunt Chloe, who had recovered somewhat of her spirit, "what's his behavin' to you, ef you ain't gwine ter live with him?"

"Oh, I shall go on," returned the girl, with a groan of mingled aversion and despair. "Nothing can make it worse than it is in itself. I shall marry him now, no matter what I hear."

CHAPTER XVI

IT is not worth while to relate minutely how Under-hill passed the time of his brief engagement, nor to make full record of the emotions and thoughts with which he approached his very extraordinary marriage.

All that—the perpetual remembrance of the fact ; the constantly varying dispositions with regard to it ; the querying whether Miss Beaufort would hold her strange purpose to the end ; the occasional wrath at receiving from her no kindly message, or notice of any kind ; the petulant resolves to see the thing through, since it had been begun ; the desperate glances ahead at the oddest of all fashions of blighted lives ; the frequent temptations toward a breaking loose from the unnatural arrangement ; the enforced meditations upon motives of pity and honor and plighted troth ; the periods of romantic expectation, and of easy confidence, and of total indifference—all that we will leave to sympathetic imaginations, and will come at once to the evening of the wedding.

An hour or so previous to the moment fixed for the ceremony, Underhill came out of the Charleston Hotel, and set off alone down Meeting Street. At first he walked rapidly, as if he had a well-defined object in view ; but of a sudden he halted, folded his arms, and stared vacantly at the pavement. A ragged negro approached, took off his tatter of a cap with a scrape, and asked : "Does you want anythin', Boss ? I'se an erran'-boy, I is."

"Yes," said Underhill, surlily ; "I want to be let alone." Then, glancing at the fellow's poverty-stricken raiment, he threw him a wad of the currency of those days, and added, " Clear out ! "

" Wah, wah, wah ! tankee, Boss," guffawed the negro, and made his exit with another resounding " Wah, wah, wah ! "

The laughter was not unlike the " Ho ! ho ! " of Mephistopheles, and probably reminded Underhill of that diabolical merriment.

" Confound the black imp ! " he muttered ; and his face became more sullen than before. He looked at his watch, pushed on hastily down the street, and came to another abrupt halt. This time he aroused the curiosity of a policeman who was standing in the shadow of a neighboring building. The official watched him a moment, edged forward with a noiseless step, and remarked, " Foine evenin', surr."

Underhill started, turned upon the man, stared at him impatiently, and yawned : " Oh—yes—fine evening."

" Lost yer way, surr ? " inquired the guardian of the public tranquillity.

" No," returned Underhill, sharply. He was moving on, but after one or two steps he stopped and said, " Officer, how deep is the water off the Battery ? "

The star reflected with an air of perplexity, which was followed by a gleam of wariness. It is probable that the suspicion came into his head that here was a fellow, impudent enough or mad enough to try to learn from a member of the force where he might conveniently drown himself. Of course, the notion was an improbable one ; but, on the other hand, there were cases of policemen who had been humbugged by frankness and straightforwardness ; and it was highly desirable not to get a repute at the office for being a simpleton. At last he replied with thoughtful deliberation, " Well, surr, I couldn't say for sure, the tide is out just now—it's three feet or so, mebbe less."

"Is that so ? shallow as that ? " was the sulky comment.

"I might walk along wid ye, an' we might have a look," suggested the official. "My bate's down that way."

" Oh, no ! don't want to go there," answered Underhill. He faced about, as if to return whence he came, but did not stir. "By-the-way, officer," he added, " can you tell me when the next train leaves town ? "

"There's niver a train out till six of the mornin', surr."

" Oh, indeed ! " said the young man, yawning with an air of complete indifference. "Thank you, officer. Good-night."

He now set off swiftly, neither toward the Battery nor toward the hotel, but across Meeting Street and in the direction of the Ashley River. The policeman watched him for a minute, and then started in pursuit. He did not follow far in a direct line, but turned to the left down the first alley, and there broke into a double, as if to wheel around a block and head off his quarry.

Underhill walked at full speed for a quarter of a mile, and came to a halt before a small, isolated dwelling, evidently the residence of people in humble life. There was a small, bare, well-trampled yard in front of it, inclosed by a dilapidated wooden fence. At one end this fence was flanked by a shapeless thicket of undergrowth, quite characteristic of the half-depopulated and ill-cared-for little city. At the other end stood the corner building of the block, apparently a deserted grocery—no light in its windows, and no revelry at its counters. Underhill posted himself in the shadow of the thicket, and quietly watched the silent dwelling-house. He had been there several minutes when a female figure came around the corner beyond and advanced rapidly toward the gate. He stepped forward, reached the gate first, seized it with one hand, and said in a low, tremulous voice, " Miss Macmorran ! "

" Sir ? " was the reply. It was partly a query, and partly a remonstrance, or rather a reproof. The tone was very gentle, but also very grave.

" Only a moment ! " he begged. " Just one word, Miss Macmorran ! "

" I can not talk with you, sir," answered Norah, her utterance suddenly dropping to a gasp.

" Only a word of good-by. How hard you are with me ! "

" I have no right to be anything else," murmured Norah, bringing out the words one by one and with great difficulty.

" You might have had the right." He could not help saying it, no matter whether it was true or false. " Do listen to me. You might have had the right."

" Oh, please let me pass ! " whispered Norah, struggling in vain to speak aloud.

" In a moment," he answered, still holding the gate. " Can't you hear a word from me ? "

" Oh, what is the use—now ? Bid me good-by, and let me go in."

" Ah, Norah ! That is just what I don't want to do. I don't want to bid you good-by."

Something or other, perhaps an impulse of conscience, perhaps a throb of indignation, restored her voice to her for a moment. "You have no claim, Mr. Underhill, to talk to me in this way," she said aloud. Then, breaking down into a sob, she added, "It is very cruel."

"Ah, forgive me! forgive me!" he pleaded, leaning toward her and whispering with the tenderness of penitence. "I don't mean to be cruel—not to *you*. I am suffering enough myself. How can I want to be cruel?"

"You!—suffering?" was the amazed and incredulous reply.

"Yes," he insisted. "It is your fault. Why have you always kept me at a distance? Why?"

"I can't tell you. I mustn't talk with you."

"Tell me!" he implored, or rather commanded. "I insist upon it. Did you think I could never seriously care for you?"

She broke into outright crying here, but was able to sob forth, "Yes, sir, I—did."

"But you wouldn't let me be near you. You wouldn't give me a chance to speak. Why was it? Did you hate me?"

"Oh!" she exclaimed, as if in horror at the thought. "No, sir!"

"Was it the difference of Catholic and Protestant?" he asked, gently. As she made no reply, he continued, "Was it—other differences?"

"Yes, sir," said Norah, with the simplicity and pathos of a weeping child. "I didn't think you could honestly care for a poor girl like me."

"But you wouldn't give me a chance—not a chance to talk with you—not a chance to hear you sing, even, by myself."

"It was best for you I shouldn't." She had got upon the subject of duty now, and could speak more firmly and clearly. "Don't you know it was? Oh, I know it, and knew it then. It was told to me."

"What!" stared Underhill. "Did my uncle write to you?" he demanded, wrathful for a moment with the dead.

Norah hesitated. "It was told to me," she repeated. "I knew he would cut you off if you took a Catholic. Isn't that in his will? Ah, I know it is, Mr. Underhill, or you would answer. That is all," she added, endeavoring to pass him. "Now please let me go."

"Oh, you little angel, I can't!" he answered, still holding the gate firmly. "How good and sweet of you to think of me!"

He was trying to take her hand, but this seemed to startle her, and she drew back sharply. "Sir, you must *not*," she protested with really touching solemnity. "And you should not be here, either," she continued, still more gravely. "Why are you not with *her?*"

"So you know *that?*" he fretted. "Norah, I am perfectly miserable. You must help me—help me to break out of this situation."

"What! Out of your marriage-troth? Oh, sir, it would be such a sin!"

"It would be mine—all mine," he urged, seizing her hand and holding it. "I won't let you go till you promise yourself to me. I must break away from this horrible marriage, and you must help me."

"O Virgin Mother, aid me!" whispered Norah. She made a violent effort and released herself from his grasp. "Now let me go," she implored, sobbing once more.   "May God help you!   But you never shall touch my hand again.   Let me pass."

"Give me one good-by kiss, Norah," he begged.

"I must not," she answered.   "It would be wrong."

He still held the gate and gazed at her eagerly.   He was quite beside himself now with longing for this girl. He had come hither in obedience to that impulse which leads a man, on the brink of a distasteful marriage, to grasp at the temporary consolation of a tender parting from some one else.   But this passionate dialogue had made him a lover, and he was really prepared to rush into a hasty and ill-assorted marriage, not merely because he abhorred his unnatural engagement, but also because he was infatuated with the nun-like creature at his side.   If he could not have her for life, he must at least hold her a moment in his arms, and win from her a farewell embrace.   This he now strove to do, putting forth his right hand as she pressed against the gate, and passing it around her waist.   Norah uttered a stifled cry and swiftly turned away her head, so that his kiss only touched a ripple of her black hair.

"O Holy Virgin, forgive me!" she exclaimed, and, breaking the gate from his grasp, fled into the house.

At the same moment a policeman appeared, advancing on a run from the neighboring corner, and calling angrily: "Let that girl alone!   Keep away from that house!"

Underhill turned, recognized his companion of a quarter of an hour previous, and responded in a rage, "What have you got to do with it?"

"Can't you see my shield?" demanded the official, who was clearly in a furious passion, and hardly able to refrain from violence.

"When a man is talking to a young lady, what has the police to do with it?" reiterated the exasperated Colonel, advancing upon the policeman with that air of domination which is apt to come to a man with years of martial life.

"I'll tell ye, surr," returned the other, lowering his tone to a surly growl. "Me name is John Macmorran, an' that young lady is me sister."

Underhill seemed thunderstruck; for some seconds he remained speechless; at last he muttered: "Good Heavens! This is *too* much."

"That's what I say meself," responded Macmorran. "I hope I sha'n't have to take ye in charge, surr."

The miserable young gentleman burst into a wretched laugh. "Oh, no," he said. "If she has a brother on the force, that answers every purpose."

Then, while Macmorran entered his mother's house, to inquire doubtless into the meaning of this extraordinary scene, our modern Bayard, the chivalrous hero of the age, turned his back and sauntered slowly homeward.

CHAPTER XVII.

REACHING Meeting Street, Underhill discovered General Hilton, standing under one of the lamp-posts in front of the market, and peering anxiously in all directions. He crossed over, walked straight up to him, and said in a tranquil tone, which contrasted singularly with his late agitation, "General, I suppose you are looking for me."

"My dear Colonel, I am very glad to find you," returned Hilton, not forgetting to shake hands cordially. "They couldn't tell me at the hotel where you were."

"I felt too gay and festive to stay there," was the sardonic answer. "I wanted to get out and frolic!"

"What time is it?" asked the General. "I don't carry a watch in these days."

Underhill drew forth a magnificent repeater. "We have ten minutes—plenty of time to get there," he said. "General, let me ask you to accept this, in token of my profound respect, and also of my regrets for having caused you anxiety. I ought to have been at the hotel, if only on your account."

Hilton gently begged leave to decline the gift. "Not now, at any rate," he smiled. "If this marriage turns out well, as I profoundly believe it will, then you shall give me that watch, and your thanks with it."

"May the hour come!" responded the young man, with a sigh of hopelessness. "Well," he added, passing his arm through Hilton's, "I am all ready—as ready as I can be. Let us go to the place of execution."

"Ah, Colonel!" the General sighed also, as they set forward, taking the direction of Grace Church.

"I understand," said Underhill. "This isn't talking like a Bayard, is it? Well, I have found—I have just now clearly discovered—that I am not a Bayard. I have been behaving, during this last *mauvais quart d'heure*, like a perfect blackguard."

"I can't credit it, Colonel. You couldn't behave like one for fifteen minutes together, if for one."

"I don't believe, General, that you have ever known what it is to be driven to desperation."

"My dear fellow, this is the dark hour before the

dawn," said Hilton. "I can remember enough of youthful feelings to comprehend that it must seem very somber. I remember, also, hours in which I have myself been very desperate. Never mind. A gentleman does his *devoir* all the same."

"*Noblesse oblige*—a gentleman must," repeated Underhill. Then he added with a smile, "So you can say that to a Yankee?"

"To any brother soldier—to any good soldier—Yankee or Southern—I can say that."

"Good Heavens! I wish it was war again," broke out the Colonel. "I wish there was somebody to fight —instead of this."

"There is no one," Hilton answered, gravely. "Miss Beaufort hasn't a male relative left." It was characteristic of the Southron that he should think at once of the duel, and suppose that his interlocutor had alluded to that method of settling fastidious questions.

"Ah, if she had!" groaned Harry, coming to a halt. "I should rather like to be shot."

"But you can't be, Colonel—unless you shoot yourself," responded Hilton, halting also, and watching him anxiously.

Underhill looked up in his face with the smile of a man who assents to an overwhelming argument. "No," he said, "I must be married, instead of buried. *Parole d'honneur!* I remember now that I gave it. I forgot it once this evening."

"Yes—word of honor!" murmured Hilton in a reverent tone. "Word of an officer and gentleman!"

"So be it," sighed Underhill, resuming his course. "Lead on to my nuptials," he added with a miserable laugh. "*Vive la joie!*"

They reached the vicinity of the church in time to see a group of three or four dark figures turn into the side-alley which led up to the vestry-door.

"Walking!" commented the opulent young gentleman, with an air of surprise. "Why didn't my wife drive?"

"She wished to escape notice," muttered Hilton. "She'll regret it some day, and regret all this. I don't believe a girl ever had a queer or private wedding without feeling more or less sore about it all her life."

Then they also reached the alley, pushed up it to the vestry-door, and stumbled into the shadowy church, dimly conscious of massive pillars and pointed arches, the latter being guessed rather than discerned. Two wax-candles in front of the altar faintly lighted a group which was huddled in the center of the transept. The clergyman, a middle-aged gentleman of mild expression and thin, patrician features, was listening to the whisperings of a portly and elderly lady, dressed in mourning. By the side of this last stood another female figure, tall and slender and evidently youthful, although her hair was hidden by a black veil and her face was turned away.

Underhill gripped his companion's arm, and brought him to a halt. "Which is Miss Beaufort?" he whispered.

"The youngest lady—the slender one—the crape veil."

"And the large one, I suppose, is her aunt?"

"No. At the last moment Mrs. Dumont's courage failed her. She called it a funeral. A woman, you know —sensitive and imaginative—perhaps superstitious—she refused to see it. The large lady is a Mrs. Chester, a distant connection."

"Are there witnesses enough ? Have all the legalities been seen to ? It would be awkward for the lady, if not."

"Thank you for the suggestion," said Hilton, evidently much gratified by this sign of good-will. "Everything has been arranged."

The clergyman now came toward them with a soft and urbane solemnity. The General introduced his companion in full, as Mr. Henry Edwards Underhill, of Boston, the affianced of Miss Virginia Temple Beaufort. There was a slight touching of hands, a faint murmuring of a civil phrase or two, and then a brief, oppressive silence. Underhill turned his head, and glanced at the dimly visible figure in the crape veil. The face was still averted from him.

"All is ready," whispered the clergyman, and glided back to his place of office. Hilton took Underhill's arm, and they walked together down the transept to join the group in front of the altar. The slight grating of their feet on the bare and apparently sanded floor was the only sound in the shadowy edifice. The moment they halted there was a complete and lugubrious silence. A moment later there was a sharp sigh ; it was only the struggling, gasping breath of a woman ; but it could be heard with painful distinctness.

Underhill was now by the side of his bride, some three or four feet distant from her, and fronting the clergyman. Not until he had thus placed himself did she turn in the same direction. He glanced—he probably could not help glancing—toward the woman who uttered that sigh. Then he discovered that her face was shielded by her veil, so that he could not distinguish a single feature. Looking at her sidewise, she was a mass of funereal black, from her feet to her forehead. Her pose was that of a statue. Not once, not even in the slightest degree, did she turn her head toward the man whom she was about to marry. It was evident that she did not mean to see him, any more than to be seen by him.

The service commenced. The clergyman knew his task by heart, and it was well that he did so know it, for the feebleness of the light forbade reading. Virginia made her responses in a low, monotonous, mechanical tone, without a tremor or any other sign of emotion. Underhill spoke in such a suppressed and unnatural mutter that Hilton stared at him with an air of surprise, and bent forward as if to see whether he were the right man. Indeed, ever since the General had entered the church, he had worn an expression of perplexity, and had stared hard and repeatedly at the bridegroom.

The service ended. The marriage-vows had been really and fully uttered and interchanged. Henry Edwards Underhill and Virginia Temple Beaufort were lawfully man and wife. That moment they separated. In obedience to a touch of Hilton's hand, the husband fell back two paces and stood motionless. The wife, drawing her veil entirely over her face, turned to the right, walked hastily by him, and, accompanied by her three friends, swept along the transept toward the vestry exit. Then, at a little distance, the two men slowly followed, and groped their way out of the shadowy edifice. The door was softly closed behind them by an invisible hand, giving a lugubrious impression of the presence of some ghostly verger. Underhill halted in the moonlight, folded his arms, drew a long sigh, and waited for his bride to pass out of sight. Meantime the General gazed at him with an air of scrutiny and bewilderment.

"My dear Colonel, when did you raise those?" he said, at last, pointing with his finger to the young man's cheek. "I never noticed before that you had whiskers."

Underhill uttered a low laugh—not quite a pleasant one to hear—rather a sardonic merriment. "Oh, it was a miracle," he said. "This has been a supernatural affair throughout. I raised them as we stepped into the church."

He lifted his hat, took off a pair of false whiskers, and put them in his pocket.

"Well, I am glad to see that it is yourself," returned Hilton. "I positively had my doubts, in there. I wouldn't have believed that such a small thing could so change a face. You had your reasons, doubtless, for the disguise."

"Of course. I had sent her my brother's picture as mine, you remember. It was necessary to look like him, or she might have been puzzled, and might have refused to go on. I had these got up some days ago. I came near forgetting them this evening, and only put them on as we entered the church."

He took the whiskers out of his pocket, waved them in the moonlight, and laughed again. "It was my only preparation for the wedding," he said. "Very appropriate! Sham marriage and sham whiskers!"

"Ah! Colonel, this bitterness will pass—it will surely pass," affirmed Hilton, laying a petting hand on Underhill's shoulder. "There will be a reconciliation. Meantime, don't murmur over your superb self-sacrifice.

It was a grand deed. I wish a Southerner could have had the honor of it."

"General, I might have escaped it as easily as not," said Harry. "I wonder I didn't think of it and do it. I had a chance, half an hour ago, to get myself arrested and locked up for the night. It's amazing that I shouldn't think to avail myself of it. My wits are not in first-rate order to-night, General. You mustn't wonder that I can't mount to your plane of discourse. Well, my wife is out of the way," he added, with a forced smile. "Come along. We'll go to the hotel and crack a bottle of champagne. I shall leave to-morrow. We'll drink to Mrs. Underhill."

"Going! — going to-morrow!" protested Hilton. "Wait awhile; wait for events. Send a message and ask an interview."

"I have had an interview to-night," said Harry, his voice trembling for a moment with anger. "She didn't look at me. I doubt whether she will ever have another chance. Come along, and let us try the grape.

> "'Come, fill the cup, and in the fire of spring
>   The winter garment of repentance fling;
>   The bird of time has but a little way
>   To flutter—and the bird is on the wing.'"

The General did not recognize the quotation from Omar Khayyam, whom indeed he had never read, nor even heard of, as few English-speaking people then had. But he seemed to be solemnized by the bacchanalian despair of the great Persian. He shook his head sorrowfully and answered in a tone of compassion: "No. Excuse me from joining you. I can't feel like champagne this evening. Good-night, my dear fellow; and God guide you and reward you!"

CHAPTER XVIII.

At an early hour after breakfast the next morning, Hilton entered Underhill's parlor and presence with an enthusiasm of greeting which seemed to indicate the inflammation of strong drink, but which really sprang from Southern sensibility and heartiness.

"Ah, my dear Colonel!" he exclaimed, seizing and squeezing both the young fellow's hands. "Colonel of my heart and soul! My superior officer in the ranks of chivalry! So you didn't at once shake off our dust from your feet? I am delighted. I wanted one more sight of your face. I come to look on you—to look up at you, Colonel—and to congratulate you."

"Don't be satirical, General," returned Underhill, rather glumly. "I am neither to be worshiped nor to be envied."

"You still can't see your own position," said Hilton. "It is a very noble one, much nobler than your wife's."

"My wife?" repeated the husband, with an angry laugh; "yes, I *was* married, I believe. I suppose I am married at this present moment. Does anybody know where my wife is?"

The General made no reply to the petulant but natural sarcasm. He simply sat down with the patient and compassionate air of a physician who perceives that he has on hand a troublesome patient.

"I did dream of something different," continued Underhill. "I did nurse a feeble, foolish hope that a Southern lady might mean something when she swore to love."

"And you?" inquired Hilton. "You could live with her?—would prefer it?—now?"

"General, I didn't take any champagne last evening," said Harry, speaking very deliberately and gravely. "I passed the evening, and a large part of the night too, in thinking and remembering. Those vows repeated themselves to me over and over. That presence haunted me. I decided not to leave here without trying to see my wife. I decided that I should prefer to live with her."

"I am glad beyond measure to know it," returned Hilton, drawing a deep breath of satisfaction. "You have given me greater pleasure than any other man could possibly give me. I repeat and solemnly affirm that you are worthy of your good fortune, and of all good fortune. You are meeting these singular and very trying circumstances in a noble spirit. If you are not a Bayard," he concluded with a smile of wonder and worship, "then we have no Bayards on earth."

"No, I am not a Bayard," denied Underhill, shaking his head sorrowfully. "I came very near breaking parole last evening. I should have run away with another woman, if she would have let me."

"I don't marvel," conceded Hilton, though he looked startled. "It must have been a trying hour. Well, I praise you all the more—all the more because you did the improbable—all the more because you had a temptation and resisted it."

Underhill paused a moment, as if pondering some fastidious subject, and then asked, "You remember Miss Macmorran?"

The General bowed urbanely, and raised his hand with the gesture of a soldier saluting a superior officer.

"I owe her a kindness," murmured Harry. "She saved me from doing a foolish and dishonorable act.

Can you help me in the matter, or rather in the manner, of paying my debt?"

"Colonel, oblige me by putting me to any trouble on your account, or on hers. She is a most admirable young lady. I don't care what her lineage is. I say —*lady!*"

"She would not accept a favor from me. I have done her no wrong: ah! yes, I have—I have pained her. Never mind—I won't go over that. But she is delicate and high-minded; she would never accept my kindnesses. Whatever is done for her must seem to come from some other source."

Then, after some discussion, it was agreed that two thousand dollars should be passed over to Hilton; that he should privately deliver it to the priest of Saint Patrick's for the use and benefit of Norah Macmorran; and that she should be led, if possible, to look upon it as the gift of the Church. With this money she would be free to go to Europe and pursue her education in music.

"That is what she wants," explained Underhill. "It is the best thing I can do for her at present. It must answer for the present." He paused, looked steadily at the General with a bitter smile, and then added, "It is a part of the money which I meant for my bridal trip, in case such a trip might be."

"The bridal trip will come," affirmed Hilton. "I promise and prophesy it, Colonel. No, doubt it depends somewhat upon yourself how soon it shall come."

"Suppose I should make a morning call upon my wife—a mere call of ceremony—and congratulation?"

"I am glad to hope and believe that you wish to see her," responded the General, disregarding the tone of sarcasm. "But let me beg of you to be considerate," he resumed, after a moment of meditation. "Don't be hasty with regard to Miss Beaufort—I mean Mrs. Underhill."

"She might fire on me, as her sister fired on Sherman's column." .

"Ah! you have heard of that? Well, now, I don't want to say a word in excuse of such an act of ecstatic madness—mere womanish excitability and hysteria, you of course understand—though our impassioned people made a good deal of it at the time. But it shows the nature of the Beaufort blood. It is a story which says, Be gentle."

"I mean to be gentle."

"I hope you do seriously mean it. I thought you spoke harshly—excuse me, I should say sardonically—a moment ago."

"Very true. Of course, I am sardonic and indignant. I had hoped—it was a ridiculous idea, General—but I had hoped for a message this morning, a message of ordinary courtesy, at least. You brought nothing of the sort, I see."

Hilton shook his head and sighed, "Alas! not yet."

"Well, who wouldn't be indignant?" demanded Underhill, striking his fist on the table. There was a pause, and then he resumed with singular tranquillity, and in a low voice : "Never mind all that. General, I have decided what to do."

The old friend of the Beauforts leaned forward with an expression of extreme anxiety.

"Last night, all alone here, I came to a resolution," continued Underhill. "I resolved to win my wife to myself, if it cost me the labor of a life to do it."

The General leaned still farther forward and grasped the young man's hand, murmuring: "Oh, God bless you, my boy! Do it! She is worth a lifetime."

"I will," affirmed Underhill, as solemnly as if he were registering an oath. "I will win her as surely as the North won the South. I will do it—I will certainly do it—no matter what it costs. If four years won't answer, I will put in forty!"

"Really, Colonel, you awe me," said Hilton, dropping back in the chair and studying the young man's face. "You are the North incarnate."

"And my wife is the South."

"Yes—a woman," sighed the General, "a generous and impassioned woman. The South has been just that, and only that, all my lifetime. I see it now."

Underhill rose and walked the room in silence for a minute or two. When he resumed his seat, he asked quietly, "Shall I have your help?"

"Yes—loyal help," fervently promised Hilton. "In this fight I am a Union man, heart and soul."

"I expected as much of you, General; still, I am greatly obliged. Well, the first service that I want of you is that you should bear a message to my wife."

"Colonel, I will bear it. I earnestly hope—excuse me for presuming to counsel—I earnestly hope that it will be a kind one."

"She won't think it kind, I suppose. You have brought up your young people as madmen and madwomen. They look upon an extended hand, if it is a Northern hand, as an insult."

"Alas! what could you expect? We were beaten and humiliated; we were beaten in peace and beaten in war—terribly humiliated in both. Please to remember,

7

moreover, that in this particular case there have been special reasons for bitterness."

"Yes, I remember. I am sorry for it. But there are special reasons for good-will, too."

"Colonel, I admit it fully and gladly ; and I believe that the good-will is sure to come."

"The message is this," said Underhill, after a moment of reflection. "Tell her that I have given her my hand, and I now offer her my heart."

"Ah ! my dear fellow," exclaimed the General, rising in such enthusiasm and haste that his wooden leg nearly gave way under him, and putting his hand on the young man's shoulder, as much to find support as to bestow a caress—"ah ! my noble friend, you have won *my* heart, at all events. That message I will bear at once, and I hope not unavailingly."

"Let me know the answer, whatever it may be," called Underhill, leaning out of the door after the departing veteran.

"You shall see me again to-day—within two hours, if possible," promised Hilton as he tramped down the resounding hall.

CHAPTER XIX.

WHILE the General was making his way toward Aunt Chloe's shanty, the inhabitants thereof were packing their small properties and otherwise preparing for a migration to the venerable town-house of the Beauforts, abandoned some two years ago to the occupancy of Confederate military officers, and, since their removal, abandoned to rats and cockroaches. Virginia's purpose was to gradually refit and refurnish it, and recommence therein the honored plenteous existence of other days. Why should Beauforts relinquish the family mansion, or depart from the sacred sand and muck of Charleston?

The household was a remarkably cheerful one this morning. There was a continuous tinkle of feminine prattle, mingled at times with hilarity. Obviously, the change from pinching poverty to full-handed wealth was enough to efface, at least for the moment, many a somber recollection, and every kind of foreboding. The two ladies were gay, in spite of bygone bereavements and disasters, and in spite of the thought that their present prosperity had come to them from the Yankees. The occasional remembrance of Mr. Underhill, even, could not banish smiles from Mrs. Underhill's lips. Only Mauma Chloe, that veteran grumbler, that maroon-colored accusing angel, showed an intermittent disposition to murmur and upbraid.

"We shall soon be out of this wretched den," said Mrs. Dumont, striving in vain to be dignified, and not to smile all the time. "Only half an hour more, and we shall be in the dear old mansion again, the house where Beauforts have lived and died for a century."

"You hasn' been so powerful mis'able *yere*, Miss Anna," retorted Aunt Chloe. "Yous enj'yed you' health an' swallered you' vittles like a wil'-cat."

"I *have* been miserable," insisted Mrs. Dumont, with great cheerfulness. "Don't tell that story to a born lady who remembers that she has lived and slaved like a sand-hiller."

"Sand-hillers dŏu' work ef dey kin help it. Well,

you *has* worked dat way—worked bekase you couldn'
help it."

"We don't want to be reminded of it, Chloe,"
laughed Virginia.—"Never mind, Aunt Dumont, we
have come into our own again—or somebody else's own."

"You hasn' got all you' own, Miss Ginny," grumbled the Mauma. "Dōn' seem to be no husban' 'bout,
's he oughter be."

"I wish you wouldn't be harping on that," said the
bride, with just a momentary shade of gloom on her
face. "It's quite enough to pay such a price for comfort, without being reminded of it every ten minutes."

"A husban's a mighty handy thing to have roun' a
house, an' mighty comfo'ting, too, fur a body as has
sense. You jess try yourn a month, honey. Ef you
gits tired on him, you kin quit agin, like niggah-folks.
'Tain't nohow fair play, dis yere 'rangement. You gits
a heap, and he gits nothin'; you's better off, an' he's
wuss off. An' you calls it good luck, an' goes roun'
a-smirkin', like a niggah dat's stole a sheep an' got somebody else in jail for it. Wonner what de raal ole-time
Beauforts 'd say to 't? Dey useter talk a heap 'bout
fair play, d' ole-time Beauforts did."

Virginia seemed to be stung at last, and with a slight
stamp of her slipper (the once bare foot was in a lovely
slipper now) she ordered Chloe to stop scolding.

"Spiled baby," muttered the old woman, meantime
petulantly cording a mattress. "Doos she s'pose d'whole
yea'th is gwine ter shet up bekase she stomps her foot?
Other folks 'll talk ef I don't. Spiled baby!—spiled
her myself—couldn' help it—she was so putty."

Presently Virginia heard approaching footsteps.
"There comes somebody," she said. "Remember, Chloe,

you are not to speak of my wedding, except to General Hilton. It's to be hushed up as much as possible."

Then Hilton entered, and saluted everybody in his most cheerful fashion, his face radiant with content over the reëstablished fortunes of the Beauforts.

"The evil days are over," he smiled. "What a pleasure it is to think of you once more as being in circumstances of comfort—yes, and of opulence ! You are situated as Beauforts should be—as Beauforts are accustomed to be."

"Ah, yes !" answered Virginia, gayly. She was young and could not help being elated by prosperity, nor help showing her gladness. "Isn't it a relief? Isn't it delightful ? "

Presently she began to talk of the family debt to Hilton. "I must begin to settle with my creditors," she said. "I owe you over twenty thousand dollars. I want to pay at once."

"You can't," the General laughed. "Your principal, you must remember, is trusteed, and you can't touch it. Your income is thirty thousand dollars, payable in semi-annual installments—fifteen thousand every six months. That is your situation financially."

"Oh, dear ! Well, but I can pay you ten thousand pretty soon, can't I ?—and ten thousand more when I get my next installment. In a year I can pay up everything : that is, all the money—never the obligation."

Mrs. Dumont, poor woman, greatly terrorized by the bygone poverty, looked scared at the thought of parting with such a sum so soon. "Isn't there one objection to being hasty about this ? " she asked. "Suppose Mr. Underhill should hear of the payment ? Isn't there some danger that he might think the General had favored the marriage in order that Virginia might be able to settle with him? A Yankee, you know, would judge from a selfish point of view."

Hilton smilingly waved away the supposition. "Not this Yankee," he said. "As for the debt, I am in no hurry. I am safe, and can wait. But as for Underhill's suspicions, he knows all about my claim. I told him of it myself; I couldn't in honor do otherwise. Moreover, the Colonel is incapable of a mean judgment. A more high-minded young gentleman I never met."

"Dar, now!" exulted Aunt Chloe. "D'ain't nothin' so mean 'bout dem Yankees. Ef dey was mean, why didn't dey take us fur dar own niggahs, 'stead o' givin' us our freedom?"

"You've got us there, aunty," the General laughed. "As for this particular Yankee, you will respect and admire him—when you come to know him!"

He seemed to be addressing Virginia, and that young lady looked rather startled, not to say annoyed. "I *never* shall know him!" she retorted, hastily. "What do you mean?"

"Of course, she never will know him," echoed Mrs. Dumont, though not with her niece's energy.

"Now, General, don't tell me that you are beginning to take this man's part," implored Virginia. "If you have brought me any message from him, you and I will have a quarrel."

"My child, do be more calm," lectured Mrs. Dumont, who had a talent of good advice, and never buried it in a napkin. "Always remember what you are."

"She ain't no Beaufort," snapped Aunt Chloe.— "Miss Ginny, remember dat you is a Underhill."

"I command you never to call me by that name again!" ordained the bride, her cheeks glowing.

The General glanced smilingly and patiently from face to face during this dialogue. At last he said: "I noticed as I came in that there was a hack at the door. Perhaps I am interfering with the family pleasures. Ah, butterflies of fashion! A hack already!"

"Dear me!" exclaimed Mrs. Dumont, recollecting, no doubt, that the vehicle was to be paid for by the hour, and still troubled by a feeling that money was very precious. "Chloe, you and I must be off.—Do excuse us, General; we are going to the dear old mansion; we are moving out of this place—wretched hole!"

Uncle Phil and the coachman soon charged the hack with packages and bundles. Then the General gave Mrs. Dumont his arm, and gallantly escorted her to her seat, followed by Aunt Chloe. As the two women drove away, they looked out of the window of the ramshackle conveyance with smiles of satisfaction which were really pathetic.

"Ain't dis yere like d' ole times!" chuckled the Mauma, who evidently considered Beaufort prosperities as her own, whether in the past or the present. "It's nigh upon three yeahs sence we's rid in a coach."

The General lifted his hat in stately farewell to Mrs. Dumont, and returned to the cabin to deliver Underhill's message to Virginia.

"What have you got to say to me?" she demanded, after one glance at his thoughtful face. "I won't hear it."

"My dear young lady, I am bearer of a word to you from—"

"I won't hear it—I won't hear it!" interrupted the girl, making a gesture of stopping her ears.

"I think you ought to hear it. Don't refuse when you are ignorant of its tenor, and even of its subject."

"He was to let me alone, and I was to let him alone. That was the understanding. Still," she hesitated, "if it concerns business—"

"It concerns the marriage."

"Then I don't want to hear it. Please, my dear, good old friend—please don't try to force it upon me."

"I think you ought to accord some weight to the opinion of an old friend and a South Carolina gentleman. My opinion is, that you should listen to the message."

"Oh, dear!" groaned Virginia, in whose eyes real gentlemen, Southern gentlemen, were great beings. "I want to do what a lady should, however disagreeable it may be. Well, if I ought, I must. What is it?"

"Let me beg of you in advance to note one thing—a lady and a Beaufort should note it: This young man has put his happiness at stake, if he has not absolutely sacrificed it, in order to give you this fortune. For your sake (and he owed you nothing, remember), he has sacrificed a liberty and opportunities which a young man must necessarily hold very dear. It was a most noble action. I doubt if ever a Beaufort did a nobler."

Virginia had the susceptible conscience and the tender feelings of youth. Her face expressed conviction of wrong, and her lips quivered with a sense of humiliation, as she answered, "What are you siding against me for?"

"My dear child, I am not siding against you; I am not condemning you."

"You are. You intimated that there was one Beaufort less magnanimous than this Federal officer. I wish you would speak out. Am I a mean woman for taking this money?"

"The lawful owner of it meant it for you. You did right in taking it. But ought you not to go further? He had other wishes."

"I could give it up rather than scorn myself," sighed Virginia.

"And send your aunt back to ironing rather than scorn yourself? Besides, the marriage was yesterday, and not to-morrow."

"Oh, dear!" the girl repeated, her mind reverting to the scene of her bridal. "What a horrible evening it was! I wonder I slept after it."

."Keep the estate, of course," pursued the General. "It was meant for you, and you terribly need it. But you ought to keep the man also."

"I've got to keep him," said Virginia, with a simplicity which would have been amusing, only that she suddenly broke into sobs. It was necessarily a terrible thing to a young woman to lose every hope and imagination of hope as to ever marrying any one whom she could love. "I'm as much bound and chained as he is," she went on, as soon as she could speak. "More! He can get a divorce. He can go to some of those horrid Northern States, and get a divorce for abandonment."

"He is a gentleman; there is no doubt of that," said Hilton. "Suppose he doesn't choose to dishonor himself, and publish his dishonor to the world?"

"Ah—well!" sighed Virginia, in the tone of a woman who gives up a hope—a shabby hope which she was ashamed of. "Then he means to hold me? Well,

he can. I sha'n't ask for a divorce. No South Carolina
lady ever did. There are no divorces here, thank
Heaven ! "

"I take it for granted that you have no such purpose," returned the General, very gravely. "It would
not be suited to a person of your blood."

"You needn't fear," declared the girl, reddening.
"I shall keep for life the exact agreement that I made.
I shall remember what I am and who I am."

"Will you kindly and considerately hear the message which I have thought it right and decorous to
bear ? "

"I must, if you bring it," gasped Virginia.

Hilton paused a moment, and then said, with a tender and touching solemnity, "Mr. Underhill' charged
me to say that he had given you his hand, and that he
now offers you his heart."

Virginia sprang to her feet, and recoiled two or
three steps, as if from the offer of a serpent. Her face
was crimson all over, her eyebrows were joined in a
straight line, and her eyes were dilated, black, and
sparkling. She looked as terrible as a beautiful young
woman well can.

"His heart ? " she demanded, in a kind of scream.
"What does the man mean ? How can he give me his
heart ? He has never seen me. He must hate me—as
I hate him. We shall always hate each other. We are
enemies for life."

"Think of it," urged the General, in a low, quieting
voice. "Think of it by yourself, and as kindly as you
can."

"I will *not* think of it ! Oh, my dear friend, I can't.
How can I ? Remember my brothers and my sister.

How could I live with him ? Do advise with him ; tell him all about it ; tell him it can't be. I don't want to be harsh with him. Tell him I thank him—thank him on my very knees—for what he has done for me. But he wouldn't be happy with me. I couldn't make him happy. He couldn't make me happy. Tell him that—do ! "

"Ah, dear ! " sighed Hilton, very sadly. "Is this final ? "

"Yes—oh, yes ! Have pity on me and say so. Persuade him that it is final, and that he musnt't try to change it."

"I am greatly disappointed and grieved," said the General, rising to go. "But I will honorably tell him what you have said."

"Oh, thank you ! What a weight you take off my heart ! "

"To lay it on his," murmured Hilton. "Well—now we have done with the subject—for the present."

"For ever," insisted Virginia. Then a new thought seemed to strike her, and she asked, with eager interest : "Where is he ? What is he going to do ? Does he mean to stay here ? "

"I understand that he is disposed to remain for a time," stated the General.

"Oh, dear ! " exclaimed the girl. "This breaks up all my plans. I am so disappointed ! I had hoped and trusted that I was to be free and undisturbed. I wanted to reoccupy the old mansion. But, if he stays here, that ends everything. I can't meet him —I can't, you know. I must go to Europe and hide there."

"It is very sad," groaned Hilton, as he opened the

door. "Well, my kindest wishes to you, and my advice whenever you want it. Good-by, my child."

"Good-by," answered Virginia, and sat down in the old rush-bottomed chair, crying bitterly.

CHAPTER XX.

THE immediate result of Underhill's offer of his heart was, that his wife gave up the stately project of abiding in the mansion of her forefathers and made a hasty hegira to Europe.

She led away into the desert of earth (afar from the Arabia Felix of South Carolina and the Mecca of Charleston) her aunt and her two faithful adherents, Mauma Chloe and Uncle Phil. She would not pass through the triumphant and barbarous North; she revolted from the idea of taking a Northern line of steamers. It was dreadful even to think of seeing hordes of Yankees, and of sitting cheek by jowl at table with abolitionists, and of being easily tracked by one's Bostonian husband. For the sake of securing all possible secrecy and tranquillity, the romantic evasion was made by a fruiterer to Havana, and thence by Spanish steamer to Cadiz. Afterward came a leisurely, a marvelous, an unexpectedly comforting saunter through Spain, Italy, and Switzerland, ending, as the European journeyings of Americans must, with an entry into Paris. We shall find them amid the clocks and mirrors and other knickknackeries of a handsome apartment on the second floor of the Hôtel du Louvre.

Virginia, who has just returned from a drive through

the glamour of Parisian squares and architecture and triumphal columns, is exclaiming and repeating: "I am so glad we ventured to come here! What a wonderful, beautiful, bewitching city!"

"It is a Babylon," declares Mrs. Dumont, who can not forget the poverty-stricken sanctity of South Carolina, though she has obviously done much expensive shopping of late, and is arrayed in rather Babylonish garments. "God will visit it some day with the besom of destruction," she adds, rolling up her eyes at the crystal chandelier. "Such pride and luxury will surely bring judgment."

"My dear aunt, you have called every city that we have seen a Babylon," laughs Virginia. "Every place bigger than Charleston you have set down for a visitation."

"There is no use in any place being bigger than Charleston," says Mrs. Dumont, with firmness and solemnity.

"Except for the purpose of holding more people," is the comment of a young woman who has evidently learned to like big places.

"The greater the city, the greater the iniquity of it," affirms the elder lady, refusing to smile or be comforted. "I recoil from masses of people. I abhor a crowd. A man ran against me in the street to-day. Of course, he touched his hat and begged pardon; but still one doesn't like to have one's ribs joggled by a perfect stranger. There is too much of our fallen humanity here. Soul and body are alike in danger amid such a multitude. I am filled with terror and grief when I think of Paris. I feel like a prophet of old, looking for the coming of the spoiler."

"Perhaps we are a little envious, aunt. It *is* rather humiliating to find that Charleston is only a hamlet."

"It is a ruin," cries Mrs. Dumont, proudly.

"I hope that doesn't prove that it has been a sink of iniquity."

"Virginia! You shock me. What do you mean by such wild talk?"

"I dare say the Yankee preachers make that inference quite seriously."

"No doubt of it. Shame on them! The hypocritical inquisitors!"

Virginia yawned—actually yawned over the question of North and South, including the desolation of Charleston. It seemed fearfully possible that absence from home and much gazing upon the great, fascinating world outside of South Carolina had begun to lull to sleep her once wakeful local patriotism.

"I can't seem to care so much here," she yawned again. "Paris is so beautiful—so absorbing and fascinating!"

"Virginia, you must not forget your country. If South Carolina is nothing, we are nothing. It is the home of the Beauforts and of chivalry."

"Not now, dear aunt. There are no more Beauforts, and there will soon be no more chivalry."

"Oh, dear!" groaned Mrs. Dumont, smiting her breast and turning up her eyes. "All our heroes gone! All our grand hopes dashed! We were to have had a chivalry of title. It would have come in time. The first families only, of course—the rice and long-staple cotton families. I am sure nothing could have been more natural and proper. The Beauforts and Dumonts, for instance, were not only great planting people, but they were undoubtedly noble before they crossed the Atlantic. It would have been as proud and grand a peerage as any on the face of the earth ; I mean morally and intellectually. Of course, there would have been no castles. It would have been an aristocracy— as your father and Mr. Dumont used to say—like that of Cincinnatus, who plowed his own fields. True nobility lies in noble blood, and in that alone. Your uncle often uttered those very words."

"And the noble blood has been all spilt," sighed Virginia. "Oh, the dreadful subject ! I used to want to talk about it. Now I don't."

"I wish we had some friend to speak to of our sorrows," said Mrs. Dumont. "I would not have them die out of mind. It would be like suffering the tombstones of one's family to go to decay. General Hilton will soon be here, with his sublime wooden leg. What a sad pleasure it will be to meet him ! I would rather listen to the thump of a Confederate soldier's stump than to an opera. By-the-way, Virginia, you must resume your music. When do you propose to begin ? "

At this moment Aunt Chloe entered the room, fat and jolly in face and neat in costume, though still queer about the head in consequence of a high-colored turban.

"Well ! this is pretty behavior," exclaimed Mrs. Dumont. "We expected to find you here to take off our things when we got in. Virginia had to pull off my bootees, my feet were so swollen ! Where in the name of wonder have you been ? "

"Laws a massy ! dunno," returned Chloe. "Jess allowed we never should git back yere agin. Ye see, me an' Phil we went over to dat other big hotel—dat are one right crost de way—"

"She means the palace of the Louvre," suggested Virginia.

"'Specs likely," assented the Mauma. "But we allowed it was a hotel, an' reckoned we might see some 'Mericans 'bout ; an' so, 's everybody was gwine in, we went in with the crowd. Laws a massy ! sech a lot o' stone gods an' picters an' all sawts o' things— rooms an' rooms an' rooms an' rooms full of 'em—never s'posed dar could be s' many rooms in one house, nor in one town—kinder seemed sometimes 's though we'd got to another city. An we got los'—jess entirely los' —like chil'n in de wood—could'n' find our way out no- how. Tell ye, we was skeered ; we walked an' walked an' walked ; reckon we walked mo'n forty mile ; did so, Miss Ginny—need'n' snicker. Tell ye, dat ar hotel is bigger inside dan it is outside—bigger'n all Charles- ton. Well, finally we met up with a man looked like he was one of our folks ; an' Phil says to him, says he, ' Boss, kin you speak English ? ' An' he 'lowed he could. An' so, as he was a-gwine out, he shown us the do', an' tole us which way to travel, fur we was clean turned round, an' did'n' know where to go no more'n a cat what's been kerried away from home in a meal-bag an' had his feet buttered. An' so heah we is. But dat ar hotel is jess wonnerful. Dar's mo' stone gods in it dan dar is folks in Charleston. Is so. You ask Phil. Doos dese yere French people wusship 'em, Miss Ginny ? "

"No, aunty ; they keep them as curiosities," briefly explained the young lady. "There are just such gal- leries in several places where we have been, only you didn't happen into them."

She had laughed heartily and in quite a girlish way over Chloe's adventures. There was far more gladness in her mirth than during the old Charleston days—the sad, fierce days after the war, when her blood beat only with grief and vindictiveness.

"Aunt Dumont, you and I have been here a week and haven't seen the Louvre yet," she went on. "It is a perfect shame. It looks as though we were barbarians."

"Barbarians!" bridled Mrs. Dumont. "I don't see so much civilization and refinement in blasphemous pictures and naked images. Beauforts have got along, and have been gentlemen and ladies, without all these dreadful things which one meets in the public places, making a decent woman ashamed to go out. Your uncle used to tell Mr. Allston, the painter, that he trusted the age of art never would come in South Carolina. And it never has. Your uncle was generally correct. Barbarians, indeed! I don't yet look upon myself as a Vandal. You must remember, too, that our time has been completely taken up with practical and pressing matters. Just think how much shopping and fitting we have done in the last week!"

"We must go to the Louvre to-morrow," said Virginia, with her characteristic decision.

"Well—if we must," sighed the senior lady. "I suppose I shall have to see all the vanities of this great Babylon—see them and lament for them, because their day of wrath will come. If Charleston could be visited with chastisements, what will not happen to Paris?"

"Aunt, you are always opening the sealed vials," Virginia smiled. "At any rate, Paris won't be bombarded by Gillmore," she added, with a transient frown of somber reminiscence. "There is a pleasure in thinking that some places are beyond that man's reach."

"Wretched Vandal!" hissed Mrs. Dumont.

"Does you mind, Miss Anna," asked Aunt Chloe, "how one o' dem rotten shot upsot Phil's watermillion-table, an' sont de watermillions a-flyin'?"

"I saw it myself," returned Miss Anna, sternly. "War in all its horrors! The crimson pulps of the melons covered the pavement. I thought they were pieces of Philip."

"An' nex' day we scooted up country," pursued Chloe. "Was skeered some all de way, I was. Didn' know jess how fur dat ar swamp-angel could kerry."

"It is a perfect nightmare yet," shuddered Virginia. "Do stop talking of it! I want to be happy while I am in Paris."

"Goody gracious me! I mos' done fo'got suthin'," said Aunt Chloe, presently. "Dar was a man down-stairs, Miss Ginny, ast me what you' name is."

"What man?" demanded the young lady, coloring with anxiety. "What sort of a man? A Yankee?"

"Reckon 'twan't no Yankee, bekase he spoke French; only we could unnerstan' him, bekase he spoke it like it was English."

"Oh! broken English; one of the clerks, I suppose," guessed Virgina. "I hope you didn't tell him my name was Underhill."

"Tole him I wasn' clar jess yet, an' I'd step up an' ast you. 'Specs likely dey're boddered 'bout it. Ye see I calls ye Miss Ginny; an' dat ar carrier-man he seen Beaufort on your trunk an' he called ye Miss Beaufort; an' so dey're boddered."

"And it was Underhill on the passport," interjected

Mrs. Dumont. "I wonder what it is on the hotel-books?"

"Man said 'twas Beaufort," stated Chloe. "Wanted ter knew ef 'twas right."

"Let it stay Beaufort," muttered Virginia.

"But your letters, my dear—your business letters?" suggested the aunt.

"They come through our banker. He knows that there is an Underhill among us. The letters won't go astray. Do, for pity's sake, let me be a Beaufort some-where!"

"An' play 'possum?" demanded Aunt Chloe, with arms akimbo. "An' git you'self co'ted, like you was a young lady?"

"I won't be courted, you old goosey," said Virginia. "You needn't stick out your neck and hiss at me."

"But the passport, my dear!" urged Mrs. Dumont. "The hotel people had the passport, and probably the police saw it. We shall surely get into some dreadful muddle."

"We must change quarters, then, and see what that will do," returned Mrs. Underhill, who was evidently bent on getting herself called Beaufort once more. "We'll run about to-morrow and look up an apartment. Indeed, we must get out of the hotel, if I mean ever to pay up General Hilton."

"An' call you'self Miss Beaufort?" persisted Aunt Chloe.

Virginia hesitated a moment, and then answered resolutely, "Yes!"

"Dar'll be some judgment on dese yere doin's," prophesied the old woman. "You wait an' see. De Lawd ain't never in no hurry to shoot, but he's mighty sartin to hit. Better keep away from him, ef you kin find out how to do't. Dŏn, see how you dast go to church. Grasshopper mus' be mighty drunk when he walk home by hen-house."

CHAPTER XXI.

An apartment of reasonable cost, size, and garnishment was secured in a street running parallel with the great avenue of the Champs-Elysées ; and Virginia entered it as Miss Beaufort, not indeed positively asserting the name, but as it were permitting it to fall back upon her.

Then followed three months in Paris, without any noteworthy incident beyond a patient application to French and an enthusiastic study of music. Meanwhile there was of course a pleasant, humdrum routine of shopping, walking, and driving, followed perhaps in the evening by cheerful theatre-going, or ecstatic attendance on the opera.

What spare hours our young lady found at home were mainly given to books of verse, both French and English. Not only was she at the age which most adores poetry, and which is disposed to accept a poet as akin to the demigods, but there were wounds in her heart which demanded the consolations of that soul's cup-bearer, the imagination. Her past had been blighted by bereavements, and her future by an enforced self-sacrifice. That detested marriage of hers, be it observed, was equivalent to a disappointment in love, and seemingly a disappointment for life. It was no wonder that she read poetry daily, and with passionate enjoyment and admiration.

Very much of the verse of the time was curiously new to her. After the fashion of the best families of South Carolina, the Beauforts had deigned to own few books which had not been read and approved by their ancestors, such as the works of Shakespeare, Milton, Addison, Pope, Johnson, and Hannah More. Byron and Shelley had been sternly forbidden to Virginia by a Puritan mother and a Roman father. Scarcely anything more modern than Cowper's "Task" had been placed in her girlish hands. It is an almost incredible yet entirely positive fact that the Brownings and Tennyson were revelations to this young lady, who looked upon herself as a result of the highest culture of the century. In other directions than poetry, moreover, her education had been limited. The South had poured its every dollar into the ravenous vortex of civil war, and even its female schools had been broken up by the dropping away of impoverished scholars. Virginia, left alone at the beginning of the struggle with an elderly and much-troubled father, had not recited a lesson nor picked up a text-book since she was sixteen. No marvel that she was hungry to read, and that her eagerest craving was for poetry, the natural food of intelligent and fervid youth.

Acquaintances she did not seek, and for a time none intruded upon her. Huge and miscellaneous Paris, perhaps, took some note of the young lady, always more or less veiled, who never drove out except in a close *coupé*, and never walked without the accompaniment of a mature friend or a negro attendant. But Paris regarded the phenomenon composedly, and made no effort to invade its privacy. As for the American colony, our Beauforts knew that it consisted mainly of Northerners, and they consequently wanted nothing to do with it. The colony, on the other hand, never troubled its manifold head about them, at least so far as could be discovered.

It was a lonesome, and at times a slightly dreary, existence. Distinctly dreary it was to Mrs. Dumont, who could not speak French, knew naught of the joys of music, and had small taste for reading anything but sermons and the prayer-book. It fretted her, moreover, to perceive that Beauforts were not sought after by Paris, and to suspect that they were not reverenced outside of South Carolina. She began to nourish plans for getting into the native society, and, more particularly, into that of the Faubourg Saint-Germain. At last she energetically opened the matter to her niece.

"I think we ought to see somebody," she said. "Not Americans—there are no Americans here whom we want to know—I mean European somebodies. We really ought to visit and invite a little."

"I don't think I ought," was Virginia's judgment. "What can a woman situated as I am do in society? It wouldn't be decent in me to try to be a butterfly of fashion."

"But French society is grave," urged Mrs. Dumont. "It is sad and grave, like our own. I don't mean the imperial hurly-burly, but the old legitimist circle. You would find it just suited to your tastes and feelings, Virginia; and you certainly speak French well enough to be at ease in it."

"But how are we to get into it? The Faubourg Saint-Germain is very exclusive."

"France is the country of our ancestors, my child. The Beauforts were French; so were the Dumonts, and both high blood. No one in South Carolina would consider it singular or unsuitable to see you married to a French noble of the old stock."

"What an idea! I am married already—to my sorrow."

The aunt remained silent for some moments, wrapped in profound meditation. At last she said: "We don't hear a word from that man. It is borne in upon me that he is getting a divorce, as Yankees frequently do, when they are not grubbing for dollars."

"I don't suppose a noble of the old *régime* would take up with a divorced American; do you, Aunt Dumont?"

Even Aunt Dumont seemed to give it up, now that it was put to her in that way. There was another period of musing, and then she brought forth the astounding suggestion, "It might be that Mr. Underhill could become a noble."

"What!" responded Virginia, opening her eyes very wide.

"With his military rank and his great fortune, you see," explained Mrs. Dumont. "As a soldier he would be considered all right here. I should think he might easily buy a title of this corrupt empire."

"And then what? Would you have me live with him?"

"He wouldn't be a Yankee any longer, you know. He would be a Frenchman."

"My dear aunt, I should think you were dreaming with your eyes open."

"It's no great wonder if I am," declared Mrs. Du-

mont, yawning with an air of extreme *ennui.* "My
life is every bit as stupid as a sleep. One can't
doze for ever. The very next Southern lady I meet,
whether at the banker's or Galignani's, I shall speak to
her."

The result of this desperate resolve was an acquaintance with a pretty and apparently wealthy young widow
from Baltimore. Mrs. Fitz James had been a year or
so in Paris, but did not object to new intimacies. She
was very social, very lively in disposition, prattled much
and gayly and heedlessly, and had a slight air of being
over-Europeanized. The suave polish of Baltimore just
saved her from being a hoyden in manner, but probably
nothing earthly could have saved her from being a hoyden in spirit. In person she was a small and plump
brunette, with an oval face, regular features, and melting black eyes.

The comparatively grave Virginia, an earnest soul
by nature, and matured by early sorrows and agitations,
did not much fancy the mercurial widow. But Mrs.
Dumont would not be denied all human converse : she
urged that Marylanders were Southerners, and must be
treated accordingly ; she insisted on making a lap for
the kitten-like Mrs. Fitz James. Moreover, the latter
took a sort of passion for Miss Beaufort, as she called
our heroine ; she adored her complexion, her dresses,
her voice, and her execution ; in short, she coaxed her
way to an intimacy.

One day she rustled into Virginia's apartment in the
company of a gentleman. "My *dear* Miss Beaufort !"
she laughed and buzzed. " *So* delighted to find you !
Let me introduce my brother, Mr. Frank Hedstone. So
glad to make you acquainted !—This is Mrs. Dumont,

Frank—a lady of the old *régime*. Make your reverence to her."

"Great pleasure—quite honored," murmured Mr. Hedstone, in a silvery voice, and with a very soft, sweet demeanor. "I have the best of sisters, ladies. I begged hard to come here, and she hadn't the heart to refuse."

He closely resembled his sister : he was small and dark, with an oval face and bright, black eyes ; his manner, however, had more tranquillity and insinuation. His black hair had vanished from his forehead, and yet he could not have been above thirty. There was something in his expression which bespoke dissipation, or at least a considerable degree of moral laxity.

"How could I refuse a brother?" giggled Mrs. Fitz James.

"Or any other gentleman?" added Mr. Hedstone, teasingly jocose in a brotherly way, but very silvery and quiet withal.

"Ain't you ashamed, Frank !—He's always bantering me. Well, I have a right to like gentlemen ; we are commanded to love our enemies. My dear Miss Beaufort, how are you? That grenadine is *so* becoming! I wish I had a slender figure. How well you are looking! I never see you out, and I know why. You just stay at home and work at keeping yourself fresh."

"I don't think of it," returned Virginia, laughing, but protesting. "I stay at home to study French and music."

"She is at work from morning till night," put in Mrs. Dumont, with the natural cluck of the last Beaufort hen over the last Beaufort chicken.

"Ah, Miss Beaufort !" sighed Hedstone. "I had

8

hoped that time hung heavy on your hands. I had hoped that I should be welcome."

As Virginia did not reply instantly, Mrs. Dumont interfered to say that Mr. Hedstone was quite welcome. "And Mrs. Fitz James also," she added. "South Carolinians always accord a welcome to—"

"To true Southerners," she would probably have said ; but Mrs. Fitz James could not wait for her to finish. "O Miss Beaufort!" she broke in, "let me say, before I forget it, that I have found you a professor—such an elegant, charming, dear little man—quite the gentleman, I assure you. You can discharge your German boor now. I beg leave to insist upon it."

Mrs. Dumont, by dint of being spry about it, found a chance to say, "I am glad you have found a gentleman for her."

"*Gentilhomme!*" nodded and smiled Mrs. Fitz James. "*Vrai gentilhomme*, Mrs. Dumont. Noble blood—ancient house."

"Capital little fellow, too, De Bethune is," fluted Hedstone. "Shares my admiration for my sister, and of course deserves my good word, as well as hers."

"Do hush, Frank!" giggled the lively widow. "Mrs. Dumont won't understand your babble.—It's nothing of the sort, Miss Beaufort. I'm chiefly interested just now in a Colonel Peyton—a new acquaintance lately come from Virginia ; I'll tell you about him some time. As for De Bethune, I like him too ; who wouldn't? He is a noble—oh ! a real one—no doubt about that—an awfully old house.—What was the story, Frank?"

"One of his ancestors was made Seigneur d'Aumale by Richard the Lion-hearted," stated Hedstone.

"Cœur de Lion! time of the Crusades!" exclaimed Mrs. Fitz James. "Wasn't that splendid?"

"Indeed it was," said Mrs. Dumont, almost awe-stricken. Then she looked puzzled, and asked, "But why does he teach music?"

"Oh! he is so fond of it," rattled the unreflecting widow. "Perfectly enthusiastic."

"But they lost the title, Lotharinga," explained her brother.

"No, they didn't lose it—not at all," asserted Lotharinga.

"Yes, they did, centuries ago," insisted Hedstone. "There's no such title as Seigneur d'Aumale. It went to some other family, I'm not sure what one, except that it wasn't Hedstone."

"Was it the house of Guise?" asked Virginia, who had just finished Macaulay's "Battle of Ivry," and so knew something about the first Duke of Aumale.

"Precisely," said Hedstone, bowing with gay reverence to so much learning. "It went to the great house of Guise, and became a dukedom, and is so still, as I remember, now that I bend my mind to it."

"Wasn't that splendid!" exclaimed Mrs. Fitz James.

"Well—not for the De Bethunes; was it?" questioned Virginia.

"Why, no—come to think of it—not for them," laughed Lotharinga. "But all the same, the professor is a noble, you see. And he is such a charming man! Such a refined, pensive expression! Such elegant, soft manners! You don't see anything of exactly that type in our plain country."

"I assure you that in South Carolina—" began Mrs.

Dumont, only to be stopped off by that canary of a Lotharinga.

"Oh! you must take him, Miss Beaufort," she twittered. Then came a bird-like giggle, "Ha! ha! ha! I don't mean as a husband, but as an instructor. Dear me, how you blush!—How she blushes, Mrs. Dumont! I would give anything for such bewitching innocence and sensibility."

"Alas!" smiled the festive brother. "The down once gone from the wings of the butterfly—"

"Do hush your poetry, Frank! I never had any wings to speak of.—Well, there is some truth in it. It hardens one awfully, Miss Beaufort, to get married. You don't know anything about it. — There you go blushing again, in the very loveliest fashion! South Carolina must be a nunnery, or garden of Eden, or something of that sort."

"Lotharinga, you would make a statue blush," said the genial Hedstone.—"Miss Beaufort, please don't judge me by my sister. I am as full of seriousness as she is of frivolity."

Meanwhile, Mrs. Fitz James's expression bespoke meditation. "But I don't see why you shouldn't take the professor," she presently added, nodding her saucy little head. "I don't see why you shouldn't take him, in the full sense of the word. You have lots of money. You could buy back the title, or buy some other."

Virginia's cheek flushed deeply with embarrassment, and perhaps also with vexation.

"Now don't say nonsense!" twittered Mrs. Fitz. "You can afford it, and I can't. My dearest millionaire, I admire him excessively; but I give him up to you, all for his good."

"I am not a millionaire, and I don't propose to be a duchess," said Virginia, in the tone of one who means to close a subject.

"You shall do just as you please about it," laughed the undisturbed Lotharinga. "Well, I have finished my business.—Come, Frank, let us go. You've got your *entrée* here now, and you mustn't be tiresome on your first call, as I know you want to be."

CHAPTER XXII.

Two or three days later the Baltimoreans came again to smile and prattle in Virginia's parlor.

This time Mrs. Fitz James was diffuse on the subject of that Colonel Peyton whom she had alluded to in her last visit.

He was a "perfectly charming man," she declared and reiterated. "Very handsome : that is, not so superhumanly handsome—not an Apollo Belvedere, you know. I really think De Bethune has more classic features. But the Colonel is so noble in manner ! so full of moral dignity ! It is enough to turn any woman's head to hear his noble talk. I won't try to give you an idea of it ; I get foundered on those subjects right away. But what I admire most is his figure : just tall enough, and so strong and vigorous ! He's a great deal better built than poor De Bethune, whose legs are really too pitiable—made to get about on, rather than to look at—like so many Frenchmen's. I proposed to him— that is, to the Colonel, you know—to come here."

Mr. Hedstone glanced sidelong at his sister, as if to see whether she were telling the truth or not.

"But he seems shy," continued Lotharinga. "Shy or sad. I sometimes think he has a sorrow at heart. He certainly is pensive. I do believe there is a mystery about him—don't you, Frank?"

"Very gentlemanly, intelligent fellow, the Colonel," said Frank, who seemed to be a man without jealousy, as well as without sentiment.

"Oh! what are you talking about?" protested Lotharinga. "I asked you if you didn't think there was a mystery about him. You've no more poetry in you than a watermelon. Well, of course he's gentlemanly and intelligent. Most Virginians are gentlemen, and all Peytons, I suppose. It's a fine old name, isn't it? I thought it had died out. Who knew that there were any Peytons left? Well, I'm glad there's one extant—this one."

"He may be of a cadet branch of the old stock," suggested Mrs. Dumont, in the tone of a person who wants to seem to know something of a subject. The genealogy of patrician American families was of course a topic worthy of her mightiest intellectual efforts.

"I really don't know anything about it," confessed Virginia, seeing that Mrs. Fitz James's eyes wandered dreamily from her aunt to herself.

"Oh! well, it doesn't matter about family," said Lotharinga, with a levity which made Mrs. Dumont stare at her in disapproving amazement. "One can't care much what such a man's descent may be. He bears his pedigree in his face. There's only one thing about him I don't quite like. He wears his hair drawn straight forward, and cut square across his forehead, like the

children in the Tower. It makes one want to get a
brush and comb, and set it to rights. But it's such a
fascinating face, all the same ! I wish you could see
it. Blonde ; exquisite complexion ; features handsome
enough for a man—*I* say ; long, yellow mustache ; and
that fine, pensive air ! "

"Won't that do, **Lottie** ? " laughed Hedstone. "You
are laying on the color pretty thick. I am getting uneasy. Nobody talks about me in that way."

"We speak favorably of you here, Mr. Hedstone,"
said Mrs. Dumont, doing the honors of the apartment.

"So glad ! " smiled the *bon garçon*. "I hadn't
hoped it, but I had longed for it."

" Oh ! I like him better than De Bethune," continued
Lotharinga, dreamily, still referring to the mysterious
Peyton. "On the whole, my dear and too lovely Miss
Beaufort, I don't think I shall bring him to you. I
don't know what might happen."

" By-the-way, we had something to say about
De Bethune," interjected Hedstone, who perhaps
thought that his sister prattled too much concerning
Peyton.

"Oh ! exactly," nodded Mrs. Fitz James, turning eagerly in the new direction, the volatile little canary.
"My dear Virginia, I want you to take him. He knows
music as well as your German, and he doesn't smell of
beer and cheese."

"I have already parted from Herr Koerner," said
Virginia, gravely.

"Oh ! something happened ? " guessed and giggled
Lotharinga. "Was he too assiduous ? Of course he
was. Those professors are so tender ! I had a regular
scene with one. He was a Neapolitan. I believe the

Neapolitans are particularly *sensible*. Frank had to
be called in to make him go away.—O Frank, what
fun!"

"Don't enlarge upon it," implored Frank, blushing
a little for his sister. "Mrs. Dumont is studying
you."

"Not at all," protested Mrs. D., though indeed
she looked rather solemn, as if saying to herself that
Baltimore ladies were not Charlestonian. Then she
added, "I usually sit with my niece during her les-
sons."

"Quite proper," giggled Mrs. Fitz. "Such a face,
and such a fortune! She needs watching."

"I suppose Mr. De Bethune speaks only French,"
said Virginia, who seemed a little fretted by this babble.
"I don't yet know the language so very well."

"Dear me! didn't I tell you?" cried Lotharinga.
"He speaks English. His family was loyal to the Plan-
tagenets, and so forth, for centuries; and he says that
he considers it the duty of a De Bethune to know English; he said it laughing, to be sure, but I think he
really meant it. Besides, he has taught in England,
and among the nobility, too. Oh! he is just what you
want, I assure you. My dear, will you see him?"

"I think I had better," returned Virginia, after a
glance at her aunt, who nodded affirmatively.

"So glad!" exclaimed Mrs. Fitz. "So obliged!
I knew you would. Well, you must get yourself
ready in soul to meet him, then. I told him to look
for me here. I took that liberty. You must know
that I always have two or three *protégés*. I am one
of those women. I can't help being busy—and use-
ful, ha, ha, ha! By-the-way, he ought to be here.

Perhaps he has lost the address.—Frank, run out and see if he is in sight."

Mr. Hedstone, with the readiness of a man trained to oblige, took his hat and went forth on his mission. Then there was a conversation between the ladies concerning French society, receptions at court, and imperial gayeties. Mrs. Fitz James was in the midst of a story of Compiègne gossip, when Hedstone reappeared, urbanely ushering in the noble teacher of music. He was a man of something over thirty, with a handsome face of the massive classic type, a dark and healthily pallid complexion, brilliant black eyes, and carefully dressed curling black hair. His figure displayed the broad shoulders, powerful bust, and disproportionately short, slender legs, so common in Western Continental Europe. In expression and manner he was singularly gentle, even more so than the honeyed but also more dignified Hedstone.

Mrs. Fitz James sprang up, shook hands with him cordially, and presented him as her dear professor—her *très cher Seigneur d'Aumale.* Then she added : " Come, Frank ; our duty is done.—Good-by, my dear Virginia ; come and see me every day.—Mrs. Dumont, please remember me oftener.—*Au revoir, mon cher Seigneur d'Aumale.*"

"Ah ! Mrs. Fitz James, you are always joking," smiled the Professor as he bowed her out.

The moment the Baltimoreans had departed, Mrs. Dumont turned with rustling graciousness to De Bethune, and, making him a salutation which might almost be called a reverence, begged him to be seated. A gentleman whose blazon dated back to Richard the Lion-hearted was clearly worthy of even the distinguished consideration of a Beaufort. "Mrs. Fitz James," she smiled, "has told us the interesting story of your high lineage."

He gave her a glance of surprise, but answered readily and sweetly, "The lineage may perhaps be high, madame, but I personally am very lowly."

"Of course, all families are liable to reverses of fortune," said Mrs. Dumont, consolingly. "We know it only too well. But under any circumstances of adversity one has a right to be proud of honorable descent."

The Professor, who clearly did not desire to talk of his ancestors, made the best of the situation by bowing.

"We think a great deal of these things in South Carolina, sir," persisted the good lady.

"Mrs. Fitz James seems to think a good deal of them," he smiled. "She questioned me very sharply about the prefix to my name. At last, to amuse her, I told her what I know, or suppose I know, of its origin and its presumed founder."

Virginia, who could not help being interested, said in a querying tone, "The Seigneur of Aumale ?"

"So I understand," he replied, carelessly. "Alas! it was six or seven centuries ago."

"It seems to me that I should assert myself," was Mrs. Dumont's spirited counsel.

"Pardon me. I have nothing to assert. It is hundreds of years since there was a title in our branch of the Bethunes."

"But when a gentleman is sure that he belongs to an old and noble French family !" said the worthy lady.

"Pardon me again," bowed the Professor. "It is Flemish. I am a Belgian."

"Oh! well, that might make a difference," hesitated the *grande dame* of South Carolina. The Beauforts, she of course remembered, were French, and Huguenots to boot.

"The highest title I can claim is Professor of Music," De Bethune continued, turning to Virginia with a bow and a smile.

"Mrs. Fitz James was very kind in asking you to call," she replied, seeing that he positively did not want to discourse further of his lineage.

Then followed a practical and business-like conversation, which ended in engaging the descendant of the Seigneur d'Aumale as a singing-master. With this result he looked more gratified than could fairly have been expected of the inheritor of so much grandecism. It seemed likely that pupils were rare with him, and revenues limited. But when Virginia seated herself at the piano and gave him an exhibition of her voice, he clearly forgot his own affairs in admiration and professional enthusiasm.

"It is a remarkable organ," he said, closing his hands and bending toward her with an air of deference. "It is a *very* remarkable organ," he repeated in a whisper which was nothing less than reverential.

Aunt Dumont bridled and rustled with family pride. Then she remembered her patriotism, and said, "Such voices are very common, I assure you, sir, in South Carolina."

De Bethune opened his eyes in wonder, but he bowed acquiescence, all the same. "It is a highly favored region," he replied. "I should like to go there.

By-the-way, did you say South Carolina? I have another pupil from that city."

" It is a State, sir," remarked both the ladies at once.

" Ah, pardon me ; I am ignorant of your geography. This lady also has a fine voice—I don't think as powerful as Miss Beaufort's, but still a very fine voice. Her name is Macmorran ; and she is a most agreeable young person—very nun-like and modest."

The two ladies glanced at each other with faces of interrogation and of alarm. It was some seconds before Mrs. Dumont mustered resolution enough to ask, "Is she Irish ?"

" American, she told me," stated De Bethune. "Black hair and very black eyes, just what I supposed to be American. Besides, her first name is—is Norah, which sounds American, surely."

" We are not acquainted with her," said Mrs. Dumont. "She is not in our circle," she added, on reflection.

Then there was more music, and the pupil sang out of tune—so much so, indeed, that the Professor looked surprised and troubled.

The moment he was gone, Virginia exclaimed, " Now the marriage will be out."

" We can get that girl's address and see her," replied Mrs. Dumont. "Perhaps she wouldn't mind keeping your secret—if you want it kept."

CHAPTER XXIII.

During the afternoon of the next day Professor De Bethune was at the apartment of Norah Macmorran. It was a single plain room, musty in atmosphere and scanty in furniture, with a bed more or less hidden in a curtained alcove ; one of those horrible ambushes where nightmares lie in wait for the sleeper. Before a piano sat Norah, just finishing a piece of music, and looking up anxiously at her teacher with the query, " Was that better, sir ? "

" Yes," he said, in his habitual tone and manner of gentle deference. "It was not only better, but it was exceedingly well."

A smile of joy forced its way into the seriousness and plaintiveness of Norah's face. "Oh, sir ! " she replied, coloring slightly, "I am so glad ! "

"You are very anxious to be a great singer ? " he asked, smiling also, very sympathetically and kindly.

"I am anxious to earn my living, sir."

"You are a high-minded young lady," he said, with an air of surprise and admiration.

"How could I wish not to earn my living, sir ? "

"I alluded to the avowal of poverty. It isn't everybody who is brave enough and self-respectful enough to avow that."

"I have always been poor. I am used to it. I never was so well off before as during this year."

"Ah ! you have had a stroke of good fortune ? Perhaps there will be more. You deserve them."

"It is the Church, sir. The Church is supporting

me here—the congregation of St. Patrick's, in Charleston."

"I have another pupil from Charleston—a very beautiful voice, too—a Miss Beaufort."

Norah, who had been gazing at the floor during most of this dialogue, raised her eyes with an expression of startled inquiry.

"She is with her aunt, a Mrs. Dumont," continued De Bethune. "Did you ever hear of them?"

"Miss Beaufort?" asked Norah, her face a little paler than usual, and her eyes drooped again.

"Yes, that is the name. Did you ever hear her sing?"

"No, sir," murmured Norah. She remained silent a moment, and then timorously queried, "Is the aunt Mrs. Dumont?"

"As I told you—Mrs. Dumont and Miss Beaufort. I hope you will hear the young lady some day; it is a great pleasure."

"And does Mrs. Dumont call her niece Miss Beaufort?" persisted the puzzled and troubled girl.

"She calls her Virginia. There is an old negress in the family who calls her Miss Ginny. But the name is Beaufort; I know it from the people who presented me there; moreover, she answers to it."

"Oh, perhaps it is a sister," Norah thought, aloud.

"Whose sister? Pardon me. I fail to comprehend."

"I don't know," was the embarrassed reply. "Perhaps these are not the ladies. Is she very—handsome?"

"Quite beautiful. You will see her, I hope. I took the liberty of mentioning you to them, and they seemed interested. Last evening, too, I received a message from Mrs. Dumont, asking for your address. I presume that they purpose calling."

"Calling?" repeated Norah, in unconcealable worry.

"I hope I have not annoyed you," said De Bethune. "They are really ladies, and moreover very agreeable ladies, especially the younger. I am sure you will like them."

"And there is no—gentleman?" asked the girl, anxiously.

"Not one," he smiled. "You are very shy, Miss Macmorran. I admire you none the less for it."

"Thank you, sir," murmured Norah, with frank and sweet simplicity, though she still seemed occupied and intimidated.

"You don't fear me?" added De Bethune, in a tone of almost tender inquiry.

"You were recommended to me by the convent," the girl answered, blushing. "Besides, I *must* see you."

"I am glad you must," he said, gazing at her with obvious admiration.

"They are very grand people in their own country," resumed Norah. "I don't see why they must call on me."

She looked appealingly at De Bethune here, as if hoping that he would be her friend in the matter, and prevent the dreaded interview.

"My dear young lady, an artist is an artist," he said, cheeringly. "Miss Beaufort is apparently a very superior young person, and no doubt has the respect of talent for talent. She treated me, a poor professor of music, with courtesy and kindness. I think you may look forward with composure to meeting her."

Then a gentle rap was heard at the door, and he inquired with a bow, "You permit me to open?"

"If you please, sir," whispered Norah, visibly disquieted and apprehensive. Her naturally pale face turned completely colorless when De Bethune gave entrance to Mrs. Dumont, and that stately dame, rustling in stiff silken raiment, marched up to her with an outstretched glove.

"I am glad to see you again, Miss Macmorran," said the unwelcome visitor, with one of those counterfeit smiles which we all know so well. "The moment I heard of your being here, I determined to call."

Norah had risen, and she took the proffered hand; but her lips merely moved and quivered when she tried to speak.

"I want you to be acquainted with my niece," continued Mrs. Dumont, in a hurried, embarrassed tone, for the interview agitated her also. "You and she have the same tastes. Mr. De Bethune has told us of your beautiful voice and execution.—They ought to sing together, oughtn't they, Mr. De Bethune?"

The Professor assented in a few complimentary words, and then, after a puzzled glance at Norah's discomposed countenance, made his urbane adieus, and vanished.

Under the pressure of extreme necessity the girl now regained her powers of speech. She hastily dusted a chair with her handkerchief, offered it meekly to the visitor, and murmured, "Won't you sit down, ma'am?"

Mrs. Dumont seated herself and drew a long breath. Her respiration was affected by the ascent of several stairways, and by the worrying nature of the business in hand. Of course, she remembered her suspicions that there had been a love-affair, and apparently a soul-stir-ring one, between this young woman and the husband of her niece. Of course, too, she was not quite sure that the entanglement, whatever it might amount to, had not continued to the present time. For all she knew to the contrary, Underhill might even now be in Paris, and still devoted, in some fashion or other, to Miss Macmorran. Yet about him she must perforce talk, and against him she must declaim and plead. She must ask, too, for a favor which she did not fully desire. She must implore secrecy for Virginia's marriage, when at heart she felt that such secrecy was wrong, and more than doubted whether it were even worldly-wise.

"My dear—I came partly on business—I want a kindness of you," she began, hesitatingly. "You know who I am?"

"Yes, ma'am," was the meek reply.

"You heard, I believe, of my niece's intended marriage?" (Norah nodded slightly.) "To a Mr. Underhill?" (Another poor little nod.) "There were circumstances which enforced the marriage," continued Mrs. Dumont, with a sigh. "But they could not make it pleasant—you hear me?"

Norah's eyes had been on the floor, but she raised them an instant and gasped, "Yes."

"Ah! dear—it was a sad marriage—a funeral," Mrs. Dumont sighed again, recollecting, no doubt, the black-crape dress and the darkened church. "I hardly know how to go on. But the long and short of it is, that they couldn't live together; they separated immediately."

Norah lifted a pair of astonished eyes, and a flood of color rushed into her cheeks. There was something like a passion of resuscitated hope in the gesture and expression; but it was trampled out immediately by conscience or reason, and the face became as nun-like as before.

"It was not a divorce," explained Mrs. Dumont. "It couldn't be a divorce—only a separation. Well, they are living apart ; that is the whole of it. I thought it best to tell you everything."

Norah said nothing, but she glanced piteously at her visitor's face, and the look seemed to ask, "Why ?"

"I want you to keep our secret," resumed the elder lady. "You will do us a favor, a very great favor, if you will not mention the marriage."

"What !" said the amazed girl, startled into the power of speech. "Do you mean *never ?*"

"Not for some time—not while you are in Paris—unless we advise you to the contrary."

Norah pondered a moment, and then replied, hesitatingly, "I think I can promise you."

"Oh ! do," urged Mrs. Dumont, in the faint tone of one who implores with a doubting conscience. "Thank you, my dear. We shall be under great obligations. If we can ever do you any kindness in return—"

"I need nothing," said Norah, supposing that money favors were meant—the natural supposition of a child of poverty. "But I will promise—since you wish it so much."

"Indeed we do ! And now you must call on us," added the *grande dame* with an effort. " By-the-way, please remember to speak to my niece always as Miss Beaufort, or Virginia. She prefers her own name, under the circumstances. I don't know that you can blame her for loving it. It is an honorable name. You may be sure that she will bear it worthily. She has no mean or unworthy purpose in this secrecy—only safety from

persecution, and tranquillity. So we can rely upon you
can we? You will not allude to the marriage, nor mention that dreaded name?"

"Oh, no, ma'am!" said Norah, with an earnestness
which confessed that the name was a terrible one to her
also.

Mrs. Dumont glanced at her significantly; she in
part comprehended the girl's emotion. But it would not
do to inquire strictly, or in fact to inquire at all, into
the causes of it.

"I shouldn't want even Mr. De Bethune to know of
the marriage," she added, reverting to her own proper
affair.

"I won't mention it to him, nor to any one."

"So much obliged to you, Miss Macmorran!" smiled
the lady of the old *régime*. "Well, now—" Here she
hesitated a moment; she was going to say a very great
thing—"now you must be our friend," she concluded,
with heroic resolution.

"Oh, thank you, Mrs. Dumont," stammered Norah.
"I suppose," she presently continued, "that he never
comes there?"

"He? Who? Do you mean her husband? No
indeed, never! She trusts never to meet him again in
this world. Well, now, I am so glad I called on you!
You must be our friend; you must call and see us," repeated Mrs. Dumont, firmly. "Will you come and sing
with Virginia to-morrow—at three, say?"

Norah, who would have given a world to refuse,
tried to show some willingness, and did succeed in
forcing a piteous smile as she answered, "Yes, Mrs.
Dumont."

Then the visitor, drawing a long sigh, as if she had

performed a very distressing duty indeed, gathered herself rustling out of her chair and blandly took her departure.

CHAPTER XXIV.

We shall obtain light upon some of the personages and circumstances of this history by going back to Mrs. Fitz James and her brother at the moment of their exit from Virginia's parlor.

The genial and chatty couple had scarcely closed the Beaufort door behind them, when Hedstone turned petulantly upon his sister, and demanded, "What are you throwing that girl at that Belgian's head for?"

"Of course, I wouldn't do it, Frank, if anything better could be done," whispered Lotharinga, eagerly and placatingly. "But what can *you* do, with a wife in America? If you could get a divorce—if there was any chance of it—" She hesitated a little, and then asked, "*Is* there?"

Mr. Hedstone's intonation was quite surly as he answered, "Not on *my* side." After pondering a moment he added, still more surlily, "My wife could get one—and won't."

"O Frank! don't go on with the subject," said the sister, flinching and coloring. "It's not pleasant to hear about. I don't see how you could be so imprudent as to put yourself entirely in the wrong. It always was so. There's ill-luck in our family."

"Your own match doesn't appear to have been made in heaven, my poor sister," returned Hedstone. The speech and the tone in which it was uttered were urbane enough; but either Lotharinga had an evil conscience, or she habitually expected sarcasm from her brother; she flinched and colored again.

"Mr. Fitz James was a great sufferer," she murmured. "I've no doubt it was a relief to him to get off his bed and into his grave."

Hedstone laughed outright. "I rather think so," he said. "Poor old fool! what a time he had of it!"

"I had a hard time, too," gasped the widow, ready to cry with humiliation and anger. "I think you ought to have pitied me, especially when you had crowded me into it—the whole family coaxing, and crowding, and bullying!"

"Well, it *was* pitiable," conceded the brother. "What can a young lassie do wi' an auld man? You deserve every cent you got by it.—But now, as for this Beaufort affair, what are you driving at? The girl could do better than take De Bethune. She could have Peyton, for instance," he added, with a malicious smile.

Lotharinga tossed her small head defiantly, something like a pretty heifer that threatens hostilities. "I don't know whether she could or not," she said. "He isn't so easy to catch with mere money. He has enough of his own, I think."

She pondered a bit, glanced at him investigatingly, and continued: "I'll tell you what I am driving at. Miss Beaufort is a millionaire, and De Bethune is of noble descent. If they get married, and she can manage to buy a title for him, then we shall know at least one noble. That will be a beginning. We shall get into the aristocratic circle."

"Oh! I see," grinned Frank; "and then you can make a strike for yourself. Well, it may work—by bare possibility. She can't buy a title, but she can buy an estate, and that may bring a courtesy title. It may work. I won't try to hinder."

"Don't, Frank! We don't want any more gabble and scandal about the Hedstones."

By this time they had got out of the house and reached Lotharinga's *coupé*. Hedstone helped his sister into the vehicle with an air of affectionate deference, and touched his hat in response to her lively and good-natured smile of farewell. One would have said that he was one of the best and sweetest of brothers.

Then he picked up a cab and drove to unknown regions. If he played there, as it is to be feared that he did, his ventures were probably fortunate, for when he appeared in Lotharinga's rooms, some three days later, he was in high good-humor, and his banter was all of the pleasant sort. In actual fact, and notwithstanding his occasional bitterness and sarcasm, he seemed to be at bottom a fairly loyal and affectionate relative, and rather proud of his sister's prettiness and small clevernesses.

"What are you up to now, old lady?" he asked, watching her with a smile as she stood before a pierglass, carefully arranging a rose-bud in her black hair. "Who are you setting that trap for? Is it still the Colonel?"

"Mind your own business, Frank."

"Thank Heaven, I haven't any!"

"It's such a shame, in a man!"

"It's no stigma in Paris, and not much of a one in Baltimore."

"You perfectly pester me with hanging around my rooms. I wish I wasn't so agreeable."

"Dear old lady! you don't mean to be. You simply can't help it. You are so amusing that it makes you agreeable in spite of yourself."

"It must be awfully amusing to sit and gape at one's own sister. You must be hard up for amusement."

"I see. There's somebody coming this morning, and you want me out of the way."

"Go and watch some other woman—do! Go and sit up with Miss Beaufort."

"I thought you didn't want me to sit up with her."

"Of course, not on your own account, Frank. But you might talk with her about De Bethune, and say a good word for him."

"Oh! *that* never will come to anything. The girl is green and uncultivated, and rather heavy company; but she is solid and sensible, and devilish aristocratic, too; she's not going to snap at a poor professor of music; it doesn't stand to reason."

"He's there every day; and that tells. And he's begun to adore her; and that tells. And they're mad about music together; and that will tell. I think the marriage is very likely to come about, and I know it's our policy to help it along. Do, for pity's sake, go and see her, and say something handsome about him!"

"Yes: you want me to be off; want the deck cleared for action—passengers go below. Who is it? If it's the right man, I'll vanish. Is it Peyton?"

"What if it is?"

"Oh, well, if it's the Colonel, I'll oblige you. I've

fallen in love with Peyton myself. I'd rather have you snare Peyton than all the other twenty."

"What twenty?" demanded Lotharinga, pettishly.

"Why, the twenty men of all nations—Americans, and Englishmen, and Frenchmen; Parthians, and Medes, and Elamites—whom you are trifling with at present."

"Don't be a bore, Frank. There's nothing funny about such exaggerations—what people call American humor. I haven't above five or six men on hand; and they are trying to flirt with me—not I with them."

"Yes, it was the lamb which troubled the water, and not the wolf," returned Hedstone, soberly. Apparently, he would have preferred that his sister should coquette less and with fewer men.

"Now do be amiable, Frank, and clear out," urged Lotharinga, beginning to look cross.

"Of course, I will," answered Frank, his smile returning. "If it is the Colonel, he sha'n't be interfered with. Not only will I go out, but I'll stand in the hall, and keep everybody else from coming in."

"Frank, if you *do!* Why, it would be just eavesdropping. Just go entirely away, and don't stop till you find Miss Beaufort."

At this moment there was a rap on the door. Hedstone stepped to it in his quick, feline way, opened it and presented his hand with a smile. The hand was taken by a person well known to us—the gentleman who had married Virginia Beaufort—no other than Harry Edwards Underhill. He looked precisely as we have hitherto seen him, except that his blonde hair was combed straight down on all sides and cut across his forehead in a "banger," and that in place of his usual fashionable morning suit he wore a frock-coat, vest, and trousers of "Confederate gray."

"So glad to see you, Colonel Peyton!" exclaimed Mrs. Fitz James, rushing forward with a cheerful blush and sparkling of the eyes. "So very kind of you to remember your promise!"

"Thank you, Mrs. Fitz James," said Underhill, tranquilly. "It is a kindness to myself.—Mr. Hedstone, how are you?"

"Please excuse my brother for leaving you," put in Lotharinga, hastily. "He has pressing business on hand. —Frank, remember my directions."

"All right," smiled Frank, picking up his hat.— "Good-by, Colonel; see you again soon."

Hedstone out of the way, conversation opened vivaciously between Mrs. Fitz James and Underhill, especially on the part of the lady. It soon appeared that the acquaintance was the result of a chance meeting at the Louvre; that it was already sufficiently advanced to admit of easy and almost confidential intercourse; that Lotharinga had not the least suspicion of her visitor's being other than Colonel Peyton and a Virginian; and that she was, to say the least, very eager to monopolize and fascinate him.

"Where were you yesterday?" she demanded, in a tone of amiable reproof. "If I hadn't met you by mere accident at Galignani's, I should have passed twenty-four hours without seeing you."

"The terrible misfortune!" he laughed. "I was amusing myself with Paris. It is very alluring."

"Isn't it lovely! isn't it immense!" exclaimed Lotharinga. "Oh, if Americans knew!—they would all come here. But then it would cease to be attractive."

9

"Not if they were all like—" And here he made a bow to her, smiling the while, however, in a light way, as if to say, Don't take me too seriously.

"I wish I knew how to pay compliments," murmured the pretty little widow, with a smile of real pleasure. "You should have some nice ones, Colonel Peyton. As it is, you must be content with a nosegay."

She took the rose-bud from her hair, leaned toward him, and coquettishly put it in his button-hole, lingering contentedly over her task, looking up at him with a smile and saying softly, "I am so awkward about it!"

"You have probably had so little practice," he answered, watching her curiously and good-naturedly.

"Satirical man!" laughed Lotharinga, though she blushed, too. "Who would have thought of drawing satire from a Virginian? I weakly believed that they were serious."

"So they are. I solemnly return thanks for this embellishment."

"No, you don't. You think I do such things for other people. That is the first posy that I have put in a button-hole for years."

"Poor, neglected button-holes!" he smiled. Then, as if the subject had received attention enough, he added in a careless tone: "How do you pass all your time, Mrs. Fitz James? Do you find any society in Paris?"

"I care so little for it!" sighed the widow. "My tastes are very domestic. Of course, there is something in the social way—imperial receptions, and balls, and that sort of thing; you know we Americans can't get into the Saint-Germain circle—poky old decayed aristocrats!"

" But there is an American colony, isn't there ? "

"Too many Yankees—nearly all Yankees. Of course, you hate Yankees."

" I hardly like to say that I do," returned Underhill, with a smile which Mrs. Fitz James, of course, failed to understand.

" Oh ! you are a soldier," said the lady, glancing with flattering eyes at his gray coat. " I believe the soldiers are the most thoroughly reconstructed part of the Southern population."

" No doubt of it, Mrs. Fitz James. But, to quit that painful subject and return to Paris, are there no Southern families here—none from the Confederate States ? "

" Oh, so very few ! " Lotharinga sighed, as if the fact grieved her not a little. " I suppose they are all broken in fortune, and can't travel. I don't know of a single family from Virginia."

Underhill hesitated a moment, and then added in a querying tone, but quite tranquilly, "I heard the other day of a Mrs. Dumont and her niece."

The widow gave him a furtive glance, which, instantaneous as it was, revealed suspicion and alarm.

CHAPTER XXV.

THE instant which followed Underhill's slight but no doubt interrogative allusion to his wife was a troubled one to both him and Mrs. Fitz James.

For reasons mysterious to her, though of course comprehensible to us, he colored and looked uneasy under her transient glance of investigation. She, on her part, had a discomforted, fictitious smile, and, when she answered him, spoke with a really childlike, pitiful eagerness, all showing that, coquette though she might be, she was a loving little woman at bottom, and had already become tenderly interested in her colonel.

"They are not from Virginia," she said, hastily. "They are South Carolinians—of the old-fashioned sort, you know—awfully prim and reserved."

The information did not seem to disturb the visitor; on the contrary, he had the air of being relieved and gratified. "I know the type," he responded in a low, meditative tone. "By-the-way, what is the name of the niece?"

"Beaufort—Miss Virginia Beaufort," stated Mrs. Fitz James, and immediately asked, "Have you ever met her?"

Underhill did not answer her question; he was gazing at her in grave surprise. "Beaufort?" he interrogated, his cheek reddening again. Then, recovering his automatic utterance and manner, he added, "I thought I had heard of her by another name."

"Beaufort—Miss Virginia Beaufort. Have you ever met her?" persisted Lotharinga.

"As I was saying, I have heard of them," said Underhill, evasively. "What sort of a person is Miss Beaufort? Reserved, you say?"

Considering that he was inquiring about his own wife, and had just learned the unpleasant fact that she had dropped her marriage name, the question was put with wonderful tranquillity of manner. Nevertheless, he could not quite deceive the bright eyes of the experienced flirt who sat beside him, and who was watching him with an attention acute enough to overhear his very heart-beats.

"Really, Colonel Peyton, you are greatly interested," she giggled uneasily. "I think you must have seen her. *Have* you seen her?"

Then Underhill judged it best to admit that she had been pointed out to him by a friend.

"I think she is perfectly lovely—don't *you?*" added Lotharinga, artfully.

He dropped his eyes pensively, as if he were recalling the darkened church and his veiled bride, and responded in a dreamy way, "I didn't see her very plainly."

Mrs. Fitz James could not suppress a little smile of satisfaction. Then she qualified her statement as to Virginia's loveliness by subjoining that some people thought her handsome, and others not. "She doesn't know anything," was the next bit of information. "She grew up in South Carolina during the war. No schooling; no accomplishments; no habits of society; no subjects of conversation—excepting, of course, the war— that everlasting war."

"Indeed, I am sorry to hear it," muttered Underhill, who was in reality sorry, as we may imagine.

"Oh, well, perhaps I am a little hard on her," resumed Mrs. Fitz James, at bottom a good-natured creature. "She is studying French and paying attention to music. She is trying to learn something."

"Music?" queried Underhill, who was, as we remember, an adorer of the melodious art.

"Yes, that's her strong point; she sings pretty well for a novice."

"I am exceedingly fond of singing," said the Colonel

in a wishful tone, which was equivalent to asking an introduction to Miss Beaufort.

Apparently Lotharinga took alarm again. "Oh! are you?" she answered, sweetly. "Then you ought to hear Miss Macmorran. I'll present you to Miss Macmorran."

"Miss Macmorran?" repeated Underhill, no doubt considerably dismayed.

"Yes! Miss Norah Macmorran. I met her at the Beaufort rooms. They seem to be quite friendly. It's rather curious. She's Irish, of course, Miss Macmorran is. It's rather curious they should be acquainted with her. By-the-way, I don't know that they are so very intimate," added the hasty and heedless little prattler, suddenly recollecting the facts of the case. "I've only seen her there once, and that was yesterday. But she sang for us; and oh! it was lovely—very well done indeed. I must look Miss Macmorran up and present you. Did you ever hear of her? She's preparing for the opera, I suppose. I didn't know but you might have heard of her. Gentlemen sometimes keep track of these professionals, don't they?"

Underhill seemed absent-minded, and made no direct response. Presently he resumed, "I suppose you have heard Miss Beaufort sing?"

"Well, I believe I have," said Lotharinga, doubtfully, as if she were sounding her memory. "Oh! yes, of course I have—it made no great impression. Do you know, Colonel Peyton, that you have asked me a good many questions as to Miss Beaufort? You are bewitched about her; yes, you are." After a moment of watching him and pondering, she continued, "You are not the only one."

"I never spoke to her, and never saw her face," affirmed the Colonel, not quite suppressing his uneasiness.

"Very likely. She always goes veiled, and generally in her *coupé*. But you have seen enough of her—some remarkably pretty costume, perhaps—enough to fascinate you."

"That is enough sometimes," admitted Underhill, though he seemed puzzled, probably at the feminine stress laid on the word costume.

"You are not the only one," repeated Mrs. Fitz James.

The husband could not help looking interested in this bit of news about his wife.

"She is very much adored," pursued Mrs. Fitz James, in a significant tone.

"How?" He asked the question in spite of suggestions of prudence and delicacy; he undoubtedly asked it before he had time to reflect upon it.

"And I think she likes it," affirmed Mrs. Fitz James.

There was a moment of silence. If the lady had glanced at her visitor, she would have seen a perturbed countenance. But her eyes were fixed on the floor with an air of meditation which was significant of invention.

"Mind, now, this is confidential," she resumed. "Oh! there is nothing wrong about it. A girl has a right to take a fancy when she is well courted."

Underhill made a strong effort to smile, and was able to say, "You tantalize me, Mrs. Fitz James."

"Of course I do," she laughed. "It must be quite unbearable to a man who has seen her drive by. Well, there isn't so very, very much to it—nothing declared about it yet, I fancy. But there's love at the bottom;

at least, I think so—I am pretty sure.　The happy man
is a Belgian—a Monsieur De Bethune."

"Horrible!" muttered Underhill, with feelings which
we can understand far better than could Mrs. Fitz
James.

"Not at all," she laughed.　"Not in the least bit, I
assure you ; on the contrary, it's quite delightful.　He's
a charming man, and of the very loveliest lineage, too—
one of the sweetest old genealogies in Europe.　The
Seigneur d'Aumale, we call him ; and I'm sure it's a
very nice title, if it *is* extinct.　His ancestor received
the fief of Aumale from Richard the Lion-hearted.
How can it be horrible?"

It may be imagined how hateful and tragical all this
cheerful levity was to Underhill.　He dropped his eyes
under those of his unconscious tormentor as he murmured the piteous evasion, or protest, "But a Catholic
and a foreigner!"

"Dear me, what difference does all that make, especially to a young lady of high blood?" rattled Mrs.
Fitz James.　"Catholic or Protestant, it's the same re-
ligion *au fond*.　And a good little Confederate—you
ought to understand it, Colonel—a Confederate girl
doesn't object so much to foreigners.　She at least finds
them more to her taste than Yankees."

Here was another hard hit for Virginia Beaufort's
husband, and he said, "I suppose so," in such a cheerless tone that Lotharinga stared.

"You are now abroad, Colonel," she ran on.　"You
still believe that Anglo-Saxons and Anglo-Saxon ways
are finer than anything ; but you will change your ideas
before long."

As he shook his head she laughed and added: "Ah,

wait! Paris is wonderfully converting. Stay here long enough, and you will think as Paris does. You will come to think, for instance—" Here she hesitated, and then, cheering herself with a giggle, proceeded, " You will come to believe that the one great object of life is to make love."

" I don't know but I concede that already," replied Underhill, no doubt remembering his wife and his desire to win her.

Mrs. Fitz James was evidently cheered by the response. " Let me fasten your rose-bud," she murmured, leaning toward him and putting forth her dainty fingers. " It is lopping over in the most alarming manner. It would be a bad omen to have it fall out."

" Thank you," he muttered, mechanically. " I shouldn't like a bad omen."

" It would really distress *me*," she said, rolling up her melting dark eyes at him. " There—I have pinned it fast—I have secured myself against the omen."

Underhill bowed his thanks, and then glanced soberly about him, apparently looking for his hat.

Mrs. Fitz James was clever enough to divine his purpose, and to invent a pretext for prolonging the interview. " Dear me, I quite forgot," she laughed. " We were to go over to the Louvre again. You promised to put me through a study of those Dutch extravaganzas, and show me why they amount to something in art."

Underhill had an air of not remembering the agreement, but he bowed civilly and responded, " I am at your service."

Lotharinga sprang up gayly, ran into her dressing-room, and presently returned with a hat on and a shawl in her hands. " Please put this on me," she said, coaxingly. "These French maids are such truants—gone just when you want them."

Underhill had distinctly seen a *bonne* through the crack of the dressing-room door ; but he of course arranged the shawl around the plump shoulders of the little lady. In the midst of the delicate labor she stepped back a pace as if to make his task handier, and pressed lightly against his arm.

"Mercy, how awkward I am ! " she smiled, looking up archly ; but although her cheek was very near to his lips, they did not meet.

"There—thank you—am I all right ? " she added, facing him and then turning herself about for inspection. " I trust entirely to your eyes."

He quietly expressed the opinion that he had put on her drapery as well as a man could.

" As well as an unmarried man could," she laughed. "Some day, it is to be hoped, you will know how to do it even better."

Then, taking his arm, she led him away to the quietest rooms of the Louvre.

CHAPTER XXVI.

As we already know, the advent of General Hilton had been for some time expected and desired by Mrs. Dumont and Virginia, two somewhat lonesome women, who of late had been kept very short of human converse, and who were downright hungry for that of South Carolinians and old acquaintance.

At last he came, his wooden leg gallantly storming

the lofty Parisian stairways, and his tall figure looming vast in a London suit of shepherd's plaid, selected perhaps because of its resemblance to the Confederate gray. Aunt Chloe and Uncle Phil were the first to meet him, and they welcomed him with an enthusiasm tropical enough to ripen bananas.

"Laws, Masr Gin'ral! Ain't we glad to see ye! Bin hopin' fur ye dese yere six weeks. Have so, fur true." Such was the substance and general purport of the first prolonged outcry of salutation.

"Couldn't get here any quicker, old folks," answered Hilton, cordially shaking the black hands. "Too many fine things to see on the way. Wasted some time in England, trying to find out where the Hiltons came from. How do you two like foreign parts?"

Uncle Phil. "Like 'em firs' rate, Boss—heap sight better'n Charleston."

The General. "Better than Charleston? Old reprobate! hoary apostate! Have you turned your old back on your country? You don't get any sweet-potatoes here."

Uncle Phil (suiggering). "Da's so, Boss—nor hoecake, nuther. But we gits 'long mighty fine on white bread an' chickin. We has good eatin', Boss."

Aunt Chloe. "Never lit on no better, Masr, not in no times. An' y' know cookin' has kinder died out in Sou' Carliny sence d'wah. Crow an' corn dōn' grow in same field."

The General. "Oh! shut up about the war. I'm going to forget the war. Where are the ladies?"

Aunt Chloe. "Yere comes Miss Ginny.—Clar out, Phil! Dōn' you an' me be bodderin' roun'." (*Exeunt Uncle Phil and Aunt Chloe.*)

Virginia arrived with rustling and laughter, a tempest of silk and of glad girlhood.

"Oh, my dear General! my dear old friend!" she exclaimed, clutching the hero's mighty arms and kissing his leathery cheek.

"Ah, my child!" returned Hilton, obviously much affected. "Rose of Charleston! flower of the lowlands!" he repeated, holding her by both hands and gazing at her noble face with the frank admiration of an elderly man for girlish freshness and beauty. Then he led her to a sofa, placed her upon it tenderly, seated himself in front of her, and studied her in silence.

"Well, what do you think of me?" Virginia laughed, joyously. "Have I changed?"

"Only for the better," declared the General. "Greatly for the better, and still the same. Still like your family. Beaufort all over. Ah, Beaufort—Beaufort!" he murmured in a caressing tone, letting his lips dwell lovingly on the word. "There never was a family like it—not on this side the water."

"This side, General?" asked Virginia, with another gay laugh. "Do you remember that you are in Europe?"

"No," he said, smiling. "I am in South Carolina. A South Carolinian is always in South Carolina. When he says *this* side of the ocean, he means *his* side."

"And the Atlantic is bounded on the east by the old country, where the South Carolinians came from, and on the west by the country where they live now."

"That is our geography, my dear. I wonder you should laugh at it. You have lost a little of the pristine spirit. At home you wouldn't have joked on these matters."

"It is a shame," said Virginia. "But I can't help it. It is so bewildering to travel! Europe is magnificent, General, and Paris is bigger than Charleston."

"Yes, and I want to protest against it; I want to form a league against it. Can you guess how the sight of this old-world splendor affects me? It is beginning to Americanize me. I want a vaster South Carolina than I was contented with once. I want to spread that name all over the United States, and look upon the whole republic as South Carolina. We are not enough alone to match ourselves against Europe. We want the help of every man of our race on the other side of the Atlantic."

"O General! — ah, General! You are more perverted than I. You are becoming a Federalist."

"It is a great country, my dear. I feel mightily protected with an American passport in my pocket. *Civis Romanus sum.* What a country it is! A wave of its hand sends imperial France out of Mexico. What other state in the whole world orders Napoleon away from its borders?"

"My good old friend, you are turning traitor to Jefferson Davis. Would you dare talk in this way to Robert E. Lee?"

"My dear, on my way North I saw him—the lovely old Christian hero! He said very much these same things to me. He is submissive, sublime, beautiful! He bows to the will of Providence. He honestly accepts the government which God has given him."

"Ah, dear!" sighed Virginia. "The soldiers have abandoned the fight, and only the women continue it."

"The women and the politicians—the politicians on both sides: may God confound them! I don't mean

the women—God help them ! They have sore, wounded
hearts, and they can't forget all in a moment."

"Never !—I never can forget !" declared Virginia.
She spoke energetically, but not quite with the old ran-
cor.

"I don't blame you," said Hilton, gently. "Nevertheless, may God aid you to forget ! You will find a
blessing in forgetfulness. I have come to the opinion
that true policy, as well as true magnanimity, consists
in forgetting our enmities as faithfully as we remember
our friendships."

"Ah, well !" responded the girl, drawing another
sigh, a slightly weary one, as if one might tire of the
subject. "We won't dispute about it. I can't agree
with you, but we won't dispute."

Hilton waved his hand, as if bidding farewell to the
ugly reminiscence, and then glanced about the apartment. It was the first Parisian suite of rooms that he
had seen, and he was evidently pleased with its furnishings and knickknackeries.

"You are finely off here," he smiled. "How many
pretty things !"

"I am ashamed of my luxury when I think of our
poor people at home," Virginia said. "At all events, I
have the satisfaction of being out of debt to South Carolinians. I am proud and glad of having paid you,
General. Excuse my mentioning it."

"Mention it as often as you please, my child," he
laughed. "I like to hear about it. It is an immense
pleasure to be worth money again."

Then followed a brief dialogue, from which it appeared that Virginia had devoted a certain sum to the
relief of Charleston's poor, and that the General had

distributed it for her. He told a pathetic tale of widows, orphans, and disabled soldiers.

"Oh, dear! I ought to go back," groaned Virginia. "But I am afraid of meeting—"

"Your husband," said Hilton, looking her steadily in the face, as if he meant to impress her with the title and its claims.

"I hate the word," the girl broke out. "Please don't use it. We never mention his name."

"I had hoped that somewhat of that feeling might have passed away," returned the General, softly. He glanced about the fine parlor again, and added: "It seems to me that, under the circumstances, it ought not to last a lifetime. May I tell you, my dear, that, when I distributed your gift among our poor friends, I almost felt it a duty to inform them that, after all, it was Yankee money?"

"Oh! why do you throw that in my face?" demanded Virginia, fairly flinching in body as well as in spirit.

Hilton remained pensive a moment, and then asked, "Can you tell me where he is?"

"No!" was the quick and almost angry reply.

"I had hoped you could. I have lost track of him."

"What in the world do you want to keep track of him for?"

"He has done some fine things. He, too, has given large bounty to the Southern poor, and I am the only person who knew whence the mercy came."

"I wish you hadn't told me that," murmured Virginia. "What do you want to make me uncomfortable for?"

"So you can give me no news of him?" the General repeated, almost disconsolately.

"No, not a word—thank Heaven! I can't help saying so."

"I hope sincerely that nothing has happened to him."

Virginia colored with sudden excitement, and asked eagerly, "Has he really disappeared?"

Thereupon Hilton told what he knew. He had written to Underhill two months ago, and got no answer; on his way to Europe he had sought him in Boston, but without success; he had found numbers of his friends, but all were ignorant of his whereabout.

"Yankee friends!" sneered Virginia. Then she added in a tone of argument, "You can see that he has no real friends."

"He has *one*," affirmed the General, slapping the knee of his amputated leg so emphatically that the girl recoiled, looking awed, hurt, and humbled. "Well," he resumed, "I could learn nothing of him, except that he had been heard to talk of a trip to California and China, and that he was gone."

"I hope he is at the antipodes, and likes it," muttered Virginia.

"I hope he is safe," replied Hilton, gazing at her gravely—so gravely and indeed reprovingly that she felt driven to add, "Of course, I don't wish him any harm."

"Certainly not," said Hilton. "He has done you what good he might, and as little harm as possible."

"O General! I had expected a friend, and here you come as a foe!" was the half-mournful, half-petulant response. It was clear enough that the young woman had been somewhat wearied and fretted by the persistent presentation of the excellences and the claims of her husband.

Hilton divined this, looked about the room for a new topic, and, perceiving Virginia's piano, asked for a song. But just then De Bethune arrived to give his lesson in music. The hostess received him so graciously and cordially that the old friend bent his solemn gray eyes upon the new one with studious inspection. De Bethune, on his part, was tremendously impressed at being presented to a General ; he looked so wonderstruck and made a bow so full of reverence that Hilton stared at him in surprise. A minute later, standing beside his pupil at the piano, he whispered to her : "Pardon my moment of confusion, Miss Beaufort. I never before met a general officer. I really could not talk."

She was already running her fingers through a prelude, and she merely replied by a little laugh of surprise. The General, meanwhile, reposed his vast length upon a sofa, waiting anxiously for the voice which he loved. He noted the smiling confidence between the two others, and he was undisguisably ill pleased with it. His suspicion, of course, was that this foreigner, this bowing and smirking and cooing Frenchman, was trying to pay court to Mrs. Underhill. He staid through the whole music-lesson like a duenna. Then, when Mrs. Dumont came in from a shopping raid, he caught an opportunity to grumble at her for leaving her niece so much alone. A long confabulation on Southern matters and Charlestonian gossip did not fully restore his equanimity, and when he left the Beaufort rooms he still wore a brooding and anxious countenance.

CHAPTER XXVII.

For a week or so the General was prodigiously occupied with Paris, as Americans are apt to be when they first reach that city of splendors and delights.

He took a cab by the day, and drove everywhere and saw everything ; he was perpetually in a cab, or a gallery, or a church, or a theatre. He began his inspection of the marvelous capital in the company of Mrs. Dumont and Virginia, but, finding that they wearied a little of twice-seen sights, he magnanimously continued the labor alone—not always alone, either, for, as he was a social, urbane, personable man, genial in deportment and attractive in appearance, he drew to himself quite a number of chance acquaintance. Yankees made up to him, and only guessed little by little that he had been a rebel, and parted from him with wonder that they could be sorry to lose sight of a rebel. Englishmen cottoned to him, and fairly loved him when they learned that he was an ex-Confederate, and almost bowed down to him when they heard him called General. A German count was delighted to practice upon him his moderate stock of English, and a custodian who could not understand a word he said showed him the private rooms of the Tuileries.

Among these picture-gallery intimates was a pretty little black-eyed lady, whom he nearly stumbled over in one of the dimmest passages of the Louvre, and who received his apologies with such a winning smile and ready sparkle of small-talk, that he at once addressed her as a countrywoman, and strolled on with her for half an hour, gathering conversation and companionship out of various schools of painting. The result was that the two exchanged cards, and the General called next day on Mrs. Fitz James, and the acquaintance became permanent. On his second visit he learned that she had quitted her private apartment for the Hôtel du Louvre. Betaking himself thither during the course of the day, he found the little lady attired as if to go out.

."I have come at the wrong moment," he said, glancing at her hat. "Don't let me detain you."

"You always come at the right moment, General," smiled Mrs. Fitz James. "Gentlemen are apt to. Do sit down. Some friends are to call for me, but meantime I want somebody to talk to."

"I wonder at your leaving your pretty rooms," remarked Hilton. "Do you like hotels best?"

"Oh! sometimes," vaguely answered the lady, who had a reason for her change which she did not care to avow. "You are at the Hôtel Castiglione, are you not?" she rattled on. "It is a quiet little place, and very handy to the theatres. But why not come here? I always did like the Hôtel du Louvre. The service is so good! A lady likes to be waited on. Then the palace is close by. I adore the galleries. And then the shop— the Magasin du Louvre—it is right under us. You don't care for shopping, I suppose. But we do—we silly women. I can lull myself to sleep with thinking of the sweet things down below me. By-the-way, I am going out with your lovely friend and pet, Virginia. Isn't she superb? *I* think so. We are to go to a private concert—something very choice and *recherché.* I wish I had a card for you. But De Bethune could only get three; so we must leave you out. Of course, he did what he could for Virginia. He is *ravi de Mademoiselle Virginie,* and no wonder. I sometimes wish he could find a success there. Isn't he charming?—and such a lineage, too! One seldom hears of anything as old as Richard the Lion-hearted. It is a real pity that such an elegant man of such high descent should have neither title nor estate. A fortune would mend all that. What do you think, General, of trying to get Virginia for him?"

"Preposterous!" exclaimed the old friend of the Beauforts, angered as well as confounded by this babble, and not able at the moment to decide whether he should or should not reveal the fact of Virginia's marriage. Presently he remembered his manners, and added hastily: "Excuse me. I know the young lady well. It isn't possible that she could take an interest in him."

"I know her too," laughed Lotharinga, tossing her saucy little head, brimful of coquetries and suspicions of coquetries. "A woman knows a woman better than a man can. Virginia and I have been rivals for De Bethune; that is, in a composed, decent, friendly way; nothing at all emotional, you understand — no transports of jealousy. But I have given him up to her— since I met you, General," she added with another silvery laugh.

The General did not respond to her jocose compliment, not even by a smile. In spite of his habitual urbanity and his efforts at self-control, he had somewhat the air of being indignant, and also anxious. Perhaps it occurred to Lotharinga that he was in love with Virginia himself; at all events, after one bright glance at his solemnized face, she changed the subject.

"Oh! I forgot," she said; "have you seen Colonel Peyton?"

"Colonel Peyton?" repeated Hilton, absently.

"Ah, you haven't met him, then? He is a Virginian; and such a superb gentleman! just the Virginian type. I want you to meet him. I know you will be delighted with each other."

"Where is he staying?" asked the General, who could not help being interested at last by the name of Peyton, so redolent of Southern aristocracy.

"Here—at the hotel," hesitated the widow, coloring a little, and letting her gaze wander. Even a man might guess that she had come to reside in the Hôtel du Louvre for the sake of being under the same roof with that wonderful Virginian. Hilton looked at her, dropped his eyes considerately to the floor, and quietly murmured that he should be much pleased to meet the Colonel. Just then a servant brought in a card, and Lotharinga rose with a smile of apology.

"I must go," she said. "The carriage is waiting. Don't give yourself the trouble to go down with me."

Knowing well that his escort would be a detention, the wooden-legged hero only went with Mrs. Fitz James as far as the head of the stairway, and there bade her adieu with a ceremonious bow. Then, after the rustle of her swift descent had flitted out of hearing, he limped slowly earthward, muttering aloud, "Frivolous, dangerous rattle-pate! Very bad company for my pet!"

On the landing of the second flight he halted, and stared with a puzzled air at an ascending figure. It was a blonde young man, dressed in a complete suit of Confederate gray, with his yellow hair combed straight and cut square across his forehead. His eyes were bent upon the stairs, and he did not see the General.

"I beg your pardon, sir," hesitated Hilton. "Is this—isn't this Colonel—"

Before the mystified man could finish his query, the other looked up, smiled familiarly, put forth his hand and replied: "Yes, it is Colonel Peyton. How are you, General?"

"Good Heavens! You don't mean—why, God bless my soul!" exclaimed the amazed Hilton.

"Yes, I am Colonel Peyton," returned Underhill. "I'm in disguise," he added in a serio-comic whisper. "Come into my room, and I'll tell you all about it. . . . Yes, I am Mrs. Fitz James's Colonel Peyton," he continued, when they were alone. "I am playing the Confederate hero. I am planning to make my wife's acquaintance."

The General gazed at him a moment with a perplexed countenance, as though he either disapproved morally of the stratagem, or doubted its success. At last, with an air of suspending judgment, he simply replied, "She just drove away from the door, I believe."

"I saw her: she is very beautiful—very!" said Underhill. He remained pensive an instant, as if recalling the image to his mind, and then added: "She looked me straight in the face. Ah, General! it made my heart beat horribly."

Hilton leaned forward in his chair, seized the young man's hand, and wrung it hard. "You have my utmost sympathy," he declared. "What can I *do* for you?"

"Keep my secret, at least for a while. Help me on with it, if you feel that you may. Learn, for instance, to call me Peyton."

"Secret!" exclaimed the General. "What secret is there about it? Here you are going around with

your own face on. I should have known you at once
but for your new way of brushing your hair."

"Exactly. You would have known me, if you had
known me. A very slight change in a face will puzzle
a man, especially when he meets the face unexpectedly.
As for my wife, she wouldn't know me in any shape,
unless I should put on false whiskers."

"And you propose to make her acquaintance under
a feigned name?" asked Hilton. "It strikes me as—
dangerous."

"It strikes me in the same way. She may discover
the trick, and be angered by it. But what else can I
do? She wouldn't see me under my own name. I
wrote to her once, and the letter came back indorsed,
'*Not found.*' She passes, it seems, as Miss Beaufort."

"Ah, you know that!" sighed the friend of the
Beauforts. "I am sorry."

"It wasn't a pleasant discovery. Still, I have
made up my mind not to be disgusted, and not to be
balked."

"Don't be balked, Colonel," begged the General.
"Go on, for your own sake, and for hers," he added,
remembering the alleged courtship of De Bethune.

Underhill noted that his visitor looked wearied and
worried, and, remembering his taste for strong liquors,
offered to ring for brandy.

"No, thank you," was the unexpected reply. "I
have stopped all that. Prosperity has returned to me,
and I don't need drink as I did. I rarely touch anything stronger than claret."

"Is there anybody about my wife who knows me?"
the young man resumed.

"No," said the General, and then groaned out:

"Yes, good Heavens, yes! Miss Macmorran is here, and visits them."

"Ah, dear!" said Underhill. "It would serve me right if she should do something to hurt me."

Thereupon there was a long conversation about Norah Macmorran, ending in an agreement that Hilton should see her, confide to her the whole story of the rejected husband's plot, and beg her not to disclose it.

"I think she will try not to meet me," Harry sighed. "She has good reason for wishing never to see my face again."

"She is a noble girl," answered the General. "I believe she will assent heartily to a project for bringing man and wife together. As for her calling you Peyton to your face, I hope she won't be forced to try it. I don't see how I can do it myself."

"You *must* do it, my dear friend," urged Underhill. "Can't you stand by a fellow who is in love with his wife—in love with a Beaufort?"

"Yes, by Jove!" promised the General. "I'll call you Peyton, if I never look man or woman in the eye again."

"And you will introduce me?"

"O good Lord! My dear fellow, I couldn't do it."

"I'll beg Mrs. Fitz James to present me."

"No, not Mrs. Fitz James," said the General, eagerly. "Better get her brother to take you there."

"Why not the sister?"

"I don't like that little—witch. Excuse me; I hope the epithet doesn't annoy you: but I can't like her. The fact is, Underhill—Peyton I should say, and will—the fact is, I don't want you with her. She is cracked about you."

"Oh! don't fear Mrs. Fitz James, General," the young man replied, gravely. "I am in love with my wife, and I never shall be in love with any one else. I don't know that I can get Mrs. Fitz James to present me," he added. "I have been hinting at it for a week, and she keeps evading it."

"Jealous," suggested Hilton. "Well, if she won't, try her brother ; and, if he fails you, come to me."

CHAPTER XXVIII.

IT must be understood that, while the General could make a call or two on Mrs. Fitz James, and could do a tourist's full duty by the sights of Paris, he did not fail to see much of his two old friends, the last relics of the Beaufort lineage.

He liked them and admired them more than ever. At home he had sometimes been tempted to consider Mrs. Dumont rather dull, if not positively light-headed ; but in a foreign land, and comparing her with people who could not speak his language, she seemed as solid and bright as a gold eagle. In fact, the worthy lady had really and greatly improved during the last half year or so. Prosperity, physical well-being, and tranquillity of feeling had restored to her reasonableness of temper and of opinion. She no longer raved and glared like a sailor going mad with hunger and despair on a wreck. She had regained the natural urbanity and

10

dignity of a Beaufort, and was as sensible in her views of life as her circumstances required.

As to Virginia, the General fairly reveled in her graces, and hardly knew which to admire most, her cleverness or her beauty. "Good Heavens, how the child has grown!" he said to the happy aunt. "She is a foot taller, mentally and morally, than she was a year ago. She was a little like a noble savage then. Now she is fit to be a queen of civilized men. She knows things that I don't. I am positively gathering information and ideas from her. What a gift she has in languages, for example! She speaks French like a native—better than the natives—more distinctly and comprehensibly. There must be such a thing as descended faculty. My belief is, that a person of old English stock couldn't learn French in that way."

"The practice in singing helps," explained Mrs. Dumont, who had not found that her French blood gave her much command of the tongue. "At least, that is what Virginia says. She says that Mr. De Bethune is her teacher, both in music and in the language."

The General became absent-minded, and presently grumbled, "I don't quite fancy that obsequious fellow."

"You surprise me," protested Mrs. Dumont. "Mr. De Bethune is what I call an elegant gentleman."

"Oh, is he?" growled the hero. "Well, perhaps, I have too lately come from South Carolina to be a good judge of gentility."

Mrs. Dumont looked hurt and little less than indignant. "I admit that he has not our manner," she bridled. "He has a softness of address which Carolinians at first might be apt to consider effeminate. But it is very common here, especially among the higher classes. One soon comes to like it. For instance, it gives me great pleasure, General, to note Mr. De Bethune's exceedingly respectful manner to *you*," concluded the lady with personal pungency.

"That is just what I object to," insisted Hilton. "He has the style, if you will allow me to say so, of a negro body-servant. I don't want to be cringed to in that way by a white man."

"It's your title, General; it's your honorable title. You don't understand what it is in Europe to be a general. It is something like being a duke. I believe military rank is about as highly considered here as nobility. Mr. De Bethune has remarked to us more than once that you are the only general he knows."

"He must have kept pretty lowly company," was the sulky comment of the ex-brigadier. "He had better move to South Carolina and get used to generals."

"I trust you will forgive him for being respectful to you," retorted Mrs. Dumont. "We admire him for it."

The gentleman turned a glance of inspection upon the lady. Probably it struck him all at once that De Bethune might be the favorite of the aunt, instead of the niece. At all events, a pleasanter expression came into his eyes, and he answered in a placating tone : "Oh, very likely I do the young man injustice. You know him better than I."

Then Norah Macmorran dropped in, and Virginia made her appearance, and the two girls sang together. The South Carolinian hidalgo was very polite, almost reverentially polite, to the poor Irish girl. He rose on his wooden leg when she entered, and shook hands with her cordially, and helped her to a chair. Mrs. Dumont was so astonished that she came very near staring.

The General, of course, did not explain that, aside from respecting Miss Macmorran, he earnestly wished to gain her good-will, with a view to securing her secrecy in the matter of Virginia's husband. When she left, he opened the door for her in his grandest manner, and also escorted her homeward as far as the Champs-Elysées. There, in the solitude of vast monumental spaces, he gently told her of the presence and plan of Underhill.

Norah walked by his side, her eyes bent on the pavement, her pale cheek a little paler than usual, and her whole soul listening. She was a most pathetic figure, and Hilton could not bear to look at her. At the last, when he had ceased speaking, she drew a deep, desperate gasp, and asked in a palpitating voice, "Will he go to her rooms to see her?"

Judging by the expression of the General's countenance, it would have been possible for him to cry with pity. Nevertheless, he remembered his anxiety for Underhill's success, and he answered in a tone of business-like firmness: "Yes, he will go there to see her— under a feigned name, you understand—the name of Colonel Peyton. If you should meet him, will you kindly remember to address him by that name, or at least to avoid mentioning his true name?"

"I shall not meet him," said Norah, in an almost inaudible monotone.

The General took her hand with such a fervor of manner as if he were on the point of kissing it. He did not raise his eyes to her face; indeed, it would have been useless to do so—the face was turned away.

"I am very much obliged to you, my dear and sweet young lady," he said. "If we can bring this husband

and wife together, I think we shall be rewarded in our souls. I trust and pray with my whole heart that you may be."

"I thank you, sir," replied Norah, still speaking in the same low monotone, but not without a touch of tenderness, as if it were of gratitude.

"Good-by, my dear and good child," said the General.

"Good-by, sir," softly answered Norah. And then, without looking each other in the face—so fearful was the one of showing and the other of seeing pain—they parted.

An hour or two later Hilton met Underhill, and learned that during the following morning he was to be presented at the Beaufort apartments by Mrs. Fitz James.

"Ah!" he exclaimed. "The little flirt is to accomplish some good without knowing it. But, Colonel, can you do it? It will be worse than storming a battery."

"I am terribly frightened—I admit it," the young man confessed. "But it must be done."

"To think of that perverse child scaring two veteran soldiers nearly to death!" said the General. "Well, I'll be there—I'll be there before you ; and I'll call you Peyton, if it chokes me. At twelve, you say? I'll be there when you arrive, and speak to you like a man."

At the appointed hour, next day, the General was in the Beaufort parlor, holding bland converse with the destined victim of his well-intentioned guile. He had summoned up all his courage, and he looked as steady as a veteran battalion. The discourse turned upon Norah Macmorran.

"I think she is as lovely as her voice," said Virginia, with honest warmth. "I think she is thoroughly good."

"Charmingly, touchingly good," answered the General, remembering the pathetic scene in the Champs-Élysées.

"She gets that sweetly modest way from the Sisters," added Virginia. "A great many Catholic girls have it. It is a sincere expression, too, in Norah's case. I believe it really represents her character."

"I think a great deal better of the girl than I did at first," put in Mrs. Dumont, with a certain air of condescension, very proper in a Beaufort. "I had a prejudice against her for a time. But she is a good child."

"I wish I were young enough to marry her," declared the General. "I think as well of her as that."

"Don't take her away from De Bethune," Virginia laughed. "I believe there is a chance of a match there, if you won't interfere."

"Is there!" exclaimed Hilton, delighted with the idea, and delighted that she should seem to like it. "Hope he may get her. He's a nice fellow."

"I thought you didn't admire him," innocently remarked Mrs. Dumont.

"Oh! he improves on acquaintance," said the General, with equal simplicity. "I don't feel sure, however, that he is good enough for Miss Macmorran. She is very lovable. I must say that I like that nunnery manner. I wish the monastic orders had the schooling of some of our Protestant hoydens. There is Mrs. Lotharinga Fitz James, for example—"

"Hush!" interrupted Virginia. "Some one is in the passage."

In fact, there came a light tapping at the door. The

General, who expected Underhill, turned an alarmed face in that direction; but the visitor proved to be merely the genial and silvery Mr. Frank Hedstone.

"Ladies, your most obedient," he smiled and bowed in his mock-ceremonious way.—"*Mon Général, salut au héros*—in plain English, Hail to the chief!—Miss Beaufort, where is my sister? Any other person will do as well who can lend me twenty napoleons."

"We are afraid you will spend them, Mr. Hedstone," said Virginia. "If you would only keep them in your pocket till the time for repaying them— Do you really want twenty napoleons?"

"Thank you," he laughed. "But I won't take them from *you*. On reflection, I prefer family gold."

"Your sister would have been very welcome," put in Mrs. Dumont. "Why didn't you bring her yourself?"

"Another gentleman was to do that," said Hedstone. "A brother seldom gets the privilege of being an escort."

"Not when the sister is pretty and admired," Virginia smiled.

"Yes, it's the plain sisters, I suppose, who are fond of their brothers."

"I don't think a girl who has been correctly educated would ever be indifferent to the company of a brother," affirmed Mrs. Dumont, a lady who never uttered a joke and rarely understood one — a lady who had no conception of the number of jokes in the world.

"But where is Lotharinga?" asked Virginia. "Did you really expect to find her here?"

Hedstone looked surprised and then amused. His

clever sister had promised to give the Beauforts notice
that she would call on them with Colonel Peyton, so
that they might not fail to be at home. She had promised this, and had not done it. But her stratagem had
failed ; the Beauforts had not chanced to go out : the
Colonel would see Virginia.

"I am not sure that she will come," said the brother,
on due reflection. "But I had looked for it."

"She is very much occupied, I believe, with some
Virginia gentleman," remarked, or rather queried, Mrs.
Dumont.

"Oh, yes, she is making a conquest," Virginia added,
gayly.

"I think a conquest is being made," said Hedstone.
"I am not sure that it is Lottie who is making it."

The ladies smiled, but they stared also. How could
a brother thus joke about his sister, even though she
were a widow and a gay one ? They seemed to be saying within themselves that no such reckless speech had
ever been uttered in the Beaufort family. Meantime
the General furtively glanced at the door, as if he feared
that Underhill would never come, and that he might
even have been run off with by Mrs. Fitz James ! Of
a sudden he heard the penetrating tinkle of her voice
in the hall ; and his eyes turned upon Virginia with an
expression of anxiety near akin to fright. If ever he
had been so scared in battle, he certainly could not recollect it.

CHAPTER XXIX.

ALTHOUGH Mrs. Fitz James had not wanted to bring her Colonel to see Virginia, there was no sign of this unwillingness in her face and manner when she dashed into the Beaufort parlor. Her eyes sparkled and her lips radiated smiles as she kissed the two ladies, nodded to the General, made a mouth at her brother, and turned to her companion, all in the twinkling of a will-o'-the-wisp.

"My dears, this is Colonel Peyton—Virginian, patriot, and poet," was her gay introduction.—"Colonel, this is Mrs. Dumont, and this is Miss Beaufort."

Underhill, standing near the door, bowed gravely and in silence, first to his wife's aunt, and then to his wife. He was at the moment very handsome, and they must have thought so. He was quite pale; his eyes settled upon Virginia with impressive earnestness; his expression had the pathos of longing and anxiety. Not until he had turned to Hilton was he able to utter a word. Then, extending his hand, he simply said in a low voice, "I am glad to meet you."

"Glad to meet you—Peyton," stammered the General, repeating the salutation mechanically, but managing to get in the right name.

Mrs. Fitz James glanced uneasily around this scene of mysterious but discernible emotion. Mrs. Dumont gazed with innocent, cordial respect at a gentleman who wore the gray and who bore the honored name of Peyton. Virginia was also greatly interested; she had already heard from Lotharinga that the Colonel was a poet; and to her mind there was no other title on earth so fascinating as that. Moreover, there must have been a potent flattery—unconscious, perhaps, but none the less ingratiating—in the discovery that this man faced her with respect and even with agitation. Her expression was that of one who wishes to say her kindliest, but who can not think of the right phrase.

Mrs. Dumont graciously came to the rescue ; she seated the visitor and made him quite an oration. She said that she was glad to see him ; that she was always glad to see Virginians ; that she was particularly pleased to meet a person of his name ; that she was honored by a call from a gentleman who had worn the gray. Underhill was too much bewildered to note her harangue precisely, and he could only respond to it by bowing repeatedly and smiling patiently. Thereupon the good lady guessed that he was still suffering from his wounds, and insisted with fervid sympathy that he should take a certain large easy-chair.

"Don't assign it to *me*," said Underhill, who had courteously risen when she rose. "Here is the General, who is far worthier."

They were the first words that he had uttered, and they made an exceedingly favorable impression. Virginia smiled in his face with bright approval, and impulsively signed him to a seat near herself. He took it, and then spoke to her, for the first time in his life, unless the marriage-vows might be called discourse.

"You are very kind to receive me," he said in a murmurous monotone, the voice of a man striving to hide emotion. "I am a stranger to nearly everybody in Paris."

"I am most happy to receive any Confederate soldier," were the first words of the Southern wife to the Northern husband.

Underhill hesitated, and no wonder. It was very difficult to talk at all, under the circumstances; and it was especially difficult to make suitable response to such a welcome. After pausing for a moment, he added dreamily and soberly, "So you are devoted to the lost cause?"

"I lost too much with it not to be devoted to it," she said, with honest seriousness.

He raised his eyes and looked her full in the face; he seemed to be studying her, and also approving. "That is a noble sentiment, allow me to tell you," he declared. "Most people hate the vessels that have shipwrecked them."

Mrs. Fitz James turned to Hilton, and whispered—loud enough for Underhill to hear: "Isn't that splendid? He's a poet, you know."

The General mumbled something about some people living poetry, and then hemmed loudly, as if ashamed of himself for not being able to talk.

"Colonel," said Virginia, "I don't think a sailor hates his ship, even if it has wrecked him."

He smiled with an air of being pleased with her cleverness; he had perhaps been fearful of finding his wife stupid.

"You are quite right," he answered. "There were no passengers at the South; everybody belonged to the ship's company."

"Except the mountain mutineers and the bomb-proof skulks," put in the General, finding at last something to say. "Of the two, I liked the mountain-men best."

"Horrid wretches!" exclaimed Mrs. Dumont. "Lying out in the woods, and shooting at our patrols!"

"But they fought, madame," insisted the old soldier, as if fighting covered a multitude of sins, which indeed was his gospel. "They fought like wolves. They didn't disgrace the name of Southerner by squatting in the grass like turkeys."

"It's a satisfaction to think that the grass waves over a good many of them!" declared Mrs. Dumont. She did not utter the bitter words rancorously, but rather as if she had got into a way of saying such things during the war, and continued to do it from habit rather than from feeling.

"Ah, Mrs. Dumont, you and I didn't have our fight out," smiled that light mocker, Hedstone. "I am very warlike to this day. All good Baltimoreans are."

"Isn't he shameful, Colonel Peyton, to make fun of his own city?" giggled Mrs. Fitz James.

But the Colonel did not hear her. During this brief dialogue about the war he had been furtively and intently watching his wife. It was necessarily a point of great interest with him to learn whether she still sympathized passionately with the old Confederate *furor.*

Mrs. Fitz James rose in a pet, rustled over to Hilton, and dropped into a chair by his side, saying, "Come, General, you and I will have a *tête-à-tête.*"

"With all my heart," returned Underhill's friend and confederate. "But I have no small talk; you must entertain me. Do let me lead you to the piano and beg of you a Scotch ballad. I can't understand Virginia's learned music—Wagner's stuff and that sort of thing—very pleasant to wagoners, I dare say."

"Oh! well," muttered Lotharinga, discontentedly, but suffering herself to be beguiled. "I can't play, you know. But I'll murder something."

Then Mrs. Dumont, either because she felt bound to

do the hospitable to Mrs. Fitz James, or because she had discovered that the noble Virginian stranger wished to converse with her niece rather than with herself, suggested to Mr. Hedstone that they two should step over to the musical end of the saloon and help make an audience.

"What! to hear my sister play?" he smiled. "Well, anything for a joke."

Thus it happened at last that the guileful Underhill had his unsuspecting wife a little to himself. For a time, however, the conversation was far from agreeable to him; it seemed impossible to drag it away from that old and angry subject, the war. Virginia still had the siege of Charleston much at heart, and she told him a good deal about the perils and hardships of the beleaguered citizens.

"You must have found it very trying," he said, eager to have her speak of herself.

"I didn't," she replied. "I always hoped to beat."

He strove to smile, but he looked anxious. There was a tone of pluck and pugnacity in the speech which made him fear that he should never win her.

"But oh, what a disappointment!" she added. "What a wretched end it all came to!"

"Would you prefer to talk of something else?" he asked, hopefully.

"I am always coming back to that doleful war," she answered. "It is like a nightmare; one struggles out of it only to drop back into it: it seems as if it would last all one's life."

Of course, he wanted to argue against giving up to the nightmare. "Perhaps it would be well to make an effort to diminish the strength of the recollection," he said. "It is unwise to live constantly in the past, especially when it has been an unhappy one."

"I can only forget it in music," sighed Virginia. Then, looking up at him with bright interest, she added, "And you, I suppose, forget it in poetry."

"I am not really a poet—Miss Beaufort."

It evidently cost the husband an effort to call his wife by this name. General Hilton heard it through the tinkling of "Annie Laurie," and looked around upon Underhill with a cautious but cheering smile. The hero was clearly not attending to Lotharinga's melodies.

"Mrs. Fitz James has spoken to me about your verses," Virginia continued, timidly but eagerly. "She tells me they are beautiful."

"Well, that is the name for them. They are verses, and nothing more. They have measure and rhyme."

"I wish I could see them," returned the girl with a longing intonation which was really childlike. "You are the only poet I know. Do you ever write about the lost cause?"

"Naturally—a little. It is not an alluring subject. I prefer to turn away from it."

"I should think indignation and grief would bring inspiration. Of course you are indignant and grieved."

"There is something potent in an accomplished fact. When a thing is done—"

"Yes, I know it is done," interrupted Virginia with something like vehemence. "We are crushed completely and for ever. I never quite realized it till I got over here and looked at the whole ruin from a distance."

There was a brief pause in the dialogue. Meantime the music continued to clatter from the other end of the long room. The astute General, now in full possession of his wits, would not suffer Mrs. Fitz James to quit the piano, and kept begging for one and another well-worn air. What the playing lacked in time and tune it made up in duration and racket. Underhill and his wife had been obliged to lean toward each other to hear each other's words. The situation tended to intimacy, and they were already on a friendly footing.

"Still, I should write about the lost cause, if I could write," resumed Virginia. Then, with a smile which was both an apology and a beseeching, she added, "Will you show me something about our great struggle?"

"It will be much meaner than the struggle. But I will venture to show you something."

Virginia's eyes sparkled with pleasure and with longing. "I want a great favor," she said. "I want you to write a piece for *me*. My professor shall set it to music, and I will sing it."

"I shall be most happy," promised Underhill, his face flushed with joy. "What shall it be? Have you any particular subject at heart?"

Virginia's brow crisped slightly; she was thinking of her dearest brother. "Yes," she answered. "Pickett's charge at Gettysburg."

"It was a superb feat of arms," said the ex-Colonel of Union volunteers. "I saw it, though I didn't take part in it. I can write about that."

"Oh, when?" asked the eager rebel and fervid adorer of poetry—"when shall I see it?"

"As soon as I can do it. Verses come uncertainly—at least to me."

"Do they? Why, of course they do. Inspiration must."

"You *will* make a poet of me," he smiled.

"I must! I do so want a poet—a great poet of the Southland—to mourn for our overthrow, mourn suitably for our dead. I want such a poet that the whole world will turn and hear."

"Alas!"

"Why do you say 'alas'?"

"You haven't found him."

"How do I know? I will see. Promise to bring me the verses."

"Of course I promise it, and with a great deal of pleasure. I will bring them to-morrow evening, with your permission—that is, if I can finish them."

"I see that you are thinking of them now," said Virginia, gazing at him with a kind of delighted awe, which would have amused him under any other circumstances, but which now gratified and fascinated him. They were leaning toward each other and looking steadily in each other's eyes, like two familiar and dear friends, almost like two lovers. Indeed, his gaze became so fervent that Virginia colored a little and presently drooped her lashes floorward.

At this moment Mrs. Fitz James stopped playing, whirled about on the piano-stool, and faced them. "There!" she exclaimed, petulantly. "I have drummed and thrummed enough—all I am going to.—What in the world are you two talking about? You look like a couple of conspirators.—Colonel Peyton, I am sorry to tear you away, but I must go. I have a horrid, hateful headache. I didn't sleep two hours last night."

"Don't go," begged Virginia, as Lotharinga rose

and shook out her raiment. "You haven't been here ten minutes. I haven't had a word with you."

"I've been here an hour, and I'm cross. We shall have words if I stay any longer. Playing always does infuriate my nerves."

"But you gratify our nerves, Mrs. Fitz James," urged the General, who was most anxious to prolong the interview between the two young married people.

"Yes, I soothe you to sleep, I suppose," snapped the unhappy little lady, taking Underhill's arm.—"Come, Colonel, say good-by. I know you are sorry, but I can't help it. You can happen in some other time."

Underhill turned to his wife and shook hands with her, saying in a tone which evidently surprised her, "Good-by, Miss Beaufort."

Hedstone, who had financial business with his sister, as we remember, followed the departing couple. The General was left alone with Mrs. Dumont and Virginia. There was that moment of prudent silence which follows the closing of a door on visitors. Then Underhill's accomplice glanced from face to face of the two ladies, and smilingly inquired, "Well, how do you like my friend Peyton?"

"He is a noble specimen of a Virginian," declared Mrs. Dumont.

"I like him very much," said Virginia.

"I knew you would," responded the General, his smile nearly turning to a laugh.

CHAPTER XXX

DURING the next day Virginia received and declined a pressing invitation from Mrs. Fitz James to attend the Grand Opéra. As evening drew near, she directed Aunt Chloe to admit no visitors but General Hilton and Colonel Peyton. When darkness fell, she seated herself at a window looking out upon the street, and persisted in reading there by the far-away gas-jet of the center-table chandelier, glancing from time to time at the dimly illuminated pavements below. At last, rising with a hasty rustle, she said, in an elated voice, "He is coming—I know his walk!"

Mrs. Dumont looked up with an air of astonishment, slightly mingled with uneasiness. Her niece familiar already with the gait of this acquaintance of a day! It was almost unbecoming in a Beaufort ; it was almost alarming in a married woman. Oh, if something would happen—if there could be somehow a release from that unfortunate marriage—if there could arrive some day a worthy nephew-in-law, whether French noble or Southern gentleman ! But in the mean time all possible reserve and decorum must be observed by a lady of the Beaufort race. Such were the natural and unavoidable reflections of a well-descended and highly proper aunt.

"I shall be so disappointed if he hasn't brought his poem !" continued the frank and impulsive young woman. "I hope he has brought some poem—don't you ?"

"My dear, you are addled about poetry," said Mrs. Dumont. "Well, I suppose people are, at your age. I remember reading 'Young's Night Thoughts' over and over, when I was a girl."

In due time Underhill made his entrance, and was welcomed by his wife as Colonel Peyton. "I am so much obliged to you for not forgetting your promise," she added. "I hope you remembered the whole of it."

She almost watched his pockets, like a child hoping for a cake. If she looked him in the face, it was unobservantly. The eagerness was for the poem, rather than for the poet.

"I have been lucky," he answered, smiling at her interest—it was so *naïve,* and yet so gratifying. "I had an inspiration, as you would call it." Then, as she seated him in a chair by the lighted center-table, he asked: "Are you going to set me at my task at once? I would rather hear you play and sing."

"I want the poem first," said Virginia, laughing and blushing at her own tyranny, but meanwhile arranging the gas-jets for him. "After that I will sing as long as you wish."

"Please remember that I am not a poet—only a versifier," begged Underhill. "Accept the modest apology of a humble author," he added, looking in her eyes with a smile. He seemed, by-the-way, to be quite at ease with his wife. No doubt, he believed that he had already made an agreeable impression.

"Go on; we are waiting to hear," was Virginia's only response. Then Underhill drew forth his sheet of note-paper, and in a firm, manly voice read his ballad of

"Pickett's Charge.

"The war had robbed the cradle,
    The war had robbed the grave,
And boys with ringlets golden
    Bore bayonet and glaive,

And grandsires flung their olden
    Thin hair to battle's wave,
When Pickett charged the folden
    Pale mists where slaughters rave.

" He trode the smitten valley,
    The mountain's hissing glade,
Right through the cannon-thunder,
    Right through the fusillade,
Till rank tore rank asunder
    With bayonet and blade—
Till Earth rose up in wonder
    To see the death he made.

" Five thousand were his heroes,
    Three thousand those who bled;
They marched without a shiver
    To join the knightly dead;
They crossed the ghostly river
    With swift and steady tread;
And fame shall shine for ever
    Around that column's head.

" The war had robbed the cradle,
    The war had robbed the tomb,
And men whose hair was hoary
    And youngsters in their bloom
Went shouting through the glory
    Which folds where cannon boom,
When Pickett charged the gory
    Sublimities of doom."

When Underhill looked up from his reading, Virginia's head was drooped and one of her hands was over her face. When she spoke, it was simply to say in a low, broken voice, "O Mr. Peyton!" Then, with a sobbing burst of "I can't help it!" she rose and hastened out of the room.

Mrs. Dumont glanced after her, wiped her own eyes for a moment, and whispered, "She lost a brother there —my youngest nephew."

"I never guessed that," murmured Underhill, in a tone of compunction. "Pickett's men were Virginians."

"He was a staff-officer," the aunt sighed. "He would join in the charge. A Beaufort must, you know."

"It is very sad," replied the young man, looking anxiously after his wife.

Just then she reappeared, advanced excitedly to the table, picked up the slip of manuscript and kissed it. "It is an epitaph," she said. "There will be more than kisses on it; there will be tears." Next, fixing her wet eyes on him with an air of wonder, she asked, "Oh! how could you write it?"

"As I told you, I saw the charge," replied Underhill, after a moment of hesitation. "It was a noble feat of arms."

"Yes—oh, wasn't it?" exclaimed Virginia, her eyes flashing with something like exultation, notwithstanding the tears in them. "'And fame shall shine for ever around that column's head!'" she repeated. "I do thank you so earnestly, Colonel Peyton! Your verses will help it to shine there."

"No," he responded, shaking his head and smiling.

"They *will*," insisted the excited girl. "It is a noble poem. I know it is. It touches my heart."

"You are to sing it for me, you know," he reminded her.

"As soon as it is set to music, and I have learned

it," she promised.   "Oh, I shall sing it, and you shall hear me ! I feel just now as though I never should want to sing anything else."

It must have seemed to Underhill that he was making a conquest of his wife. He looked so gratified and also so fascinated that it is a wonder she did not suspect his identity. Possibly she might have divined him, but for a fixed belief that her Yankee husband was a dreadful creature who necessarily regarded her with ill-will, and whom she would instinctively fly from at the first glance.

"I should like to have you give me back that manuscript, some day," he ventured to add. "You have made it precious in my eyes. I never had such a tribute before."

Apparently Virginia took some slight alarm from the fervor of his manner. "I want to copy it first," she replied simply, and immediately changed the subject. "The whole war ought to be written over with song," she declared. "Was there ever such another theme for verse? I should think it would inspire every poet of the South to do wonders. Isn't it a glorious subject? You couldn't write in this way about Yankees?"

Underhill pondered. Should he say Yes, or No? Should he speak against Yankees, or for them? These questions and hesitations would naturally flit through the mind of a man in his position.

"I might," he at last replied ; and then came this sharp dialogue :

Virginia. "What !   About those cowards?"

Underhill (quietly). "Were they cowards?"

Mrs. Dumont. "Certainly they were, and Vandals to boot."

Underhill. "My dear madam, do think how impossible that is. How could a land of brave men be overrun by cowards?"

Mrs. Dumont. "Well, I don't know, I'm sure; unless there was some Yankee trickery about it."

Virginia. "Colonel Peyton, you astonish me. I admit that what you say seems rational. But how can a Southerner say it?"

Underhill (smiling). "Why not? Why shouldn't a Southerner say something rational?"

Virginia. "I don't know what to make of you—to write so eloquently—and then joke!"

Underhill (pensively). "I find that I can write with sympathy on almost any subject, if I think of it long enough."

Virginia (after a long gaze at him). "Oh, it must be the impartiality of genius. I have read of that somewhere. Like Shakespeare and Homer. They write kindly about both sides—heroes and villains—Greeks and Trojans. It must be the impartiality of genius."

Underhill (amused). "Not in my case; it can't be that. [Seriously.] I suppose it is the impartiality of a soldier. A soldier learns at last to worship valor, no matter where found."

Again Virginia studied him with a perplexed gaze. She evidently considered him a puzzle, and held that he could not explain himself, or at least did not. At last she recommenced her questioning. "But how can you *begin* to think sympathetically of a hateful subject? Tell me. I am insatiably curious about poetry."

"Oh, a line comes—I don't know how or why—and then its fellow comes. Pretty soon the interest, the sympathy, awakes. I take another man's place and divine his feelings. After a while I am eager to finish the work ; I can't let it alone till it is done."

"Ah, dear ! I wish I could do it," she sighed. "Poetry is my adoration and my wonder. But you ought not to degrade it," she added, with a vehement shake of the head. "If ever you do write a nice poem about our enemies, I don't want you to show it to me."

Underhill waited a moment, as an archer waits for a gust to pass before he shoots, and then asked, "Hadn't I better show you just one—merely as a curiosity ? "

Virginia fell back in her chair and reflected, before she answered. "Well, perhaps—when I am more prepared to bear it—just one," she finally said. "It *would* be a curiosity."

Underhill watched her with a tranquil expression of grave interest. He had by this time got used to his situation, and was able to study her calmly and intelligently. Presently he ventured to put her a personal question : "What do you mean by saying that you may be more prepared to bear it ? Are time and distance telling on the old feelings ?"

"Yes," burst out Virginia, almost angrily. "Isn't it horrible ? It is like forgetting the dead ; it *is* forgetting them."

"It may be best," he replied, gently. "Probably it is best to remember chiefly living facts and living men."

"How can it be best when it is shameful ?" demanded the passionate child of the South. "It is shocking to think of forgetting my State—its heroic ideas and sorrowful failure—its thousands of martyrs to liberty, and its innumerable mourners. What a disgrace and wickedness to let all that fade out of one's mind !

And yet, distance does fade it, and the splendor of Europe helps, and the lapse of time also. It is unpardonable, and still I can't help it."

There was more of this fervid reminiscence and self-condemnatory confession. There was an eager talk about the war, and about the growing torpor of memory concerning it, all considerably cheering to Underhill. At last he remembered that he had made a long call, and with extreme unwillingness he rose to depart.

"What, so quick!" exclaimed the frank young woman. "I had a dozen questions to ask you. You must call again before long, to answer them."

Then, as soon as he was out of hearing, she snatched up his verses and declaimed passionately:

> "They marched without a shiver
>   To join the knightly dead;
> They crossed the ghostly river
>   With swift and steady tread;
> And fame shall shine for ever
>   Around that column's head!"

CHAPTER XXXI.

DURING the next week the Colonel was two or three times at his wife's apartments. He called, on various pretexts—once to leave somebody's poems, once to ask whether De Bethune had yet found an air for his ballad, and once to bring a bouquet. No account will be given of these agreeable but indecisive interviews, fur-

11

ther than to say that he succeeded in making himself a most welcome visitor.

Meantime the pretty Baltimore lady was a real perplexity to him. At no time of day and in no part of the Hôtel du Louvre was he comfortably sure that he would not either meet her or get a billet from her. Of course, he had pungent reasons for desiring that between her and him there should be nothing more than civil acquaintance. In the first place, it troubled his now sensitive conscience to remember that he, a married man, was passing himself off upon her as a bachelor. Furthermore, there was danger that the least show of intimacy would be reported to Virginia as courtship, and would lead her to regard him as a serious suitor of Mrs. Fitz James, or as a flirt. Finally, he was in the state of mind of an ingenuous boy who is in love ; he did not want to be liked by anybody but the right person ; he positively hated to be liked by the wrong person.

The result was, that he carefully dodged the goodwill which followed him. One day in particular, when he had received an invitation from Virginia to call in the evening, he kept out of the hotel from morn till dewy eve, and later. He made a tour of the sights and wonders of Paris. He took his noonday meal in a retired restaurant of the Latin quarter. At last he chanced into the Luxembourg, and there stumbled upon the colossal apparition of General Hilton, posted between Müller's "Calling of the Condemned" and Couture's "Decadence of the Romans," and surveying them alternately with an air of noble indignation. The high-minded hero, it must be understood, was as yet inclined to judge a picture by its subject rather than by that merely adventitious circumstance, the handling of the artist.

Underhill briefly narrated the substance of his latest interview with his wife. The General rejoiced, uttered favorable auguries, and then broke into wonder. "My dear fellow, I don't see how you can do it—how you can face her," he said. "Merely to hear about it turns my brain. The evening we were there together gave me the nightmare. Well, some men have all kinds of courage. I believe you would have made a great general—you have the coolness and the stratagems."

"I have the courage of desperation," returned Underhill. "There is nothing to be done but what I am doing."

"Alas! no—but the end justifies you," declared Hilton, who was still troubled by the deception involved in the means.

Then the coloring of the "Decadence" caught his eye once more, and drew from him a discourse which would have astonished Monsieur Couture. "I can't help thinking, sir, that the age of art is an age of corruption," he said, with noble severity. "There was no art in Sparta, sir ; none in Rome during her grandest days ; none in the forest cantons of Switzerland. I thank Heaven, sir, that we have none in South Carolina ! "

"You needn't fear any, for some time to come," returned Underhill. "Art doesn't spring up in thinly settled agricultural districts. It needs cities."

"Just look at that picture—the 'Decline of the Romans,'" continued the General with increasing vehemence. "Do you call that civilizing and refining and purifying ? It is a spectacle of crapulence and indecency. And here is this other—this 'Calling of the Condemned'—the triumph of the plebeian over the patrician —of brutishness over refinement ! They are both, to my eye, abominable paintings. Why do artists select such subjects? Here is an orgy of drunkenness, faced by an orgy of cruelty."

The younger but more experienced critic of art turned from canvas to canvas. "Excuse me for suggesting that you have missed the lesson of the pictures," he said. "The one is a protest against unbridled Cæsarism, and the other a protest against unbridled democracy. I presume that they were placed opposite each other by design. It is as much as to say, 'That leads to this, and this leads to that.'"

The General seemed much struck by the commentary; he stared backward and forward with great interest. "I think you are right, Colonel," he conceded at last. "There is a moral there, and a tremendous one. By Jove! it takes practice to really see a picture, as well as to run a plantation, or shoot wild-turkeys."

The dialogue lingered for some minutes around the subject of art. A rosy and pursy little Englishman, apparently of the London shopkeeper breed, who had heard the two men call each other General and Colonel, sidled somewhat nearer to them and listened with furtive respect, as if sure that the opinions of persons of such rank must be well worth attention. His wife, a lady of remarkable presence in the way of breadth, followed his movement with the ponderous deliberation of a merchantman drawn by a tug-boat, and turned her moist blue eyes with something like awe upon the lofty figure and haggard features of Hilton. Three cherry-cheeked daughters, obedient perhaps to some parental signal, took out note-books and began writing or sketching. Presently the General became aware of the proximity of this group, without in the least suspecting its simple interest and reverence. He made a gesture of apology, and drew Underhill to one side.

"We were in the way of those ladies," he whispered. Little did he guess that he had deprived those ladies of an unusual treat, and that his massive aquiline profile already adorned one of those note-books, labeled in fine, sharp letters, "*The General.*"

They had scarcely quitted their reverent audience when Underhill made a hasty right-about, muttering, "Good Heavens!"

Hilton looked over the young man's shoulder, and discerned, amid the groups of picture-gazers, Mrs. Fitz James.

"What!" he whispered. "Are you dodging our little friend? I wonder which of us she is pointing for? She has been very pleasant to *me* of late."

"I suppose she is pleasant to everybody," said Underhill. "Is she coming?"

"Yes, she is coming, Colonel; we'll make an excentric retreat. We'll divide our columns and skedaddle in different directions. One of us will escape."

So far as concerned Hilton, it was easy enough to put this strategic joke into successful operation. It was Underhill whom Mrs. Fitz James wanted, and she overtook him in the most adroit manner, almost without seeming to mean it. It will be understood, of course, that he conducted his flight without much skill or vigor. I suspect that all men are ashamed to run away from a woman, and do it feebly.

"So glad to meet you!" smiled Lotharinga, either not noting the attempt to escape, or choosing to ignore it. "How lucky! Did you know that I was coming here? Do say so. I'll try to believe it. Won't you join us? My escort is a nonentity—just an Italian count whom I sometimes walk with, when I have nobody better."

She turned toward her cavalier, and gave him a fluttering smile and sparkling of the eyes, as though he were the dearest object in life to her. He was the usual Italian, somewhat low in stature, with a pallid, olive complexion and dreamy black eyes. He had halted discreetly some ten steps away, and it might be guessed that he had been instructed so to do.

"I should be most happy," said Underhill. "But your escort has his claims. He looks very love-lorn, and he will think me an intruder."

"Nonsense!" urged Lotharinga. "He isn't a bit love-lorn. Besides, Count Minuzio is a perfectly broken *cavaliere servente*, as all Italians are. Do let me introduce him. He speaks French perfectly."

"But I don't," returned the Colonel, glad of it for once. "I shall simply be a nuisance to him and a load to you. Let me make a call, instead."

"But you don't call; you never call—not even when you promise. You are the most unsocial man—a perfect hermit and anchorite."

"I'll change—I'll take to society again."

"Well, if you won't come, you must go," fretted the lady. "I almost hate you for it. No, I don't," she smiled. "Do call oftener."

Underhill slipped away from a woman who wanted to see him, only to stumble upon one who would have been most happy to avoid him. He had scarcely taken five steps among the knots of picture-gazers, and he was still within range of Lotharinga's bright and eager eyes, when he came face to face with Norah Macmorran. It is almost needless to state that both of them looked as if they would like to run away. The gentleman was the first to recover himself; he bowed with a respect which was very near to humility.

"Miss Macmorran, excuse me," he murmured. "I had no intention of seeking an interview. But, now that we have met, may I have one word?"

Norah stood, pale and still, like a marble statue of a saint, her hands folded across each other, her head inclined slightly, and her eyes upon the floor. "If you wish it, sir," was her only response, uttered in a voice which was little more than a whisper.

"I want a favor of you," he begged, remembering the proximity of Mrs. Fitz James. "Will you do me the kindness not to utter or reveal my name?"

"I should not have spoken it, sir," gasped Norah. "General Hilton told me what you wished."

He might have gone now; he might have felt sure of her fidelity; but he was still a little anxious. Strange to say, yet naturally enough, he was anxious not only for her secrecy, but also for her esteem.

"You don't condemn me for using a disguise, I hope," he continued. "You know the whole unhappy story, don't you?"

"Yes, sir. Mrs. Dumont told me about the old bad feeling. General Hilton told me the rest."

"And that I want to win my wife? Did he tell you that?"

"Oh, yes, sir," whispered Norah. "I was so glad to hear of it!" she added, with an heroic effort. "I have prayed for your success, sir."

Underhill had the air of being completely humiliated. "You noble young lady!" he murmured. "I wish I could fall down and worship you."

"Oh, no, sir!" softly protested Norah.

There were tears in the young man's eyes at this moment. Neither of them could look the other in the face.

"Well, I thank you profoundly!" he said at last. "Is there nothing that I can do for you? Can I do *anything?*"

"No, sir," returned Norah. "I am supported here by St. Patrick's Church," she added, as if to make sure he should understand that she needed no money. "I want nothing."

Of course, he did not tell her that it was he who had furnished the funds for her education. He was pondering how he could render her some present service or courtesy.

"You have not lost your way?" he asked. "You don't need a guide?"

"No, sir," she replied, with a faint smile of thanks. "A gentleman is with me," she immediately explained, coloring slightly. "It is Mr. De Bethune, my instructor in music. He just went for a catalogue. I am so curious about the pictures!"

"Oh!" responded Underhill, apparently well pleased, and glancing at her with a slight air of investigation. "I am glad you have such good company."

"He is very good, I think," murmured Norah, now blushing noticeably. "And very kind to me."

At this moment, Underhill discovered the Professor approaching from the other end of the saloon. He made him an amicable gesture, bowed respectfully to Norah, and turned away.

During the latter part of this dialogue, he had not thought of Mrs. Fitz James. But that eager-minded little lady had not forgotten him, nor failed to follow him with furtive and watchful eyes. She now left the tranquil Count Minuzio once more, and slid across the hall to Norah and De Bethune.

CHAPTER XXXII.

Mrs. Fitz James opened the interview with a genial twitter of "How do, Miss Macmorran? So glad to meet you here!" Then, turning gayly to De Bethune, "*Bon jour, mon cher seigneur.* You know Count Minuzio, don't you? Do run over and entertain him a minute. I find him an awful load, and I want to talk to Miss Macmorran."

De Bethune bowed in his urbane fashion, and went to hold discourse with the urbane Italian.

"Really, Miss Macmorran, you are much to be envied," continued Mrs. Fitz in a tone of banter which was meant to be insinuating, but which revealed a spice of petulance. "You have the most elegant men about you—Mr. De Bethune for an escort to the galleries, and Colonel Peyton catching the first opportunity."

Norah looked a good deal confused, and no wonder. She knew the Baltimore lady but slightly, and was astonished at being addressed by her. Moreover, Mrs. Fitz James's manner, which was that of a superior to an inferior, or a grown person to a child, tended to abash her. Finally, it was embarrassing, or rather it was extremely painful, to be spoken to of Underhill.

"Oh, you quite mistake," she stammered. "I met Mr.— I met the other gentleman by accident."

"What did you say?" asked Lotharinga, quickly. "I didn't quite understand."

"I said that I met Colonel Peyton by accident," returned the girl, speaking more firmly, but regarding the floor.

"I thought you began to say something else," persisted Lotharinga, watching her sharply. The hoydenish, audacious coquette was evidently puzzled by those downcast eyes and that meek face. It is likely enough that she understood them as signs of a guilty conscience.

"I am so glad you know Colonel Peyton," she resumed, after a little pondering. "He is perfectly charming. Isn't he?"

"I think he is good and noble-hearted," answered Norah, looking up with a serious countenance. It was clear enough from her manner that that was what she indeed thought of the man.

"Dear me!" laughed Mrs. Fitz. "How we women do know all about the men's hearts!"

The clever comment and the keen gaze which accompanied it forced a slight blush into Norah's pale cheek. "I have heard," she stammered, "that he gives a great deal to the poor."

She had heard it, no doubt; but, nevertheless, the speech was an evasion, and she looked uncomfortably conscious.

Mrs. Fitz James noted the expression, and was not deceived by the explanation. "I didn't suspect that you knew him," she continued. "I see the Colonel frequently, and he has never mentioned you. Let me tell you—of course you know it as well as I do—that you are fortunate in the acquaintance. He is perfectly delightful. Do you see him often here?"

"Here!" repeated the questioned girl, coloring profusely. It was a charge, as she comprehended it, that she made appointments to meet Underhill at the Luxembourg. "I never met him before in Paris," she answered energetically and incautiously.

"Oh! then you knew him in America," inferred Lotharinga, with the alert air of a coquette who scents a love-affair. "In Richmond, I suppose," she went on, too eager to wait for replies. "So you knew him in Richmond? He is very fond of music, isn't he?"

She paused upon this last question, and surveyed Norah with a significant smile.

"I believe he is," said Norah, and then added quickly, "I know he is."

"Yes, and your voice and execution must be such a treat to him!" insinuated Mrs. Fitz, beginning to show in her face more of the serpent than of the dove. "I really envy you. Of course, you couldn't refuse to sing for such an attractive gentleman as Colonel Peyton."

"I never sang for him in particular," was the stammering but honest response. "He never heard me but in the church and at concerts."

Mrs. Fitz James was not to be beaten by any such trickery as the simple truth. "I think it is dreadful," she giggled. "You are just like all these artists. I do think it is dreadful behavior. How in the world, when such a charming man calls on you, can you refuse to sing for him?"

"He never did call on me, Mrs. Fitz James." Norah said this with just a little touch of pugnacity in her tone; it was worrying to be so cross-questioned, and irritating to be an object of suspicion. Then, all of a sudden, she recollected the duty of meekness, and her eyes dropped floorward. There was an expression in her face as of beseeching pardon, and possibly she was praying for a higher forgiveness than that of Mrs. Fitz James.

Lotharinga fell back a little, like a serpent which has struck its blow, and struck in vain. She studied the chastened countenance and gently bowed figure of the pure-minded child of poverty with an almost comical air of frustration and annoyance. She clearly did not know whether to regard her as a stupid thing, or as an artful baggage.

"You astonish me," she said at last, with a little titter of perplexity. "Why, there is some mystery about it ; it is perfectly romantic and delightful," she added, falling into the commonplaces of banter. Then, turning serious and inquisitive again, "Why shouldn't he call, and why shouldn't you see him ?"

"He is a very rich gentleman, and I am a poor girl," returned Norah, simply and gravely. "It is not proper to have such calls."

For a moment, at least, Mrs. Fitz James believed in the girl's sincerity. But she was not touched—as even some very coarse kinds of manhood might have been— by a revelation of lowly-born humility and maidenly timidity. She merely stared at it, as though she had never inspected nor divined the like before, and found it a very amazing and irrational spectacle. On second thoughts, too, she burst out laughing at it.

"What ideas for Paris !" she giggled. "Don't let people hear you. They'll think you are silly."

"If any people think so for that reason, their thoughts are of no value to me," replied Norah.

Mrs. Fitz had a look of querying, "I wonder if she *is* good?" Then came another expression which signified, "What nonsense!" . . . "But you know Colonel Peyton," she said aloud, resuming her catechism. "You must have met him somewhere to speak with him. Oh, I can guess; he waited on you to the concerts, or home from church?"

She tried to win a confession by a genial smile; but, of course, there was no confession to be made. Norah simply shook her head, and responded, "No, Mrs. Fitz James, he never did."

"Then how *could* you get acquainted with him?" Lotharinga exclaimed. "Were you born acquainted?"

The joke threw the Irish girl off her guard; she smiled and replied, "The chorister introduced us."

"Oh, the chorister! Then he used to come into the choir to hear you practice? Dear me, how enchanted he must have been! No wonder. Your singing is perfectly ravishing; it's enough to turn any man's head."

Norah's face became grave again. She was obviously very anxious to escape from her worrying and little less than defamatory inquisitor. She glanced across the hall at De Bethune, as if with the purpose of summoning him; but the Professor was talking earnestly with the Count, apparently about Couture's one masterpiece, and did not happen to look her way.

"Oh, leave them alone—they are contented enough," said Mrs. Fitz, who had noted the glance. "And so it was the chorister who introduced you? I suppose the Colonel asked for the favor. Didn't he?"

"I don't know—I suppose so," stammered Norah.

"O Miss Macmorran!—O Miss Macmorran! you

know it perfectly," giggled Lotharinga. "I can see it
in your face. You blush killingly."

At last the Celtic blood of the pestered girl rose in
revolt and resistance. "Mrs. Fitz James, I *don't* know
it," she said, firmly. "I would have been ashamed to
ask. And I don't think you have a right to question
me so much."

Lotharinga looked dismayed, and then resentful.
"Oh, well—if it is a matter of feeling to you—as I suppose it is," she sneered. "Of course, I shall be silent on
the subject, if you prefer it." After hesitating a moment, she added with increased sharpness : "But I can
do you a favor, Miss Macmorran. I can give you some
information—very important information, perhaps—that
is, to *you*. There is an affair with another lady."

"Another lady !" replied Norah, still on the defensive, and indignant thereat. "How, then, can it con-
cern me ?"

Lotharinga should have seen that her thrust had not
taken effect ; but she pushed on headlong, like a fencer
who has lost his balance. "He is devoted to Miss
Beaufort," she whispered, her lips quivering with no
enviable emotion. "He is bewitched with Miss Beaufort."

Norah was at that moment nodding to De Bethune
by way of recalling him to her. Next she astonished
and routed Mrs. Fitz James by facing her with a smile
and saying placidly—"I don't wonder. Miss Beaufort
is very lovely."

"Good-morning, Miss Macmorran," snapped the
widow, turning her back rudely.—"Oh, you've got tired
of the Count," she added, addressing the Professor.
"So have I. I'm tired of everything. Good-by."

Before she had taken three steps, however, she looked around with a coaxing smile—as if suddenly remembering to flirt, even in her bitterness—and called to him : "Come and see me, *mon très cher seigneur. Au revoir.*"

De Bethune acknowledged the invitation by a gesture of thanks. But in the next instant he turned to his companion and said in his sweetest tone, " We have lost a great deal of time, Miss Macmorran."

It was evident that she understood a compliment, for she gave him a shy glance of comprehension and gratitude. Then taking the catalogue, and quickly averting her face from the nudities of Couture, she began to study with awe-struck eyes " The Calling of the Condemned," while De Bethune poured into her ear a murmurous commentary, the very tone of which —no matter what the words were—showed respect and liking.

CHAPTER XXXIII.

From the Luxembourg Underhill and Hilton went to see the tomb of Napoleon, where they had much interesting conversation with the wizened veteran of Waterloo who served as their guide, and were treated by him with immense respect in consideration of their titles.

About five they dined at the General's favorite fifty-cent restaurant in the Palais Royal, while a military band poured forth alternate marches and waltzes in the square below their window, and a hundred or two of

cheerful convives rattled knives and forks in unison.
Next came an hour over a cup of black coffee in the
Café du Pavillon, meantime studying the never-ceasing
flow of promenaders, and interchanging the usual com-
ments of the tourist.   The General still retained the
naïveté of the citizen of a small place who visits a large
one.   He was amazed at the metropolitan abundance of
humanity, and seemed to regard it as a portent of coming desolation.   He surveyed with horror a blonde ad-
venturess who had arrived from Russia to barter her
charms in Paris for English gold, and remarked solemnly, "This is a wicked city."   When Underhill asked
him if he would have cognac in his *café noir*, he replied
firmly : "No.   It improves it.   It makes it taste more
like coffee.   But I won't have it.   This people needs an
example of self-restraint."   A little later, glancing at an
American who was mixing Sauterne and seltzer-water,
he exclaimed, "Good heavens, how the French are
given over to luxury !"   Two young Wallachians, who
were somewhat flown with wine, impressed him with a
belief that Parisians drank too hard.   In short, the
General saw that France was corrupt, and sorrowfully
predicted the fall of the empire.

At last Underhill rose and said with a cheerful
smile, "I must go and dress to call on my wife."

"Ah !" laughed Hilton.   "Put on your very pretti-
est.   By-the-way, I am to be there this evening ; there
is some treat for me, I understand.   But I'll drop in a
little late ; I'll leave you the field for a time.   Be careful about Mrs. Fitz James, and don't bring her along if
you can help it."

An hour later Underhill was in his wife's parlor.
He found her radiant with beauty and content, and

ventured to allude to the fact in a complimentary way.

"Yes, Virginia seems very happy to-night," said Mrs. Dumont, glancing at her niece with pride.

"So I am," returned the young lady. "Colonel Peyton, my music-teacher has just suited me with an air for your poem. I am going to sing it to you this evening. Oh! he has just suited me," she repeated, joyously. "It is very simple—no warbling and ornament —a few notes like a trumpet—just what I wanted. I told him it must be simple, and he has made it so. It is hardly more than passionate declamation. But it belongs to the words. I know you will like it."

"Of course, I shall like my own verses, sung by you," he replied.

Mrs. Dumont gave him a glance of investigation, as if she thought his tone or manner a trifle too enthusiastic, considering that her niece was a married woman in disguise.

"Anybody would like them, whether sung or said," declared Virginia, whereupon the gaze of the elder lady was turned upon her with even more anxious inspection.

Presently Underhill inquired with natural impatience why he was kept waiting for the song.

"I want General Hilton," explained Virginia. "I sent him a note telling him that I had a treat for him this evening. I want to surprise him. He doesn't know what it is. He will be delighted. I think I shall make him cry—that is, you and I will."

"Virginia, how you prattle!" sighed Mrs. Dumont.

"I am out of my head with my song," the girl rattled on. "I am as happy as a child over it. Music and poetry have that effect on me. I forget everything else. Oh, it is a lovely song, Colonel Peyton, though I say it. I think you will be proud of your verses when you hear them to this air."

"I am proud and gratified already," said Underhill, his face flushed with gladness and his eyes bright with adoration.

After a time the deliberate tramp of the General's ligneous march was heard in the hall. "There is my old hero," exclaimed Virginia, springing to open the door for him.—"Come in, bravest of the brave."

"Nonsense!" laughed Hilton, shaking hands all round, as his custom was. "Well, here we are," he added, dropping into a seat. "Now, what is it?"

"General, it is a song," smiled the elated *cantatrice*, who was already at her piano. "It is 'Pickett's Charge,' written by Colonel Peyton. I want you to hear every word. Don't mind the music. Listen to the words."

"Ah! one of yours, Colonel?" bowed Hilton. "I shall stand at attention."

Then Virginia struck the first notes of a simple, masculine, clarion-like air, and threw the whole fervor of her powerful soprano into—

> " The war had robbed the cradle,
>   The war had robbed the grave," etc.

When she ended, the tears were in her eyes and Mrs. Dumont was sobbing like a child, while the wooden-legged Confederate General and the Yankee Colonel in his disguise of gray were hiding their faces. It was half a minute—it seemed to be several minutes—before any one spoke. Then Underhill murmured, "I am cry-

ing over my own verses—well, they are poor enough
for it."

The General turned his moist eyes upon him, and
took him gravely by the hand. "Poor!" he said.
"Colonel, I don't know whether you are a poet or not;
but what you write breaks my heart. Ah, those sublime regiments! How grandly they went to destruction!"

"Yes, grandly! sublimely!" echoed Virginia, and
then impetuously declaimed the lines:

> "They marched without a shiver
>   To join the knightly dead;
> They crossed the ghostly river
>   With swift and steady tread;
> And fame shall shine for ever
>   Around that column's head."

"Yes, for ever!" said the General, solemnly. "It
will never be forgotten—that column."

"To join the knightly dead," repeated Virginia.
"Oh, how could you find those words, Mr. Peyton?"

"What other words could he find?" demanded the
General. "They are just the words. Knightly men,
every one of them—and they joined the knightly souls
of old—all the brave who have died gloriously. Colonel, I sometimes wish I had fallen on that battle-field.
It would have been a great honor."

"Ah! there were enough without you," sighed Virginia. "I can't spare another friend, not even in
thought."

So the impassioned Southern talk went on for many
minutes. Underhill found it difficult to bear any part
in it, and naturally said little. But he was obviously

not embarrassed, and far indeed from unhappy. His eyes were fixed nearly all the time on Virginia with an expression of fervent admiration, mingled with pensive study. If she looked at him, he smiled gently and dropped his gaze, but soon raised it again to her face. He was not only fascinated by his wife ; he was desperately in love with her.

"Well, that will do for a Confederate palaver," said the General at last, glancing at Underhill as if he remembered all of a sudden his Yankeehood. "I don't want to spend an entire evening in lamenting the lost cause."

"We shall have to stop it soon, anyway," answered Mrs. Dumont. "Mrs. Fitz James is coming at nine ; and she is *so* light-headed ! One doesn't like to speak with her on a really great subject."

"Little Mrs. Fitz James coming ?" asked Hilton in mild dismay.

"So she wrote me this morning," stated Virginia. "She made the appointment. I couldn't help it."

"Colonel, we must skedaddle again," said the elder gentleman. "Suppose we jump out of the window ?"

"What, and leave us !" protested Virginia, looking imploringly at her poet. "Don't run away from my poor little friend. What if she does rattle ? You can take turns in listening to her. The disengaged one can talk to me."

Underhill obviously longed to remain ; he was gazing raptly at his lovely wife. Mrs. Dumont glanced at him, glanced at the eager face of her niece, and became very grave.

"If the gentlemen don't like Mrs. Fitz James," she

said—"and I really can't wonder they don't—I am sure they have the right to avoid her."

Thereupon the General told the tale of the attempted flight in the Luxembourg. "We made an excentric retreat," he said; "we broke for the rear in twenty directions. I thought she was after me. But it turned out that the Colonel was her objective point."

Virginia uttered a little forced laugh, and glanced uneasily at Underhill. "And you, Mr. Peyton," she asked—"you surrendered, I suppose?"

"Yes," he replied. "But I broke my parole, and here I am, instead of there."

The young lady could not help looking a trifle elated by this triumph over a rival who was at least pretty and lively, and whom she in her inexperience regarded as a woman of the world and a leader in society. Her laughter burst out again, this time in a perfectly natural argentine tinkle, significant of pure satisfaction.

Mrs. Dumont's countenance became more and more solemn. As we have heretofore been forced to acknowledge, she was a woman of but moderate intellectual parts, capable of occasionally acting with unwisdom, and liable to talk flat nonsense; but the grave and prim manner in which she had been reared, and her high ideas as to what was becoming in a lady of the Beaufort blood, put her on the plane of a judgmatical person in matters of decorum. She could see that her niece and this troubadour visitor were getting interested in each other, and she knew that it was not best that the feeling should be fostered by opportunity. Her conclusion was that, under the circumstances, he had staid long enough.

"Ought you not to consider Mrs. Fitz James?" she suggested. "If she expected you at her rooms, and then finds you here, she will be hurt."

The General, who knew the wisdom of bending before the senior womanhood of a household, rose at once. "We must bolt," he declared. "I prefer the Funambules to Mrs. Fitz."

Virginia made no further objection; on the contrary, she laughed assent. "Here is the window," she giggled. "Wouldn't Lotharinga be furious to see you jumping out of it, and running for an omnibus? I sha'n't tell her that you have been here."

"Farewell!" said the General in a melodramatic voice, striding to the door with an imitation of the gait of a stage conspirator. Underhill nodded gayly to the ladies, and followed in the same manner. The last sound he heard was the merry laughter of his wife, apparently well contented with his flight from the coquettish widow.

CHAPTER XXXIV.

Mrs. Dumont could not help laughing over the mock-tragedy exit of the two gentlemen; but, the moment they were gone, she became serious again, and recommenced to study her niece.

"What fun! Poor Mrs. Fitz James!" the girl was saying. Then, suddenly checking her laughter, she sighed, "Oh, dear! I was crying a minute ago."

"You laugh or cry just as Colonel Peyton chooses," returned Mrs. Dumont, with severity if not with injustice.

"I don't!" asseverated Virginia, coloring. "It was General Hilton who made me laugh. The idea of an honorable, simple South Carolina gentleman, who never did an underhanded thing in his whole life, putting on the airs of an opera brigand! It's enough to upset any one's gravity."

Mrs. Dumont laid a hand on her breast, rolled her eyes upward, pursed her lips, and, in short, prepared for a struggle.

"I wonder if that was all?" she said. "If the General had gone alone, and Colonel Peyton had staid to see Mrs. Fitz James, I wonder if you would have laughed so heartily?"

Virginia's sensitive pride enabled her to see the whole force of this accusation. "Aunt, what do you mean?" she demanded, indignantly. "Do you think I would allow myself to fall in love with this man, or any man?"

"My dear, you put things so violently! I wish I could ever speak to you for your own good without being answered so passionately."

There was a moment of silence, and then came a subdued reply. "Excuse me, my dear aunt. But the mere suggestion of such an idea is very fretting. It seems to throw a stigma on me. You couldn't expect a Beaufort to bear it patiently."

"I know you will always remember who you are," said Mrs. Dumont. "But you are in a very difficult situation. Oh, it is a dreadful situation!" she groaned. "I think of it sometimes, and of the possibility of gossip about you, till it seems as if I should go wild. It is such a strange situation—so completely unprecedented. No other Beaufort was ever in such circumstances.

There is nothing in our noble family history to guide you."

"I believe I always remember that I am a married woman," murmured Virginia. "I know that I do. How can I ever forget the horrid fact?"

"But here you are making a demigod of this man, and he makes a perfect goddess of you."

"Oh, no!" exclaimed the girl, blushing violently. "Don't say that, aunt. He doesn't."

"I think he does. I am an old woman, my dear— at least, I am a great deal older than you. I know men better. Never mind about your being clever. You may be cleverer in some things than any other Beaufort that ever lived. But I have been married. And a married woman, no matter if she is a foolish old aunt, understands men better than a girl."

"I am married, too," said Virginia, bitterly.

"What does it amount to? Well, it amounts to a good deal. So much the more reason for being careful."

"I have been careful."

"In future, I mean; on *his* account," pleaded Mrs. Dumont, placatingly.

Virginia turned her face away from the light as she muttered, "I don't believe he cares for me."

"He does!" firmly insisted the elder lady. "I watch him when you are not looking at him."

"I wish you wouldn't." This was said in a tone of impatient lassitude, as if the speaker found the dialogue wearisome and fretting.

"He never takes his eyes off you. He follows you about the room with, oh, such a gaze! I am perfectly sure that he is dead in love with you."

Virginia fairly shrank under this announcement. "O aunt! what did you tell me that for?" she broke out in a sort of cry. "You drive me distracted!"

"I tell it to you because you ought to know it," persisted the monitress, with an anxious and almost sorrowful glance of investigation.

The girl remained silent for a little, her eyes fixed on the carpet and her hands clasped tight. At last, looking up eagerly, she demanded: "What *am* I to do? I don't want to break with my poet—the only poet I ever knew—merely because you suspect that—that he cares for me. Oh, I wish I was divorced!"

"Divorced!" screamed Mrs. Dumont. "There never was a divorce in our family, nor in South Carolina either, except among niggers. It is a thing that niggers and Yankees do." Then, after a horrified stare of inquiry, she added, "Do you mean divorced so that you could take *him?*"

"No!" answered Virginia, stamping her foot in the violence of her denial. "But to be free—free from scandal. I foresee that my life will be one long struggle to avoid scandal."

"I am afraid so, my dear."

"I wish I was as ugly as a turkey-buzzard, and had no more voice than a screech-owl," sobbed the girl, driven into the grotesque by desperation.

Mrs. Dumont clasped her troubled bosom, lifted her somber black eyes, and meditated gloomily. "I sometimes think," she resumed in a timorous tone—"of course, it is dreadful to come to it—but I sometimes think it would be best to—to write to Mr. Underhill."

Virginia's spirit was by this time wearied with outbursts, and she did not utter the vehement dissent which

12

had been expected. She merely sighed. "If my husband were a noble Confederate soldier, I would crawl on my knees to ask him to live with me."

Mrs. Dumont looked but half satisfied with this declaration. Possibly it occurred to her that the phrase "noble Confederate soldier" might express a kindly reminiscence of Colonel Peyton.

"Of course, you would," she said. "A lady should do almost anything, rather than live separated. I am one of the old-fashioned sort. I believe that marriage should mean something. I have always said so."

The niece replied by a vacant look, as though she failed to remember the remark, but felt that it mattered little. "Are you quite in earnest, aunt?" she presently asked. "Do you distinctly advise me to write to Mr. Underhill?"

Mrs. Dumont's old vacillation as to this thorny affair returned upon her, and she evaded prompt and positive response by having recourse to her emotions. "I don't know, Virginia," she whimpered. "I want you to do what is best for yourself, and for the good name of the family, whatever that may be."

"I couldn't love him—I couldn't," said the wife in a short, dry tone, shaking her head violently as if at the image of her husband. Presently her face changed from resolution to perplexity, and she asked anxiously, "Must I refuse to see Colonel Peyton?"

"Well—no," hesitated Mrs. Dumont. "That would be rude. But do be careful. Don't let him adore you; and don't—"

"Don't adore *him*, I suppose you mean to say," fretted Virginia. "However, I will be careful. I'll talk with him as little as possible. I'll sing to him, and make him read me his verses."

"Mercy on us! do you suppose—" began the elder lady; but just then came a tap at the door, and Mrs. Fitz James rushed in.

"How do, my dear?—How do, Mrs. Dumont?" she laughed, kissing to right and left.—"I've got such a lovely air for you, my dear," she added, running to the piano. "Let me touch off the first bars for you."

Virginia hurried after her, exclaiming, "It's all in confusion; let me clear off those things."

But she was too late. The alert and inquisitive little widow had already picked up the sheet containing Underhill's ballad.

"What's this—a new piece?" she rattled. "'Picket's Charge'—words by Colonel Henry Peyton—music by L. De Bethune." She read this legend with undisguisable dismay, and with a really pitiful subsidence or collapse of utterance. Then, turning suddenly upon Virginia, but not looking her in the face, she asked: "Have you been singing it? Has he been here?"

"Yes, he and General Hilton," was the brief reply.

"And you sang it to him?" gasped Lotharinga. "Oh, how charmed he must have been!" she added, forcing a smile. "How sweet of you! Do sing it to me."

There was nothing better to be done than to sit down and execute the "Charge" with spirit. Mrs. Fitz James listened abstractedly, obviously engaged in profound and troublous reflections, but murmuring from moment to moment: "Oh, that's lovely. *Isn't* it lovely! Too sweet for anything. And he gave it to you? What a perfectly irresistible man he is!"

She had nothing to say of the heroic strife, nothing of the "knightly dead," nothing of the clarion music. When the song was ended she at once began to talk of something else. Presently she got Virginia to essay her own *aria*, a trivial bit of love-making nonsense. But all this while it was as clear as possible that she was meditating with her whole feather-headed might. At last the attack came : she recommenced about Colonel Peyton : he was irresistible—perfectly irresistible—wasn't he, my dear ?

Virginia grew fretful under the repetition of the phrase, and finally responded with some asperity, "You may find him so, Mrs. Fitz James."

"So do other women," said Lotharinga, quickly. "I came across one of his conquests this morning. Such a pretty girl ! And such a nice girl !—as I had supposed. It is really too bad to tell on her. You must keep it a solemn secret—promise me now. You wouldn't think it of our demure little Irish thing, would you ?"

Virginia had not been able to help listening, nor could she help turning hot and red with anger. Her first impulse, no doubt, was to tell the scandal-monger that her whole story was a stupid misunderstanding or a wicked fabrication. But she was self-possessed enough, or, more likely, paralyzed enough, to remain speechless. It was the amazed Mrs. Dumont who demanded, "Do you mean Miss Macmorran ?"

"Just Miss Macmorran, and nobody else," affirmed Lotharinga, bearing on to her words significantly. "Oh, I don't know how much it amounts to," she added with the candor of a serpent. "I only suspect. But, my dears, I suspect—volumes."

Virginia still sat silent, a spot of crimson in either

cheek, and her eyes settled sternly on the babbler's face. Lotharinga's glance dropped, and then wandered away to Mrs. Dumont, like a scared loon diving in one spot to come up in another.

"I met them in the Luxembourg," she hurried on, determined to finish her tale. "They had a long and confidential talk. Then Colonel Peyton saw me and stole away. I went straight up to Miss Macmorran and pumped her. She is a sly little piece, with her nunnery face and downcast eyes and subdued voice. Oh, she was awfully adroit; she dodged and evaded in wonderful style; she was almost too much for me. But I learned something. I learned that there had been an intimacy in America."

At last Virginia spoke. She had looked once or twice at her aunt with an expression which asked, "Are you not going to stop her?" Now she broke out energetically: "Why do you go on with this, Mrs. Fitz James? I prefer not to hear any more about it."

"Oh, well—if it annoys you—certainly," returned Lotharinga, maliciously. "Let us talk of something more genteel."

But the conversation dragged, and ere long she had her cab summoned and drove home, cheered by the belief, perhaps, that she had spoiled Colonel Peyton's market with Miss Beaufort. It is entertaining, by-the-way, to think what would have been her stupefaction and wrath, could she have learned that the two supposed lovers whom she was trying to separate were husband and wife.

The moment she had departed, Virginia turned to her aunt and asked, "How are we to behave to Miss Macmorran?"

"How indeed?" answered the perplexed lady. "I can't believe ill of that modest, simple little thing. And yet, there is that old affair in Charleston, her interest in Mr. Underhill, you remember. She may be aided by rich men, and under obligations to them. Singers sometimes get on in that way, and of course get more or less entangled. It is a little suspicious—have you noticed the fact, Virginia?—that she doesn't come to see us of late—not once since Colonel Peyton appeared."

"I shall not look her up," said Virginia, after a long meditation. "But if she calls, I shall treat her well, until we learn more."

"Yes, indeed! We know nothing as yet. Mrs. Fitz James is a flibbertigibbet. I wish she would leave Paris."

"It makes my course all the easier," added Virginia, with a sigh.

"What course? What are you talking about?"

"My course with regard to Mr. Peyton."

Mrs. Dumont looked undecided, but made no remonstrance. It was clear that both ladies had believed somewhat of the gabble of Lotharinga, and that both were now convinced that it would be well to see as little as possible of the charming Colonel.

CHAPTER XXXV.

A WEEK or so has passed since Mrs. Fitz James's tattling visit. Looking into the Beaufort parlor, we find Virginia alone, bending with a studious frown over her French dictionary, while in her lap lies a volume of Thiers's "Histoire de l'Empire," a work naturally interesting to a young lady who had grown up amid battles and besiegings. Mrs. Dumont enters, drops upon a sofa with the tired air of a woman who has done much shopping, and gazes thoughtfully at her occupied, silent niece. After a little, the following conversation ensues :

Mrs. Dumont. "You are regularly unsociable to me, Virginia. You hardly speak at all nowadays. You work all the while."

Virginia (without looking up). "I *must* work. How else can I pass my time? Oh, it is *so* dreary—this foreign life ! "

Mrs. Dumont. "I wish you wouldn't study so much. That, or something, is wearing on you. You look jaded. I wish you would see more people and have some amusement."

Virginia (throwing aside her book). "How can I see more people? Nobody comes, except General Hilton and Mrs. Fitz James ; and I wish *she* wouldn't."

Mrs. Dumont (picking over the card-basket). "Has nobody been here to-day? When was this card left? Did Colonel Peyton call?"

Virginia (dryly). "I didn't see him."

Mrs. Dumont. "That makes three times—three refusals. Do you mean to cut him altogether?"

Virginia. "I wish he wouldn't call."

Mrs. Dumont. "He will soon stop, at this rate—well, perhaps it is best."

Virginia (petulantly). "Best ! How can there be any best about it? I think the whole thing is—wretched ! "

Mrs. Dumont. " But haven't you helped to make it so? You are always so headlong and so extreme, Virginia! There was no need of your breaking with this gentleman abruptly and completely. I'm sure I didn't advise that."

Virginia. " You remember what Mrs. Fitz James told us, I suppose."

Mrs. Dumont. " Mrs. Fitz James is a very frivolous, unreliable person. When you have had my experience of the world you won't believe everything that its votaries say. To be sure, it seems extraordinary to suppose that a born lady would lie. But I have sometimes had my doubts, dear, whether she is a born lady. I never heard of the Hedstones."

Virginia. " I don't believe one word of the horrid story. Mrs. Fitz James is a slanderous little vixen."

Mrs. Dumont (in a scream). " Virginia! what language! I'm sure that I never heard such language among the ladies of our family—that is, before the war."

Virginia. " I perfectly hate her. She has no business to bring her gossip here—into a Beaufort house."

Mrs. Dumont. " You are quite right, my dear. It was a great impertinence. I don't wonder you are indignant. So, then, you don't believe anything wrong of Colonel Peyton? In that case why refuse—"

Virginia (interrupting). " I don't believe anything wrong of Norah Macmorran. She is a good, sweet, nice girl, no matter if she is plebeian."

Mrs. Dumont. " So she is good and sweet. I wonder at it. She is a Catholic. It is the church of Babylon. But the girl herself is good."

Virginia. " Well, if she is good, he is good. I

don't know but that I ought to receive him. Aunt, what *shall* I do ? Do tell me something positive."

Mrs. Dumont. " Certainly. I want you to behave like a Beaufort. Remember that, whatever you decide upon, do it like a Beaufort."

Virginia (wearily). " Beaufort ! I am almost tired of hearing the word. I wish I could call myself something else."

Mrs. Dumont (rolling up her eyes). " Virginia ! You shock me beyond expression. I never heard such wild talk. One would suppose you were perfectly reckless and capable of anything."

The indecisive but enlightening dialogue was interrupted by the entrance of General Hilton. He was clearly in a sulky humor ; he looked perplexed, annoyed, and injured. Some small talk opened, but he took little part in it, and seemed to be meditating. Presently he asked abruptly and with an appearance of excitement : " What have you ladies got against my friend Peyton ? He tells me that all of a sudden he is refused here. He wanted to know of me if he had given offense."

Virginia rose, walked languidly to the piano, and commenced thrumming abstractedly. Mrs. Dumont glanced at her niece, as if for instructions, and, getting none, ventured to say, " There is some annoying gossip about Miss Macmorran."

" O aunt ! " protested Virginia, wheeling impatiently on her music-stool. " I didn't want you to speak of her."

" What *did* you want me to speak of ? " implored the bothered Mrs. Dumont.

" Oh, never mind," fretted the girl. " It is a wretched, stupid muddle, but you may as well go on, now that you have begun."

"What about Miss Macmorran?" demanded the General, indignantly, as if he would like to challenge somebody.

"Miss Macmorran and Mr. Peyton," whispered the elder lady. "A love-affair."

Remembering, no doubt, the old complication between Norah and Underhill, the General looked scared. He was so really and thoroughly dismayed, indeed, that at first he could only murmur, "I hope not." Then, recovering his courage a little, but still greatly confounded, he inquired, "Do you mean something past, or something present?"

"Both," returned Mrs. Dumont. "That is the story. I don't quite believe it; I don't want to believe it. He is too much the gentleman, I think, to care for a low-born girl. And she—well, I like her, too, and judge well of her."

"There is no love-affair between them," affirmed Hilton, who had had time to think it all over. "If it is a man who brings this story, I'll make a personal matter of it with him. By Jove!" he concluded, looking about him wrathfully, "I am not too old for that yet."

"You can't do that, General," said Mrs. Dumont, simply, and without either surprise or agitation, so accustomed was she to the idea of a duel. "It is a woman."

Then the General made a guess. "Mrs. Fitz James!" he scoffed. "What do you believe *her* for? She is a light, wrong-headed, misbelieving little baggage. Is it possible, my dear ladies, that you are shutting your doors for her sake on a dear and trusted friend of mine?"

Once more Virginia wheeled upon her pivot, but this time with a fairly cheerful face. "I want you to understand us, General," she said. "Your friend may pay attention to whom he pleases, if he won't trifle with good and poor people."

"Pitch Mrs. Fitz James's gossip out of the window," returned Hilton. "There has been no trifling here—no paying attention to anybody."

"I shall write him a note," decided the young woman, with her characteristic *vim*. "I shall ask him to tea."

The General sometimes forgot, as it were, that Peyton was Underhill and Virginia's husband; but at this moment he recalled the fact vividly, and nearly laughed in the wife's unsuspicious face. He struggled with himself, however, and merely smiled as he said, "I think you owe him as much as that."

Then Mrs. Dumont queried whether the invitation ought not to be in her name and handwriting.

"I want to write it myself," insisted the girl.— "Mayn't I, General? My aunt is always fearful I shall do something improper in a married woman."

"I don't think your husband would object to your writing that note," answered Hilton, with a grin.

"What did you say that for?" demanded Virginia, evidently both puzzled and nettled.

The General looked at her; then looked at vacancy with an air of meditation; then settled his eyes on her once more, and responded gravely, "I think you are doing something improper all the time."

"I should like to know what," was the pugnacious retort.

"Living without your husband," said the General,

firmly. "Why don't you put an end to the worrying and scandalous situation? There is no longer any sufficient reason for it. The old bitterness has faded out of your soul, at least in a great measure. Don't deny it; I can see it. Time and distance and prosperity have done a part of their inevitable work, and are sure to do the rest. You have to make a struggle to remember your anger. You talk about hating your husband, and you are merely indifferent to your marriage. What is the use of a make-believe aversion? What nobility, what sense even, is there in living a lie? It has just occurred to me that living a lie is as unbecoming to a Beaufort as telling one. Besides, you are driving your best friends into suppressions and prevarications which demean them, and which they are ashamed of. We have to call you Miss Beaufort when you are Mrs. Underhill. We have to fib and sham and lurk and sneak, for your sake."

Both the ladies seemed to be completely overwhelmed by this tremendous indictment. Mrs. Dumont looked at Hilton as a criminal might look at the State's attorney, and feebly stammered forth, "I'm sure it isn't I who uphold her in it." Virginia, reddening to her forehead, forgot to make the simple assertion that she did hate her husband, and that therefore her life was not entirely a lie. She merely said, in a hesitating and undecided way, "It shows such a lack of character to change."

"Ah, my child!" sighed the General, "you are just like all of us; you are just like the whole South. You make yourself miserable by refusing to recognize an accomplished fact."

"I proposed this separation," pleaded Virginia. "I

think it would be contemptible in me to propose to give it up."

"Look into the future," said Hilton, pursuing his advantage with something like oratorical vehemence. "What have you to hope for in life? what usage of the affections? what womanly development? what chance of happiness? Think of ten years hence—thirty years —fifty! You are preparing for yourself a lonely and melancholy old age."

"I sha'n't live to be old—I hope not," muttered Virginia.

"My child, that is wrong," put in Mrs. Dumont. "You will live as long as your Maker pleases."

"You will be a solitary, friendless old worldling," groaned Hilton, honestly and profoundly touched by the picture he was drawing, so potent was the man's imagination and so tender his heart. "Do you remember Pope's verses—'See how the world its veterans rewards: a youth of frolics, an old age of cards'—and so on?"

"They don't apply to me. Have I had a youth of frolics? I had a youth of calamities and solemnities. My life ought to be passed in remembering them. It must be sacred to them."

"You are young yet," said the General. "Pardon me for being honest and bold with you. The frolics may come."

"Never!" declared Virginia, reddening to her hair again.

"Will you write to your husband?" he asked, significantly. "Shall I write for you?"

The girl wavered in silence for a little, but at last shook her head.

Hilton surveyed her a moment, and then made a terrible home-thrust. "Shall I ask Colonel Peyton to do it?" he inquired.

There came into the girl's face an expression which was either a consciousness of guilt, or a consciousness that a colorable charge had been brought against her. She tried to show resentment, and could not ; she merely murmured, "What has he to do with it?"

"What I mean is, that you ought to tell Peyton of your marriage," continued the General. "The truth would save entanglements and misconceptions. It will bring you his respect. I am sure that you had better let him be informed. If you do not, you will regret it."

"It would be more like a Beaufort, my dear," urged Mrs. Dumont.

"Well, if I ought, I must," hesitated Virginia. She looked very undecided, however, and presently subjoined, "I will think of it."

When Hilton next saw Underhill, he said to him, "You can call on the Beauforts now." Then he burst into an uncontrollable fit of laughter and added : "I am afraid your wife is falling in love with you. She ought to be ashamed of herself."

CHAPTER XXXVI.

When Underhill next called at the Beaufort apartment, he obtained prompt admission and found his wife alone.

They were heartily glad to see each other, and could

not quite disguise the magnetic fact. In spite of Virginia's efforts at reserve—if, indeed, she remembered to make any—the interview had the air of a meeting between warm friends who are delighted to end a difference. Underhill uttered his pleasure at finding her once more with a fervor of feeling which gave the words tenfold their natural significance. Virginia's voice was just a little tremulous as she replied that it was very good of him to persist in calling despite of disappointments. Meanwhile he sat so near her, and his gaze dwelt upon her so admiringly, that ere long she began to color feverishly and to look uneasy. It seemed to her necessary that the subject of their reconciliation (so to call it) should be dropped, and that some barrier should be put up athwart this too emotional interchange of felicitations and amities.

Was it best to make revelation, as promptly as possible, of her marriage? There could be no doubt of it; the burning in his eyes told her that—the burning in her cheeks also. But how could such a delicate and embarrassing confession be accomplished? To drag it bluntly into the dialogue would look like an assumption that her visitor cared for her and needed a warning. The subject must be reached through some other subject; the revelation must glide in, as it were, by accident. Perhaps it was chance, perhaps it was a deceiving undercurrent of interested curiosity, which led her to turn the conversation upon Norah Macmorran.

"You have heard me mention her," she continued, meanwhile avoiding to look at him, lest she should see guilt in his face. "I wish you could hear her sing. She has a delicious voice and a great deal of feeling. She sometimes comes to practice with me; but I haven't seen her for quite a while. I am afraid she has had some trouble. I ought to go and look her up."

"I know her," replied Underhill, with entire composure of manner, so little did the name of Norah move him, now that he was in love with his wife. "I met her at the Luxembourg with Mr. De Bethune, a few days ago. She was well then."

His calmness, and the mention of De Bethune as Norah's escort, clearly gave great satisfaction to Virginia. She went on buoyantly with the subject. Miss Macmorran was lovely. She came of commonplace people, but she was herself very lovely. As for her singing, she was almost a great singer, and yet so charmingly unobtrusive and modest! That nun-like way of hers was fascinating, and all the more so because it expressed her character. Was it possible that she had allowed Mr. De Bethune to wait on her to the Luxembourg? Well, so she might; he was a thorough gentleman and a good man; he was fit company for a Lady Superior.

"Really, that inspires me with an audacious idea," she added, her eyes sparkling. "I want to befriend Norah; I want to get her married—if that is befriending her."

"I believe people generally think so," replied Underhill, with an imploring sort of smile.

"It may not be so—not always," said Virginia, turning grave again. "There are some unhappy marriages. I will tell you of one—some time."

She so evidently referred to her own, and was so obviously upon the brink of speaking plainly of it, that her husband trembled and turned red.

"Now, who shall the man be?" she resumed, after a

moment. "Where shall I find a husband for Miss Mac-morran?"

"Let her find him herself," he answered, incautiously. "It is the simple old way."

"It is the American way, and the good way. A husband who is found for you is a grievance and a danger."

"Always?" asked Underhill, soberly. "Not always, I hope and trust. There are many happy marriages in France, although they are usually arranged by the mothers."

Virginia shook her head gravely; she held it a hard thing to believe. "I have such a prejudice against arranged marriages!" she sighed. "I will tell you why—some day."

Once more she had made an effort to reach her confession, and once more some confused emotion had caused her to fail. It was far easier to talk of Miss Macmorran than of herself.

"What was I saying?" she muttered, after a brief silence. "Oh, I was proposing to find a husband for Norah. It won't be easy, I fear. She has no family and no money. A rich gentleman might not want her, and a poor gentleman perhaps couldn't afford her. What is to be done about it? I should hate to see her fall to some common fellow. But where is the uncommon fellow who will take her?"

Underhill liked the subject. In the first place, it was quite enough for him that his wife there was interested in it. In the second place, as we know full well, he bore earnest good-will to the modest and pretty Irish girl, and had also a feeling that he owed her reparation for peace disturbed. After pondering the match-

making problem for a little, he looked up with a smile
of satisfaction and said : "Why not De Bethune? I
thought she had the air of liking him."

"Did she?" laughed Virginia, delighted, no doubt,
with the amiable fact itself, but perhaps equally delighted with her poet's obvious pleasure in mentioning
it. It was very clear to her mind by this time that
Lotharinga's tale about a flirtation between Colonel
Peyton and Miss Macmorran was a silly or wicked fib.

"Oh, that would be so nice!" she went on. "They
are just suited to each other—both Catholics, both mu-
sicians ; and he likes her character and ways—I know
he does. He really thinks she is quite high-bred, because she has that monastic meekness and shyness, like
a *demoiselle Française.* As for her family, what does
that matter, over here? Speaking two languages, and
singing almost well enough for a prima donna, she
would be quite a star in *bourgeois* society. There is
only one difficulty : Mr. De Bethune—poor, nice gentleman—has no money ; and, like. all decent Frenchmen,
he thinks it wrong to marry on nothing ; that is, I suppose he thinks so."

Colonel Peyton—*alias* Colonel Underhill—suggested
that that was a difficulty which might be got over.
Then followed a long financial conversation of a most
opulent and munificent character. It must be remembered that both these young persons were very wealthy ;
that the lady had some thirty thousand a year, and the
gentleman considerably more. It was quite easy for
people in such comfortable circumstances to suggest ar-
rangements which would justify a poor professor of
music in marrying a penniless church-singer.

After a time it became apparent to Virginia that the

Colonel was talking as if his pocket-book were concerned in the proposed settlement.

"But this money mustn't come from *you*," she said, with her usual frankness and decision. "She wouldn't take it from you, nor would Mr. De Bethune like to have her, I presume."

"It could come from me by passing through your hands," he suggested. "Why not from me—at least in part?"

Virginia shook her head ; she alone must give the dowry. Underhill bowed to her judgment with a look of admiration followed by a smile of amusement. Apparently it entertained him to see his wife thus grandly dispensing and donating what had once been his uncle's treasure, and, but for her, would have been his own. Presently he made bold to remark that, before the match should be proposed to De Bethune, it would be well to see a lawyer and inquire into the methods and proprieties of matrimonial endowments. Virginia replied with charming simplicity that General Hilton was one of the leaders of the Charleston bar, and that she would consult him.

"The General is not qualified to act here," Underhill delicately observed, not caring to tell her that her trusted friend was ignorant of the civil code. "I think you will need a French attorney," he added. "I happen to have with me the address of one, and a very able one, as my bankers tell me. Allow me to give it to you."

He drew a number of papers from his pocket, selected a card from among them, and handed it to Virginia. She took it, thanked him with a smile, and went to deposit it in her writing-desk. The skirt of her dress caught a slip of manuscript which lay upon the floor, and

dragged it half across the room. Neither of them noticed it, and the dialogue was resumed. They had just
reached the judicious decision that nothing should be
done without legal advice, when Mrs. Dumont entered,
saluted the visitor cordially, noted the stray bit of paper,
picked it up and handed it to Virginia.

"What is this?" was the very natural question of
a middle-aged lady who had mislaid her glasses, and
could not read without them.

"Verses!" exclaimed the worshiper of poesy with
a little laugh of pleasure. "It is your handwriting,
Colonel Peyton. Did you bring them for me? Please
let me look at them."

Underhill apparently had not brought the verses for
her, and he rather allowed consent to be assumed than
uttered it. Thereupon, in a tone of rapidly deepening
emotion, Virginia read aloud the following ballad. :

"Raven Van Ross.

"'They say that the Vandals will come:.
   I would not believe it till now;
But this horrible throbbing and hum
   Is the tramp of their march drawing near,
And the roll of their barbarous drum:
   So let me remember my vow,
And hasten forth robed for my bier,
To strike at the joy of their cheer,
   To strike and leave some one dumb.

"'My lineage is gentle and old,
   And my heart is.virginal pure;
My hair is a girl's sunny gold,
   And my hand is of satiny gloss:

But no heart can more bravely endure
  The peril of life and the loss;
No hand with the pistol is truer,
  And I'll shoot the first Yankee as sure
    As my name is Raven Van Ross!'

"She speeded forth into the night,
  And saw the dark column anigh;
She stood there in delicate white,
  A woman too lovely to die—
Too precious for aught but the sight
  Of Love, and the kiss of his mouth,
And the clasp of his yearning delight;
But, maddened by echoes of fight,
  And the passionate blood of the South,

"She shot! But no death-cry replied;
  From the column responded no ball;
It trampled on massive and wide,
  From curbstone to curbstone across,
Dumb, solemn and black as a pall,
  Unknowing that close by its side,
Withdrawn from life's hyssop and gall,
Heart-broken, death-smitten, lay all
  That remained of Raven Van Ross."

A year before, Virginia could not have read these verses aloud. Now, by a great effort, she was able to finish them; but with the last line she burst out weeping violently. Mrs. Dumont, who had a tear or two on her cheeks, glanced at the Colonel as if she were moved to tell him something, but could not because of the presence of her niece. Underhill, who knew perfectly well that his poem narrated the death of Virginia's sister, watched her in silent pain and anxiety. It was a long time—that is, it seemed a long time—before any one spoke. At last the shaken girl recovered a little self-control, and, looking Underhill piteously in the face, sobbed out : "Did you know that that was my sister? Did you know her?"

"The incident was related to me," he replied, eva-sively. "It was so startling that it took possession of my imagination. I may say that I couldn't help writ-ing the ballad. But I am very sorry that I chanced to bring it here."

"How strange !" murmured Virginia. "You seem to be doomed to move me ; there is a fatality about it. Will you give me the poem? It is a companion-piece to the other ; they are both epitaphs. I wish that you would give it to me."

"You shall do as you like with it," he bowed. Then, feeling, no doubt, that to prolong the interview would be to prolong a pain, he begged forgiveness for having reawakened grief, and took his departure.

"Call again—soon," said Virginia, very gently, and he replied, smiling, "Thanks for your permission."

Scarcely had he gone—scarcely had this very kindly farewell been uttered—when Mrs. Dumont turned to her niece and asked, gravely, "Does he understand that you are married?"

"I tried to tell him—and couldn't," confessed the girl, shedding tears once more—this time tears of shame and humiliation.

"O Virginia ! Where will this end?" groaned Mrs. Dumont.

CHAPTER XXXVII

It was a period of vacillations with the usually confident and decided Virginia.

When her aunt asked her "where this was to end," she replied impetuously, "I don't care if it ends in the Seine!"

"Virginia, hush!" exclaimed the elder lady, indignantly. "I know, of course, that you don' tmean what you say. But I don't wish to hear such reckless and unchristian remarks from a person of my family."

Next morning, appearing late and pale at the breakfast-table, the unhappy child meekly announced that she desired, if her aunt did not object, to quit Paris as quickly as possible and return to Charleston.

"I dare say it is the best place for us," assented Mrs. Dumont. "South Carolinians are happier in South Carolina than they can be anywhere else. Besides, you will get rid of your present perplexities and annoyances, my dear."

Later in the day our troubled and irresolute heroine sent a note to General Hilton, setting forth that she wished to go to Milan to continue her musical studies, and asking if he could find it convenient and pleasant to accompany them thither.

The result was a prompt call from her old friend, and a vague but eager plea against the project of quitting Paris, the conversation eventually running on to the subject of Colonel Peyton, and the urgent propriety of informing him as to the marriage.

Virginia's next change of opinion and purpose will appear in a dialogue which took place between herself and Mrs. Fitz James. The tricky but honestly love-lorn

little widow called with her brother, but soon became
visibly anxious to have him take his departure.

"When are you going, Frank?" she asked for the
third or fourth time, beginning to look a little cross.

"Going where?" queried the urbane tease.

"Why, to the club—to the boulevards—wherever
you do go. You know well enough where to go when
I want you to stay."

"I thought I was wanted here—not by you, of
course," trifled Frank.—"Miss Beaufort, you couldn't
think of sparing me, could you?"

"To oblige your sister, I might," replied Virginia, in
a tone of such complete indifference that Mr. Hedstone
smiled again and bowed ironically.

"Do trot off, Frank," urged Lotharinga. "I have
something awfully particular to say to Miss Beaufort."

"It may be worth your saying and not worth her
hearing," tranquilly rejoined the brother, as he took his
sauntering departure.

The moment the two young women were left alone,
Mrs. Fitz James began to prattle about Colonel Peyton.
She talked in a hurried, nervous twitter, glancing quickly at Virginia and away again, and trying in vain to
wear a smile of light composure.

"So you have gone to seeing him again?" she said.
"Well, I don't blame you; so have I. He is too irresistible for anything. Such a man as that can do what
he pleases, and a lady must put up with it."

Virginia was apparently out of patience with the
widow, and had decided to give her a smart setting
down. "Mrs. Fitz James," she replied, looking her
straight in the face, "you are entirely mistaken in your

judgment of Colonel Peyton. He is a thoroughly high-minded, good-hearted man."

Lotharinga was not crushed ; on the contrary, she was delighted. "You don't say that he doesn't care for that girl !" she exclaimed, with a happy face. The truth is, that she had partly believed her story about the scene at the Luxembourg, and that she had been at least as jealous of Norah Macmorran as of her friend here present.

"He is a perfectly high-minded, kind-hearted man," repeated Virginia, too angry with the subject to enter into it specifically.

"I am so glad to hear you say so !" returned Mrs. Fitz James, with a smile of honest joy. "He had stopped calling on me," she rattled on. "That is, you know, he called less often ; and I suspected it was on her account. I am so glad—"

"You made me do him a very great injustice," interrupted Virginia, reproachfully, as if embittered by Lotharinga's happiness.

"What ?" queried the little widow eagerly. "Did you have a scene ?"

"Certainly not," replied our noble young South Carolinian, drawing herself up in amazement and *hauteur*.

"Oh, of course," nodded Mrs. Fitz James, not in the least hurt, so interested was she and so obtuse to scorn. "One doesn't talk outright of some things. What was I thinking of ?" she added with a little make-believe air of indifference. "I wanted to ask you something. Oh —so you have made up again ?"

The question, when it was permitted to come out, revealed deep and piteous eagerness. It was answered by a grave, settled gaze, which came from solemn trouble

13

and perplexity of spirit, but which to the poor little interrogator seemed contemptuous and very cruel.

"You are *so* reserved and proud, Miss Beaufort!" she said, or rather gasped. "I can't say hardly anything to you that I want to."

Virginia drew a long breath—the forced breath of one who struggles for speech—and then in a cold, low monotone replied, "Mrs. Fitz James, I don't mean to be uncivil."

"I wish I could understand you," complained Lotharinga, very near to whimpering. She pondered a moment, biting her restless lips, glancing uneasily about the room, griping her parasol unconsciously in her small glove, the picture and incarnation of a little soul mightily tempest-tossed. At last, speaking so rapidly and gaspingly that the words could hardly be understood, she asked, "Do you care for Colonel Peyton?"

"Mrs. Fitz James! You perfectly amaze me!" exclaimed Virginia. The query struck deep: she could not sit still under the blow; she rose and walked the room, as a worried man does. After one turn, however, she stopped in front of the dismayed Lotharinga, and said in a strong, steady voice: "Mrs. Fitz James, I can clear this up in one word. I am—married!"

"Married—you?—o—h!"

It is utterly impossible to give an idea of the intonations of amazement, of relief, and of joy with which the enamored widow uttered these three words. It is almost equally impossible to describe how much sweeter and finer Lotharinga looked than she in heart could possibly be. She was, as we already know, a commonplace, selfish, unscrupulous, and almost mean little creature. But at this moment, embellished and ennobled by love, gratitude, and happiness, she had the air of an angel, and seemed worthy of any man's adoration.

"And I am *not* married to Colonel Peyton," continued Virginia. "That settles it, that I can *not* care for him."

Mrs. Fitz did not think to dispute this inferential statement, although, alas! it might reasonably have been questioned. Just then she had no thoughts but for that surprising confession of marriage, and for the palpitating gladness which it brought her. A bystander might, perhaps, have heard her worthless little heart beat as she gasped out: "Who would have imagined! Is it possible!"

She meditated a moment, and then added, with a bright, sweet smile: "Oh, my dear friend, I am so obliged to you for telling me this! You have taken such a load off my mind! I'll be perfectly frank, now. I thought he liked you best, and—I'll tell you the whole truth, now—I perfectly worship him—there!"

She ended her confession with such a throb of emotion that her voice broke, and the tears came into her eyes.

We can imagine the feelings with which Virginia listened; but her utterance revealed naught of them when she answered. "You can inform him of my marriage," she said. "I would prefer to have you."

"Oh, thank you!" smiled Mrs. Fitz, so simply, and gratefully, and joyously, that it is difficult not to pity her, knowing as we do the hopelessness of her love. "But, perhaps he wouldn't believe me," she instantly suggested. "Everybody calls you Miss Beaufort." Then an odd expression of mingled inquisitiveness and amusement came over her face, as she added, "What *is* your name?"

"Mrs. Underhill." Virginia uttered the word with an unwillingness and pain which we can understand; but, singular as the tone was, it did not rouse the slightest interest or sympathy in Lotharinga.

"Underhill? You don't say so!" she chattered, gayly. "It seems like a dream. To think you have been married all this time! Well, life is a romance. It's stranger than fiction. I guess Colonel Peyton will think so. Won't he be surprised! He will be very much surprised, my dear, after all that has happened. In fact, I suppose, he will be incredulous, at first. He won't believe me—that is, I guess he won't. How am I to make him believe it, unless you tell him of it too?"

"I have decided to tell him the next time I see him," said Virginia. Her voice was a little unnatural, a little tremulous, as she made this promise. It is likely enough that she found her visitor's cheerfulness and eagerness hard to bear.

"Oh, thank you—thank you!" exclaimed Lotharinga, jumping up and kissing our unhappy heroine. "I see it is an effort for you to talk of it. I won't ask any questions. You have my sympathy, darling, and my best love. But of course your decision is right," she added, prudently. "A marriage, however unhappy, is always best announced. It saves misunderstandings and imbroglios."

"Don't be anxious," Mrs. Underhill could not help retaliating. "I won't forget to announce it."

Lotharinga accepted the scoff with patience, and even with sweetness. She would probably have let Virginia box her ears without showing resentment, so happy was she over the news of this matrimony, and so eager to have it made public.

"Well, I must go," she said, shaking out her dress, and surveying herself in the pier-glass. "Dear me, I'm so glad I came! Good-by, my dear Virginia—my dear, dear Mrs. Underhill," she giggled, and, with another kiss, fluttered away.

CHAPTER XXXVIII.

Shortly after the departure of Lotharinga, General Hilton and Underhill arrived, and were admitted by Aunt Chloe. There was a little anteroom, where visitors of a common class were usually detained, and there the two gentlemen chose to halt, instead of pushing on to the parlor.

"We met Mrs. Fitz James going away, aunty," said the General. "Has she told any fibs this time—made any row in the family?"

"Ruther 'specs not," replied the old woman. "We all seems putty quiet in our minds. Dŏn' rain every time pig squeal."

"Very good. Now, aunty, I want to see Mrs. Dumont on business. Ask her if she will do me the favor to step in here. Don't bring Miss Ginny along, and don't come back yourself. It's too old talk for young folks."

"Mus' be mighty ole, if it's too ole fo' me," chuckled Aunt Chloe, as she seesawed out of the room.

"I'se somethin' like a turkey-buzzard : I knows mo' dead folks dan livin' ones."

Presently Mrs. Dumont came stealthily down the passage, and entered the anteroom, with face full of expectancy. She glanced almost timorously at the Colonel, as if he were a man who held much of Beaufort destiny in his grasp, and could perhaps work mischief with her noble name, if he should violently will it. Nevertheless, she gave him her hand pleasantly, and murmured a word or two of stately welcome.

"Do me the kindness to sit down by me," the General said to her. "I have an important secret to communicate. As for the Colonel, we must get him out of hearing, and he had better step in and chat with Virginia."

Underhill bowed in silence, and took his way to the parlor. He looked as if Hilton's important secret concerned himself, and as if some decisive and terrible disclosure were at hand. His face lost color, and his eyes became solemn with anxiety, while he awaited the answer to his tap on the door. Hearing at last the words "Come in," he entered very softly, and with a bearing of apology. It was obvious that the disguised husband was at that moment very much afraid of the unsuspecting wife.

"I have ventured again, you see," he said, with an almost imploring smile. "I hope you won't tire of me."

Virginia gazed at him with the gravity and the speechless embarrassment of one who feels that an answer may amount to much, and who can not at once decide what that answer should be. Her trouble of mind, or perhaps one should rather say of feeling, must have been very distressing, for she turned quite pale.

"Are you unwell?" he asked, after one agitated glance at her colorless face.

"No, sir," she murmured. Norah Macmorran could not have been more meek in speech or subdued in manner. Presently she remembered the demands of courtesy, and added more firmly, "Please sit down, Colonel Peyton."

Underhill bowed and took a chair near her, meantime watching her with a tender interest which he not only could not control, but did not even strive to hide.

"I thought General Hilton came with you," said Virginia, who would have given anything to have some one enter and break up this *tête-à-tête*, although she had fully determined that her visitor should not depart without hearing of her marriage.

"He stopped in the anteroom to speak to your aunt," explained Underhill, tremulously, for he well knew what his friend was to reveal. "I believe he has something special to say to her."

Virginia glanced at the door with an air of inquiry and wonder. In her present agitation of mind every incident was significant. Was the General talking about herself and that lugubrious secret of hers which she found it so hard to confess? Was he, by bare possibility, making an offer of marriage to Mrs. Dumont? Well, whatever might be up, it was a private interview between a gentleman and a lady, and another lady must not interfere. She could not summon either of them to help her face Colonel Peyton.

"I suppose he will come in soon," she murmured. "When he does, I shall have something to tell you."

Underhill smiled faintly, and drew a deep breath of satisfaction, such as men draw only a few times in their lives. It was clear that she was nerving herself to reveal her marriage; and how noble it was in her, he said to himself, the love-lorn young fellow; how he admired and adored her for it!

Then came the question whether he should speak his love before she reached her avowal. Or, rather, the question did not come up at all; he did not argue it, nor even think of it: he gave way to a sudden and violent impulse. He *wanted* to speak—to say to his wife that he worshiped her—to woo her and win her and secure her at once. He had been married to her for months, and had never given her a sign of affection, nor even breathed a word of courtship. He *must* utter his heart, and utter it *now*.

"I have something to tell *you*," he burst forth. "I have to tell you that I love you with all my soul!" he hurried on, determined not to be quelled or impeded. "I do love you. It is the truth."

Virginia was so stunned and crushed and terrified that she was an object of pity. For a moment she sat paralyzed and crouching, merely able to gasp out in a stifled voice, "O Mr. Peyton!" Then, making a convulsive effort, like a person struggling out of a nightmare, she threw upon him a glance which was partly beseeching and partly horror, and strove to rise and escape.

He seized her hand and detained her by force, begging her the while, in some confused stammering or other, to listen to him.

"I can not—I must not!" panted Virginia, writhing herself to her feet. "Please let my hand go. I can't let you touch me. I am—married!"

"I want one word," he urged, rising also and continuing to hold her, in spite of her pleading accents and piteous expression.

"I can't—I mustn't hear you!" she repeated. "Have pity on me! Forgive me. I have deceived you. I never can look you in the face again. Oh, do have pity on me, and leave me for ever!"

"One word!" insisted Underhill, speaking out of a sudden sense of triumph which made him tyrannical and indifferent to everything but complete and instant domination. "I must know one thing. I have a right to know it, after all that has passed. If you had been free, could I have hoped?"

Virginia broke loose from him, covered her face with both her hands, and burst into a loud, hysterical sobbing. It was a very terrible moment of humiliation, and of extorted though inarticulate confession. However wayward and unwise her life may have been since her marriage, she was, in that abasing and torturing moment, abundantly punished.

"My dear young lady," murmured the husband, with extreme tenderness—the tenderness of sudden compunction as well as of profound love—"my dear and good little girl, you *are* free to accept me."

"What do you mean?" asked Virginia, uncovering her face and looking straight at him through her tears, as frankly as a child. "You don't know about me. What do you know?"

"I know a great deal," he replied, breaking into a laugh of happiness. "I know that my wife loves her husband!"

She stared at him in utter stupefaction, while he caught one of her hands and covered it with kisses. Then she abruptly sprang away from him, ran to the door which connected with the anteroom, tore it open, and called sharply, " General Hilton ! "

The General's tall figure and haggard aquiline countenance appeared in the doorway. He looked down upon her with a caressing smile of comprehension, and inquired, " What do you want, Mrs. Underhill ? "

" Who is this ? " she demanded in a panting voice, throwing her hand toward the supposed Colonel Peyton.

" That is Mr. Henry Edwards Underhill—your husband ! " said the General, his smile broadening to a laugh as he shut the door in her face.

Virginia stood irresolute. She heard her aunt giggle in the anteroom, and she recoiled a little from the merriment. Next she became conscious that her husband was close by her side, and that there was a sound of a heart beating terribly, either his or hers. She turned impulsively, laid both her hands on his shoulder, and dropped her face between them.

" Ah, my dear little wife ! " he said with many kisses. " Have I won you at last ? "

Virginia was crying again. She cried a good deal, but she remained in his arms. She lay perfectly quiescent, resting her whole weight on him, as if she were utterly exhausted. At last she put her mouth softly up to his cheek and kissed him.

" You belong to me, heart and soul, don't you ? " he whispered.

" Yes," she whispered back, kissing his lips and clinging there, as Southern in her love as she had been in her hate.

Then another mercurial change came. She seized both his shoulders, stood off from him at arm's length, gazed at him with an air of wonder, and burst into an hysterical laugh. "Oh, you deceiver!" she exclaimed. "It was a regular Yankee trick. Oh, you darling humbug! You are perfectly wonderful!"

It was clear enough that, when she said "wonderful," she did not allude to the trickery, but to the man. Her eyes sparkled with admiration; she was already worshiping him. Next, she was struggling out of his arms with a panting whisper of "Let me go—they are coming!"

In fact, the anteroom-door swung ajar, and Hilton towered in the opening, with Mrs. Dumont sniveling happily behind him.

"We can't hear anything through the key-hole," grinned the General. "We are dying to know how you like it as far as you've got."

Virginia dashed at him, and embraced him violently, exclaiming: "You dear old traitor! And my artful aunt, too!" she added with more kisses. "You are all Yankees together. Oh, what a trick to play on me!"

"I knew nothing about it, my child," eagerly explained Mrs. Dumont, who even in that joyous moment could blush under an imputation of Yankeehood. "General Hilton has just told me the secret. But I am truly delighted," she subjoined, pushing toward Underhill with extended hands. "It is an immense relief—and satisfaction. The ways of God are wonderful," she whimpered, as she fervently exchanged her first kiss with a Yankee.

Just then an expression of reminiscence, of regret, and of compunction, came into Virginia's face. "Oh, *now*," she sighed, clutching her husband's arms, and looking him sorrowfully in the eyes—"*now*, I wish we had had a public marriage. What a fool—what a hateful fool—I was! Do forgive me."

Woman-like, she cared much for the nuptial solemnity and parade, and supposed that he too would lament, during life, that the world had not been bidden.

"But I will make it all up to you," she continued, tightening her grasp on him. "I will be married henceforth as woman never was. You shall be contented. Trust me!"

Presently, Aunt Chloe and Uncle Phil were summoned to greet Miss Virginia's husband, and made their entry into the parlor with marvelous courtesying, scraping, and smirking.

"Is dat ar him?" demanded the old woman, staring at the newly revealed one, as if he were something extra-human.—"Masr Peyton, is you reely Masr Underhill?" she went on, shaking hands. "De Lawd be praised, though he might 'a' fotched it roun' sooner, 'pears to me.—I s'pose, Miss Ginny, you's satisfied with him, now you's got him in you' own way. S'pose you's contented, an' feels good, an' grateful. Chick'n nebber so wicked but he thinks grasshopper sent by de Lawd.—An', come to 'flect on't, Masr, I do b'lieve you's been helped. Hope you'll be helped to stay an' abide, though I'm kinder skeered all the while, too, 'less you should'n'.—Phil, come an' shake hands with him, befo' he disappeahs."

"Boss, I'se glad to see ye—I'se mos' powerful glad!" grinned Phil. "I 'specs you'll hole on now a spell, won't you, Boss?"

"I hope so, Phil," laughed Underhill, dropping the old man's hand, and taking his wife's.

"As long as I have life to hold him," said Virginia, laying her head anew on her husband's shoulder.

We have only to add that Mrs. Fitz James left Paris within a week; that a sufficient marriage settlement enabled Mr. De Bethune to wed Norah Macmorran; and that Mr. and Mrs. Harry Underhill are still living happily together.

"The affair has been a little—providential," Mrs. Dumont occasionally explains to her friends, both Northern and Southern. "But my niece has acted throughout as became a Beaufort."

THE END.